This is crazy,"

"This was supposed to be a good-night kiss."

"Who said?" He slid his hand under her blouse and touched her breast. Marina closed her eyes and prayed for control. How long had it been since anyone had touched her like this? His hand felt so good she couldn't think.

"I think, uh, you did," she managed to say. "Now I'm on your bed in a motel room and you have half my underwear off me. I can't believe this."

"Me, either," he said against the corner of her mouth. "Damn fool luck, if you ask me."

"Damn fool luck," she repeated, stalling. "Is that a Texas expression?"

"Hell," Clint said, fumbling with her blouse. "These buttons are too damn small."

"Do you always swear when you undress women?"

He lifted his head and gave her a level look "Women?"

"Well, uh, you must have a lot…" She stopped, not really wanting to know how many women he'd slept with in Tyler. He was a virile man who could certainly take advantage of those cowboy boots of his.

"A lot of what, Marina?"

"Sex," she whispered. "You must get a lot of it. Anytime you want, I mean."

He flopped on his back and started to laugh. Finally he took a deep breath and propped his head on his hand. "Lady, you have a lot to learn about me."

Kristine Rolofson is acknowledged as the author of this work.

ISBN-13: 978-0-373-82555-4
ISBN-10:   0-373-82555-2

A TOUCH OF TEXAS

Copyright © 1996 by Harlequin Books S.A.

Printed in U.S.A.

KRISTINE ROLOFSON

A Touch of Texas

**He could solve the mystery,
but not without destroying her....**

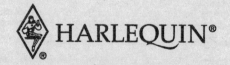

HARLEQUIN®

TORONTO • NEW YORK • LONDON
AMSTERDAM • PARIS • SYDNEY • HAMBURG
STOCKHOLM • ATHENS • TOKYO • MILAN • MADRID
PRAGUE • WARSAW • BUDAPEST • AUCKLAND

WELCOME TO A
HOMETOWN REUNION

Twelve books set in Tyler.
Twelve unique stories. Together they form a
colorful patchwork of triumphs and trials—
the fabric of America's favorite hometown.

Around the quilting circle...

"My goodness," Tessie Finklebaum declared. "The population of Tyler is certainly growing! I'm going to need ten extra fingers to keep up with the quilting."

Her friend Martha nodded her agreement and admired the pattern of pastel triangles before her. "I do love stitching the quilts for the little ones, don't you?"

The ladies chuckled and Bea Ferguson asked, "When is Raine and Gabe's baby due?"

Martha shrugged. "Late fall, maybe? I'm not sure, so just in case, we'd better not take our time with this one."

"I refuse to be rushed." Tessie sniffed. "My stitches will be uneven."

Martha rolled her eyes and changed the subject. "Any news for Judson or Tisha about rebuilding the plant? Seems like an awful lot of people are out of work."

"Not that I've heard," Annabelle Scanlon answered. "Although there have been rumors...."

"Rumors?" Tessie stopped quilting. "What kind of rumors?"

"Well," Annabelle began. "My granddaughter says the other kids think the new boy at school, John Weiss, had something to do with the fire."

"Weiss," Bea Ferguson murmured. "Isn't that the name of the pretty young woman who works for Amanda now?"

Martha nodded and Tessie said, "Sounds like she and that new principal—you know, that Texan with the cowboy boots—should be finding out what's really going on at the high school."

Martha brightened. "Oh! And they're both single, too. What do you think will happen?"

"Between a shy secretary and a handsome Texas bachelor?" Bea giggled. "Use your imagination!"

CHAPTER ONE

MARINA WEISS WAS the happiest woman in Tyler. Of course, she was the only person who recognized that particular truth. She was sure other women were happy, too. Her boss, Amanda Trask, an efficient and popular lawyer, certainly smiled a great deal. Even on days when work piled on their desks and the telephone wouldn't stop ringing, Amanda remained amazingly good-natured. Marina had met other women in town, women who were in love with their husbands and satisfied with their work and content with life in general.

But Marina knew, deep down in her Midwestern heart, that no one was happier than she was. She knew it without a doubt; she made a mental list every day when she drove down the quiet street from her house to the Trask law office. Sometimes she even walked, relishing the fact that she didn't have to watch for muggers or hug her purse tightly to her chest. She didn't have to worry about her son being threatened by gang members or her apartment being robbed. Chicago was a zillion miles away, as far as she was concerned, and a zillion miles was about far enough.

Tyler, Wisconsin, was paradise, and Marina Weiss, almost-forty legal secretary and single mother of one handsome, brilliant teenager, knew she was a lucky woman. Lucky because she now owned her first home, a sweet Victorian in the heart of town. Roses would be blooming against the white picket fence come summer.

Lucky because she lived alone with her son in a pleasant town with pleasant people and tree-lined sidewalks.

Lucky because her life finally was just the way she'd always dreamed it could be. Coming to Tyler had been the right move, she knew.

So on a lovely spring afternoon in early April, when the phone rang at her desk, Marina wasn't too concerned to learn she was wanted at the high school to meet with someone there about her son. Even when the woman calling mentioned an "incident" that needed her "immediate attention."

Marina put the telephone back in its cradle and turned to Amanda, who stood in front of her desk with a sheaf of papers.

"What's up?" her boss asked.

"I'm not sure. I've been called to the principal's office," Marina explained, swiveling her chair away from the telephone. She tucked her shoulder-length hair behind one ear and rested her chin on her hand.

Amanda chuckled. "What did you do?"

"There's been an 'incident' involving my son. The secretary said that Mr. Stanford wants to meet with me at my earliest convenience, but it's not an emergency."

"Clint Stanford isn't scary," Amanda assured her, dropping the papers onto Marina's desk. "Especially if you like handsome men with shoulders the size of Texas. He's a real charmer. Haven't you ever met him?"

Marina shrugged her own petite shoulders and reached for the papers. "I don't think so. Maybe I did and I don't remember."

"You'd remember," Amanda assured her. "He's caused quite a commotion in town. He's from Texas and he has an…interesting accent."

"Do you need these right away?"

"Not until Friday morning. That will give me time to go over them before I meet with the client Tuesday."

"All right."

Amanda hovered near the desk. "When are you going over to the high school?"

"I said I would either come over this afternoon or call back to make an appointment in the morning. It could be about Jon's transcripts, but I thought that had been resolved. I can't imagine why anyone at the school would want to see me."

"Whatever it is sounds important. Go over there now," Amanda suggested. She gestured toward the pile of paperwork stacked on Marina's wide desktop. "All of this can wait for a while. Besides, you're going to worry until you do. Do you think your son is in some kind of trouble?"

"I don't know. He's not exactly the troublemaking type." Marina's worried expression softened. "He's more into science and his computer than anything else."

"Clint's a friend of Ethan's, by the way. He seems like a pretty nice guy. If he wants to see you it must be important."

"You wouldn't mind if I took half an hour?"

"I'll dock your pay if it will make you feel better," Amanda teased, and moved across the wide, airy room to her own office.

Marina looked at her watch. "I'll try to get an appointment with him right away and be back by two."

"Marina, don't worry. That's not a problem," her boss called, and disappeared into her office. Marina picked up the phone and dialed the number the school secretary had left her. If there was something going on with Jon, she wanted to know about it. It hadn't been easy raising a boy all by herself, but she'd managed. And Jon had been an easy kid, the kind you didn't have to worry about doing anything stupid or irresponsible.

Ten minutes later she was in her four-year-old Oldsmobile heading through town toward the high school. She could have walked, she knew, but there wasn't time for a casual stroll through town, despite the fact that it was a beautiful spring day and the air smelled like flowers for the first time all winter. She rolled her car window down and took a deep breath as she turned onto Main Street. It was a quiet afternoon in Tyler, but then every afternoon was quiet in Tyler. She drove the three blocks and took a left, then parked in the visitors' lot near the high school. Swallowing a sudden nervous lump in her throat, Marina slung the strap of her purse over her shoulder and entered the wide double door of the building. A sign on the inner door said All Visitors Report to the Office, so Marina followed an arrow. An older woman smiled at her as Marina stepped up to the desk.

"I'm Mrs. Weiss. I have an appointment with Mr. Stanford."

"Are you Jonathan's mother?" Marina nodded. The woman pointed to one of the doors across the room. "Go right on in," she said. "He's expecting you."

Marina scooted around the copy machine and hesitated at the doorway of a bright, window-lined office. A large man sat behind the wooden desk, his dark head bent over a manila folder full of papers. Marina cleared her throat. "Mr. Stanford?"

Dark brown eyes met hers as he lifted his head to face her. A slow smile crossed an attractive, square face and the little lines at the corners of his eyes crinkled.

He stood slowly and held out his hand. "Mrs. Weiss? I'm pleased to meet you."

"Thank you," she said, stepping into the room. She could see why Amanda called him a charmer, accent and all. She shook his hand, wondering how hers could disappear into someone else's so easily. He stepped around his desk and shut the door, then gestured for Marina to take a seat in the chair that fronted his desk. He did look vaguely familiar, in a Western-movie kind of way.

"I'm glad you were able to get over here so quickly."

"Your secretary said it was important." Cowboy boots, she realized. The man wore chocolate-colored leather cowboy boots, which quickly disappeared behind the desk as he took his seat and faced her. Those giant hands closed the folder and pushed it to one side. "Is there something the matter with Jon?" she queried.

Clint Stanford leaned forward. "I don't know. That's what I wanted to ask you. Is something going on at home that the school should know about?"

We could have done this over the phone. Marina stopped herself from fidgeting with impatience. This big man with the soft Western drawl acted as if he had all the time in the world. "I'm not sure what you mean."

"Divorce, illness, death in the family? I know you're new to town. Any changes that would cause Jon to be upset?"

"I'm not aware of anything wrong with my son."

"I wish I could agree with you."

Marina frowned. She didn't think that Jon was having trouble with his classes. He'd never had problems with his schoolwork before, except for that one time in English. "Is this about his grades?"

"No. Your son doesn't seem to have any trouble with his schoolwork. I'm just concerned…" The principal stopped, drummed long fingers on the desk blotter and eyed Marina with concern. "Ever heard Jon talk of a kid named Brad Schmidt?"

The name didn't sound familiar. "I don't think so."

"He's a senior. He was on the science team with Jon, on the F and M project, until it was canceled."

Marina remembered the morning after the fire at Ingalls Farm and Machinery, when the townspeople had realized what losing the plant could mean to the town. And since then, that was all anyone could talk about. Amanda had spent hours trying to come up with an answer to how to rebuild her grandfather's business without the insurance money. "That's been a real tragedy. I've always thought it was a miracle that the kids weren't working there at the time."

"Yes," he agreed. "We were lucky no one was hurt. So you don't know Brad?"

"I'm pretty certain Jon's never mentioned him. What does he have to do with my son?"

"I'm not sure. There was a confrontation in the hall this morning. I'm still trying to figure out what's going on."

"Jon is not exactly the fighting type."

"Anyone can be pushed too far, Mrs. Weiss."

"And you think Jon is being pushed?"

"Or he's doing the pushing. He's the new guy in town this year. That can't be easy."

"No. It's not."

He seemed to take her reply very seriously. "Tell me about why you moved to Tyler. Do you have family here?"

This time Marina looked at her watch. She didn't want to be away from her work for longer than necessary. The law office was always busy and there were three case files sitting on her desk right now. Besides, she wasn't used to chatting with strangers about her life, so she ignored his question. "Just what exactly do you mean by a 'confrontation,' Mr. Stanford?"

"I don't know who started it, but I think someone would have gone home with a bloody nose if a couple of teachers hadn't stepped in as quickly as they did."

"Jon isn't the kind of boy who picks fights, Mr. Stanford."

The principal didn't comment on that observation. "I've called Brad's father, too. I think both of you need to be aware that there was a problem here. Both boys received detention for the rest of the week. If there is any more violence of any kind, one or both boys will be suspended. I thought it was best that you should be informed.''

Marina's stomach twisted nervously. Suspension would surely hurt Jon's chances for a college scholarship. She stood up, anxious to leave. ''Thank you. I'll talk with Jon tonight and find out exactly what happened.''

The man stood and held out his large hand. ''Thanks for coming in.''

Marina shook it briefly. Mr. Stanford was large, warm and solid; she could understand why he held a job dealing with teenagers. One look at him and a kid would think twice about taking him on. ''You're welcome. I'm sure it won't happen again.''

''I hope so, too,'' he murmured. ''Jon seems like a nice kid. I worked with him on the science team for a couple of months and—''

His telephone rang, giving Marina the perfect opportunity to back up. ''Goodbye,'' she said, anxious to leave.

''I'll be in touch,'' he assured her, seeming in no hurry to answer his phone.

''Thank you,'' Marina said, hurrying through the doorway. She walked past the secretary's desk and toward the front door, where she took a deep breath as she stepped out into the sunshine. She felt as if she'd escaped a dragon, and she didn't know why. The man was only doing his job, and if Jon had actually been involved in some kind of fight she certainly wanted to know about it. What would possess her mild-mannered son to behave so strangely?

''BAD TIMING, Ethan,'' Clint drawled into the telephone. He watched through the window as Marina Weiss crossed the parking lot to her car. She looked worried, and he didn't blame her. She also had a great pair of legs. "I was in the process of ending a meeting with a very attractive woman."

"You're always in a meeting or prowling around that school," Ethan Trask replied. "And attractive women have been making moves on you for the past year and a half without much success. Who is she? Anyone I know?"

"Probably." Marina stepped into her car and disappeared from sight. Clint turned from the window and moved to his desk. "But she wasn't interested in me. It was strictly business."

Ethan chuckled. "Guess you didn't turn on the famous Texas charm."

"What can I do for you?"

"I don't know if you're still interested, but one of Amanda's clients mentioned that he was thinking about selling some land out by Timber Lake. The house is just a fishing cabin, actually, but the property is a real gem. I don't deal in real estate, but I told Amanda you were looking for something by the lake and she told him. Are you interested?"

"More than you know," Clint drawled. "I'm having a hell of a time living in the middle of town. How do I get in touch with this person?"

"He's in Milwaukee until next week, but he gave Amanda the keys and permission to show you around. I've been there a couple of times to fish, so I think I can find it."

"Do you have time today?"

"I'll check." Clint heard his friend's deep voice as he talked to his secretary and then he came back on the line. "Sorry. I'm in court all week. How about Friday? I should be back from court by three."

"I'll meet you at Amanda's office," Clint volunteered, eyeing the manila folder on his desk. "If that's convenient."

"Fine. Amanda can handle the legal work for you, if you

decide to buy the place. She'll have to tell you the price, too. I don't have any of the details.''

Clint didn't bother to hide his excitement. ''I appreciate this, Ethan.''

''Anytime.'' With that, Ethan, one of the best-known prosecutors in Wisconsin, ended the call.

Clint replaced the receiver and opened the Weiss file again. Jon's mother worked as a paralegal and assistant to Amanda Trask. Divorced, apparently, with no mention of a father or stepfather anywhere in the picture. The boy had been enrolled in Tyler High the week before classes started at the end of August; his transcripts from Chicago showed nothing unusual. Except for his consistently high grades, he was the kind of kid you'd never notice, except that this morning one of the most popular boys in the senior class had tried to take a swing at him. It didn't make sense. There didn't seem to be any link between them, except they'd both been on the science team. The other kids watching the confrontation had looked as baffled as their principal. Come to think of it, there had been the other incident after the donkey basketball game, but Clint didn't think the two things were related.

He closed the file and gazed out the window again. This day was certainly looking up. It was April, almost the beginning of fishing season, and he had a chance to own a place out on Timber Lake. And he'd met a lovely woman who looked as if she needed his help, even if she didn't know it herself. Clint had a feeling that whatever was going on between Jon and Brad, it wasn't going to end with a few words in front of the cafeteria. Marina Weiss might not like it, but she was going to need help.

''YOU NEED HELP?'' Jon was on the porch when Marina got home.

''Bring the milk,'' Marina said. ''I can get the rest.''

Jon bounded off the porch and opened the passenger door. He grabbed the two cartons of milk and kicked the door shut with one sneakered foot. "Is that it?"

"That's it." Marina climbed the five steps to the porch, her son following close behind. He opened the screen door for her and they walked through the living room and dining room to the bright yellow kitchen. The outside of the house was yellow and so were the downstairs bathroom, the kitchen cupboards and the living-room walls. Whoever had lived here before had liked the color of sunshine. Marina was growing accustomed to the small Victorian's cheerful rooms, although she intended to paint every wall in the house ivory as soon as the weather turned sunny and dry.

"What are we having for dinner?"

"Something easy. Do you want hamburgers or meat loaf?"

"Hamburgers."

Marina dropped her briefcase on the faded yellow linoleum floor and set a paper bag of groceries on the counter. She pulled out a package of hamburger buns. "That's what I thought you'd say."

"Cool." He shoved the cartons of milk in the refrigerator and then peered over her shoulder into the bag. "Did you buy chips?"

"Not this time." She pulled out a large plastic bag of frozen french fries and set them on the counter. "We'll have fries and the rest of the salad from last night."

Jon set the table, a job that had been his since he was six. "How was your day, Mom?"

Marina washed her hands, unwrapped the package of hamburger and began to shape patties. "It was an interesting day. An *unusual* day, as a matter of fact." She waited, her back to her son while she shaped five hamburgers and set them on a plate. Jon remained silent. "In fact," she continued, "I've never had a day quite like it."

The boy sighed. "The Cowboy called you."

"The cowboy?" Marina turned around. Jon looked dejected but not guilty.

"Mr. Stanford. The kids call him The Cowboy because, well, he's from Texas and he wears really wild boots."

"I noticed. Right before Mr. Stanford started asking questions about you."

Jon's hazel eyes, the same shade as hers, widened. "You were at the school today?"

"Yep. I got a call from the office telling me that the principal wanted to see me. When I got there I learned that you'd been involved in a fight—"

"It wasn't a fight," Jon interjected.

"What was it?"

"It was, uh, just one of those things."

"That's all you have to say? It was 'just one of those things'?"

"Yeah." He shrugged, a little too casually for Marina's taste. "You know, a *guy* thing."

"And was Mr. Stanford satisfied with that explanation?"

"Not exactly." Jon grimaced. "You want me to turn the oven on?"

"Sure." She let him move away and fiddle with the top of the stove. "Four-fifty."

"I know."

"And what does the other *guy* have to do with this?"

Jon bent over and opened the oven drawer, then pulled out a cookie sheet. "You want me to put the fries on now?"

"I want you to answer the question."

"I can't."

"You mean you won't."

"Can't." He looked at his mother with a pleading expression. "Brad Schmidt is a senior. Plus he's lived in Tyler forever, he's on the football team, the basketball team and the wrestling team. He's almost six feet tall and built like a tree trunk. I don't want him on my case.''

''Who started it?''

Jon's expression clouded. ''It just happened, that's all. I have detention for a week.''

Marina wasn't satisfied with his answer. ''All I want to know is, is this the end of it?''

Jon shrugged. ''Yeah, sure. As far as I'm concerned.''

Marina gave her son a long look as he opened the bag and began to cover the baking sheet with french fries. ''I hope you're right. Mr. Stanford doesn't look like someone to tangle with.''

''He's okay, I guess.''

High praise from a sixteen-year-old, Marina observed. She decided it was time to let him off the hook. She didn't think she was going to learn anything more tonight, anyway. She reached for the frying pan and set it on the stove. ''Do you have a lot of homework?''

''Not much. I did my algebra in detention, but I've got an essay to write for English tonight. There's a chemistry test tomorrow, but that's no problem.''

''All right. I'm going to change before I start frying the hamburgers.'' Marina hurried up the central staircase and into her bedroom to the left of the stairs. She knew Jon was telling the truth—at least about the chemistry not being anything to worry about. Jon had never lied to her before, so she had no reason to mistrust his explanation of today's ''guy thing.''

Marina hung up her cream dress and pulled on jeans and an old pink T-shirt. She hoped that was all it was, merely an isolated incident between two hormonal teenage boys suffering from spring fever. She had no desire to sit behind The Cowboy's desk again anytime soon.

''HE DID *WHAT?*''

''Jon was involved in a food fight,'' the principal repeated, leaning forward across his desk. Marina couldn't believe what she was hearing, yet how could she argue with the man? She couldn't. Two days ago she'd thought she was through with visits to the high school, and here she sat. Same chair. Same room. Same man.

"What happened?"

"It involved the Schmidt boy, but so far I haven't been able to determine who started it. They're both threatened with suspension."

Marina's heart sank. She'd never had any trouble with Jon. He was the last kid she expected to cause trouble. She blinked back tears and hoped Mr. Stanford wouldn't notice how upset she was.

"They were warned," the man continued. "I told them this had to stop or else."

"Is Brad a troublemaker?"

Clint leaned back and gave the question some thought. "I haven't been here all that long, so I can't say. He's a kid who's full of himself, I'd guess. But he is popular, he's a football player and a championship wrestler. He's smart, too."

"Jon only knows him because of the science project at the F and M."

"Did Jon mention anything about problems when they were working together?"

"I don't think Brad is one of his favorite people."

"I've been trying to think why two boys would be in each other's faces. Did they like the same girl?"

Marina shook her head. "Not that I know of. Jon isn't much for dating, although I think he has a crush on Christy Hansen. Is she Brad's girlfriend?"

"No." Clint turned back to the folder that lay open on his desk. "I can give him another warning." He looked back at Marina, a sympathetic expression in his dark eyes.

"Don't worry. We'll get this straightened out, but in the meantime tell Jon to stay away from Brad and avoid any further confrontations."

"Thank you. Where is Jon now?"

"He's in the cafeteria, scrubbing the floor. Another two weeks will be added to his detention time, and if there is any more trouble, both boys will be suspended for three days. Hopefully we can avoid that."

Marina stood up and took a deep breath. Mr. Stanford stood also and held out his hand. Marina took it, but the principal didn't let go right away. "It's going to be all right," he assured her, before releasing her hand. "It's my job to make certain of that. But talk to Jon. I think there's more to this than we realize, and if it goes back to the F and M project, I need to know about it."

She lifted her chin. "Jon isn't a troublemaker."

"He has a problem," Clint said, steel edging his voice. "Which means *we* have a problem. The sooner we get to the bottom of it, the better. I've told Jon that if he needs to talk to someone, my door is always open."

"I'll take care of my son."

"You might be out of your league. You look like you could use a friend, too. Sometimes—"

"Thank you," she interrupted. She didn't need a speech about friendship from a stranger, that was for sure. She knew he was only trying to be nice, but she could handle her son all by herself. She'd been doing it for years. "I'll see that Jon stays out of trouble."

His eyebrows rose. "Good."

Marina turned and left the office. The school corridor was empty, classes having finished an hour ago. She would go back to her office and finish typing up the brief Amanda needed for tomorrow's court session and then she could go home and confront the kid who'd flung french fries in the face of a championship wrestler. For a science major, he wasn't acting very intelligently.

Marina pushed the heavy door open and stepped out into the fresh air. It had been cloudy all day, but it hadn't rained. Spring was taking its time getting to Tyler and she thought she could use a little more sunshine.

Up until now she and Jon had done just fine. She'd raised a good kid, a nice boy with a scientific mind and an easy-going personality. They'd done fine together, just the two of them. Marina had thought moving to Tyler was going to be a good thing. She'd gotten a good price for the apartment in Chicago; she'd been able to afford to buy the little house in the middle of Tyler. She liked her new job and her new boss. Now everything was unraveling.

No, it wasn't, she told herself, getting into her car. Jon might be having trouble adjusting to a new school. He might have some kind of personality conflict with the wrong guy, but everything would work out okay.

It had to. And she would make sure that it did.

"HE'S NICE, isn't he?" Amanda hovered near Marina's desk and waited for an answer.

"Who?" Marina sat down and turned on the computer.

"Clint Stanford."

"I guess so. I hope I won't have to see him again, though."

Amanda poured two mugs of coffee and pulled up a chair. She handed one of the mugs to Marina. "Forget the computer for a minute. What was it this time? I mean, if you want to talk about it I'd be glad to listen."

Marina hesitated. "The whole thing is ridiculous."

"You look like you could use a friend."

"That's what Mr. Stanford said." She took a sip of the coffee and was grateful for Amanda's thoughtfulness.

"There was a food fight in the cafeteria. Can you believe it?"

"How many kids were involved?"

"Just Jon and a boy named Brad Schmidt. Again."

Amanda frowned. "Brad's father works at the plant. I remember Brad when he was a little boy."

"He has it in for Jon, but no one knows why and Jon's not saying. And Mr. Stanford is punishing both of them."

"At least he's being fair."

"Is he?" Marina took another sip of coffee. "Maybe it was a mistake to move here, after all."

Amanda shook her head. "No way. What would I do without you? When Tessie retired I was in deep trouble." She grinned. "I'd updated my computer system and couldn't find anyone who could operate it. I'd be out of business if it wasn't for you."

Marina chuckled. "Now *that* I doubt."

"Jon will be fine," Amanda assured her. "He has a great mother. You'll *both* be fine."

"I hope you're right. I could do without any more trips to the principal's office."

Amanda's eyes twinkled. "You have to admit that he's a good-looking man."

"If you like the type," Marina conceded.

"What type?"

"You know, the Western thing with the boots and the drawl and the giant shoulders. He looks like he should be in a rodeo."

Amanda laughed and stood up. "That's bad?"

Marina shook her head and turned back to the computer screen. "I'm not saying it's bad," she said. "I'm just saying he's not my type." Clint Stanford was a stranger, a stranger who didn't know what was best for her son.

CHAPTER TWO

CLINT STANFORD PARKED his Jeep wagon behind the Trask law office and stepped out into the spring sunshine. A sense of freedom usually accompanied Friday afternoon and the end of the school week. He'd stopped for a few minutes to watch the boys' baseball team practice behind the school; he'd waved to the girls' softball team as their bus left for a game thirty minutes away.

Clint undid his tie and tossed it through the open window onto the seat. He rolled up the sleeves of his blue shirt and unbuttoned the collar. Now that school was over, he had all the time in the world. At least until Monday. He had no plans for the weekend, but that was fine, too. He could think about buying land, he could think about fishing, he could tie some flies and see if anyone was interested in a poker game.

He'd learned to find plenty of things to occupy his spare time, but he'd never quite gotten the hang of being alone. Judy's death had left a void that couldn't be filled, and he hadn't even bothered to try. He knew he should go out more, date once in a while, but sometimes that seemed to be more trouble than it was worth. Clint tugged at his collar. If he was a real smart man, he'd back off right now.

If he was a real brilliant kind of guy, he wouldn't set one booted foot into that office where Marina Weiss was sure to be working. He wouldn't sneak a peek at those legs or wonder if her skin was as soft as it looked and if the slight scent of floral perfume was as intriguing as he remembered from yesterday. If he was a bona fide genius he'd go over to Marge's Diner and call Ethan from the pay phone and arrange to meet him somewhere else. Anywhere else.

Clint strode up the sidewalk toward the law office. Hell, how could one big Texan be afraid of a tiny little thing like Marina Weiss? He could lift her with one arm if he wanted to. As he swung the door open, stepped into the wide reception area and saw Marina standing on a swivel chair watering a plant, that was exactly what he wanted to do: scoop her up under his arm and set her on the ground before she hurt herself, dammit.

She turned when he growled and, despite the fact that the chair swiveled alarmingly, hopped onto the carpeted floor without losing her balance. Clint couldn't believe she hadn't fallen. It was automatic to cross the room in three quick strides and take the watering can from her hands. "Whoa, there," he said, taking her elbow to steady her. She was small-boned and felt fragile under his hands, and the flowered dress she wore made her look as delicate as one of Aunt Martha's porcelain teacups.

"You don't have to worry, Mr. Stanford," she assured him, her voice quiet and low. She reached for the watering can and he relinquished it, but he hesitated before releasing her elbow. "I do this all the time."

"Right brave of you, too," he drawled, releasing her. "Next time use a stepladder. So you don't crack that pretty head open."

"Thanks for the advice," she said, moving away from him. She set the watering can beside the desk and slipped her stocking feet into ivory flats before moving her chair to its place behind her desk. She sat down and scooted into position. "Is there something I can help you with?"

"I'm here to see Ethan. Is he in yet?"

Marina looked relieved. She probably thought he'd come here to talk about her son, Clint realized.

"Ethan isn't back yet. He called a while ago to talk to Amanda, but he didn't mention an appointment."

"Well, it's not exactly an appointment. We're going—"

"Clint!" Amanda popped out of her office and smiled. "I thought I heard your voice. You and Marina know each other, don't you?"

"Right," Clint replied.

Marina gave her an odd look. "Yes. We met this week."

"Oh, that's right," Amanda said. "I forgot." She smiled, as if she was pleased with both of them, then turned her blue-eyed gaze on Clint. "Ethan is stuck in court."

Clint hid his disappointment and started to back up. "That's fine. We'll make it another time."

"Oh, you can still see the place," Amanda assured him with another dazzling smile. She reached into her jacket pocket and pulled out a key. "Here you go," she said, dropping a thick brass key into Clint's palm. "I wish I could go with you, but I'm waiting for a call."

Marina looked surprised. "They haven't settled yet?"

Amanda shook her head. "I'm sure it will be any minute."

"Go ahead with, uh, Mr. Stanford," Marina urged. "I'll stay as late as you want and take a message."

"I'd rather be here myself," Amanda assured her. "That way I can finish it up once and for all. But you could do me a favor," she said, still smiling. "Drive out to the lake with Clint. That way there'll be a representative from the office with him."

"I'm not sure I can remember how to get there. You drove the time we went," Marina said.

"I'll draw you a map. Is that okay with you, Clint?"

Having a beautiful woman accompany him to a fishing cabin? He didn't think he minded at all. "Sure."

Marina handed Amanda a legal pad and Amanda took a pen and quickly drew a diagram on a sheet of yellow paper.

"Turn right when you get to the lake and follow that road for about half a mile. There's a fork in the road, but you bear left and start counting mailboxes. Turn right at the fifth mailbox and follow the dirt road to the cabin. The key is for the back door, remember?"

Marina nodded. "I remember."

"I don't want to put either of you ladies to any trouble," Clint said, pocketing the key. "I'm sure I can find it myself."

Amanda shook her head. "I can't let you go out there alone. It wouldn't be…right."

Marina didn't look as convinced as Amanda did, but she pushed back her desk chair and stood. He saw her reach for a beige blazer and he quickly took it from her and held it out for her to slip into. "Thank you," she said, sounding surprised.

Amanda handed her the piece of paper with the map drawn on it. "I'll close up the office as soon as I get that call, so don't bother coming back here. And thank you for helping me out."

Marina picked up her purse. "That brief you needed to be typed—"

"Can wait until Monday," Amanda finished for her. "Have a nice weekend."

"Tell Ethan I'll be in touch," Clint said, stepping to the door and holding it open for Marina.

"He'll be anxious to know what you think of the place. We'll be home tonight if you want to call." Amanda held the door and waited for them to step out onto the sidewalk. "Have a good weekend," she said, sounding pleased with herself.

"You, too," Marina replied, then Clint took her elbow and guided her toward the path to the parking lot. He had the feeling he'd just been hog-tied, but he wasn't going to complain real loud. "My car or yours?" Marina asked when they entered the parking lot.

"We'll take my Jeep," Clint decided. "You can hold the map." He opened the passenger door and waited until Marina was settled in the bucket seat before he slammed the door shut and went around to his own side of the car. "I appreciate you going out to the lake with me."

Marina smiled and turned to him. "I don't think either of us had any choice."

He grinned. "Amanda is used to getting her own way."

"She's the boss," Marina answered, sounding amused. "She's supposed to."

Clint started the car and drove out of the parking lot to Main Street. "How long have you worked for her?"

"Since September."

"How did you end up here after living in Chicago?" He stopped at the intersection, for one of the few traffic lights in town. The two Hansen kids in a battered pickup truck waved to him, and he waved back and waited for Marina to answer the question. She sure as hell hadn't wanted to answer any of his questions yesterday.

"A friend of a friend told me about the job and about the community. I was tired of worrying about Jon's safety. It seemed like every day there was another drive-by shooting or something terrible."

"You lived in that rough a neighborhood?"

"No. The violence just kept coming closer and closer."

"And Tyler seemed safe," he concluded, knowing he'd felt the same way. The light turned green, so he stepped on the gas and continued to make his way out of town.

"Yes," she repeated. "Tyler seemed safe." After a few seconds of silence, she spoke again. "There wasn't any more trouble between Jon and that other boy today, was there?"

"No. Not that I know of." He glanced over at her and

noticed the worried expression had returned to her eyes. "You talked to your son?"

"Yes."

"And?" he prodded. "What did he say?"

"He said it wouldn't happen again."

Clint wasn't entirely sure about that, but he decided to keep his opinions to himself. "Sounds good to me," he said.

"He's a good kid, Mr. Stanford."

"I never said he wasn't," Clint drawled. He glanced over at her again. "Could you call me Clint? It's Friday afternoon and I sure hate to act official on the weekends."

She returned his smile. "All right. If you call me Marina."

He nodded. "Pretty name."

"Thank you. It was my grandmother's."

"It's unusual." He fiddled with the radio and turned on the country and western station, then rested his elbow on the frame of the open window. The air smelled like fresh earth and fertilizer. He took a deep breath. "I love Friday afternoons."

"I can tell," she said with a laugh. "You look like a man who's been set free."

"Damn right," he said. "I love my work, but..." He hesitated, remembering he was talking to the parent of a student.

"But?" she urged.

"It's a long week," he said diplomatically. "Especially this time of year. The kids start feeling their oats, especially the seniors." He wondered if she was dating anyone. Would Ethan know? Possibly. Clint tried to keep his thoughts on the fishing cabin, but Marina's presence interfered with visions of isolated fishing weekends.

"You have to take a left here," she said as they approached the highway.

It was a stupid idea to date a parent. Built-in complications, that was all it was. He could smell trouble with Jon Weiss. There was a situation that wasn't going to go away, no matter how much he or Jon's pretty little mother might want it to.

It would be better to keep his mind on fishing.

Much better.

He took his foot off the gas and eyed the building ahead on the right—the Dairy King. The parking lot was half-full and customers were coming and going. Suddenly Clint didn't feel as if he was approaching fifty anymore. It was spring and Friday, and the sun was shining and an intriguing woman sat beside him in his car. "Want an ice cream cone or a root beer float? I don't know about you, but I'm starving." He drove the car into the gravel parking area that fronted the building. "Well?" he asked, turning off the ignition and ignoring the curious looks from the crowd of teenagers near the door. "What'll it be?"

"A hot fudge sundae," she declared, eyeing the two-foot poster of a sundae posted in one of the windows. "One that looks just like that picture, please."

"Comin' up," he said, glad she'd agreed. Next time he'd see if she'd have dinner with him. He was pretty damn tired of eating alone. And it was time he got out more. He greeted each teenager by name, ignored their grins as they tried to see who was sitting in the front seat of his car and stepped up to the window to order a large root beer float and a deluxe hot fudge sundae with the works.

The word would be all over school by Monday: The Cowboy had a date.

HE WOULDN'T HAVE believed it if he hadn't seen it for himself. Jon lounged near the counter of the Dairy King, his chocolate-dipped vanilla swirl starting to melt at the edges and drip down his fingers. He stared at Mr. Stanford's familiar car and the dark-haired woman on the passenger's side. His mother and The Cowboy?

"Wonder who the babe is," the guy beside him muttered, nodding toward Mr. Stanford's Jeep. "You never see him with anyone, not really."

Jon didn't say anything. *The babe?* He couldn't think of a reason for his mother to be with Stanford. He couldn't think of a reason his mother would be anywhere but at the law office. Jon turned away and grabbed a napkin from the dispenser by his elbow. Two junior girls nearby whispered something to each other and took quick peeks at the Jeep. He tried not to stare, but he had to be sure that was his mother sitting beside Mr. Stanford, just as if she belonged there. And she was smiling, too. Like she was having a good time. That was part of the trouble. His mother, *the babe,* thought Tyler was a dream come true.

She didn't have a clue.

"I'll bet she's somebody's mother," Eddie said. "I heard he doesn't date teachers."

"How would you know something like that?"

"I hear things." The kid shrugged and ate another mouthful of his ice cream.

Jon watched as the principal approached the window and gave his order to the girl behind the counter. Then he said hello to the kids he knew, while Jon used the cigarette machine as camouflage. He didn't dare look back at the Jeep. What if his mother saw him and waved? Or worse, came over and said hello? Then everyone in school would know that his mother was the Friday Afternoon Mystery Woman, as if things weren't bad enough.

"Schmidt still on your case?"

"What?"

"Schmidt," Eddie prompted. "I heard he has a problem with you but no one knows why."

"Yeah, well..." Jon hedged, unwilling to give the kid

any information. They were in chemistry together, but they weren't friends. Jon had hitched a ride with him to the Dairy King because he'd overheard Matt Hansen telling another kid that he was stopping there after school.

"You'd better hope he doesn't show up here. Tina broke up with him again, so he'll be lookin' for trouble."

"What else is new," Jon muttered. All he needed to finish up the week would be having the burly football player try to take another piece out of him. Just for fun, of course.

Jon glanced toward Matt's truck and hoped that Christy would look his way so he'd have an excuse to cross the parking lot and say hi. Christy Hansen was beautiful. There were a lot of beautiful girls at Tyler High, but Christy was the most approachable. Or, Jon amended, she had been until the past few months. This thing with Schmidt had screwed up a lot of good things.

Not that Christy would have been seriously interested in a science student, anyway. Still, Jon was tougher than he looked; he wasn't built like a football player, but he wasn't undernourished, either. And the blue-eyed freshman hadn't seemed to mind his help with her science homework. She didn't look his way, and several kids leaned against the truck to talk to her after Matt went to the window.

"She's pretty hot, isn't she?" Eddie said, noting the direction of Jon's gaze. "You asking her out? Think she'll go out with you?"

"That's three questions," Jon replied, forcing himself to sound bored. "Which one do you want me to answer?"

He didn't reply, his attention caught by the principal returning to his car. "The Cowboy is giving his new girlfriend a sundae. That's cozy."

"Shut up, Eddie."

Matt stood by the window, collected two drinks and glanced toward Jon. He didn't smile, but he said hello.

Jon nodded. "Hey, Matt. How's it goin'?"

"Okay." The tall boy started to move away. "See you later."

"Yeah." Jon watched as his former friend grinned at a couple of girls on his way back to the truck to bring his sister a cold drink. Matt Hansen was one of the good guys, and everyone knew it.

Eddie nudged him. "You done?"

"Yeah. Let's get out of here before…"

"Before what?"

"Nothing." Jon tossed the rest of his uneaten cone into the metal garbage bin at the corner of the building. There were advantages to being invisible, and disadvantages, too. His mother hadn't seen him, but neither had Christy. If he was as smart as everyone thought he was, he'd give up on that particular fantasy—dating Matt's sister.

He took one last look at The Cowboy's Jeep as he followed Eddie to his car. What on earth was his mother doing eating ice cream with Mr. Stanford? Jon assumed it was business—his mom didn't date. But what possessed her to be seen with him in such a public place?

And what were they talking about? Jon's stomach knotted, a familiar tension since December. Mr. Stanford was getting too close for comfort, that was for sure. The less Stanford knew, the better. The good news was that the principal wouldn't learn anything from Jon's mother. Marina didn't have a clue what was going on, and that was exactly the way Jon meant to keep it.

"I DIDN'T KNOW this place was such a hangout," Clint said, as another carload of teenagers pulled into the parking lot.

"They're staring at you," Marina said, digging into her sundae. "Does that bother you?"

He smiled. "No. I'm used to it. Jon's not going to appreciate it, though."

"I don't think anyone here knows who I am."

"Except your son. He was trying to disappear before either one of us noticed him."

Marina stopped eating and looked toward the building. "He's here? Where?"

"He just left."

"With who?"

"A kid from the science club."

"I wouldn't have embarrassed him." Marina took another spoonful of ice cream. Jon would not appreciate her being seen with the principal, of all people, especially in such a public place with all these kids around. But work was work. Despite the ice cream and the casual conversation, this was still part of her job as Amanda's assistant. "I try not to do that, although with teenagers you never know. I'm glad he was doing something fun with the other kids. He spends too much time alone."

"I'm sure he'll have some questions when you get home."

Oh, she was certain about that, too. Marina looked at her watch. "Maybe we'd better get out to the cabin."

"Give me another couple of minutes," he said, dipping his spoon into the large waxed-paper cup. "We're not in any hurry, are we?"

Marina was caught between enjoying an afternoon in the country and getting home early to putter outside in her future garden. Jon teased her about her obsession with seeds and weeds, but she ignored him. She liked putting down roots in Tyler. "No," she agreed. "We're not in any hurry. I keep forgetting that. You must be quite a fisherman, since you're thinking about buying a cabin on the lake."

He nodded. "It's something I enjoy, and the thought of living out on the lake sounds good."

She ate another mouthful of ice cream coated in hot fudge before replying. "You'd actually live out there?"

His dark eyes twinkled as he looked at her. "I wouldn't mind."

"You might want to see this place before you make any decisions."

"It's that bad?"

"Well…" Marina hesitated, trying to remember the exact details of the lakeside cabin. She didn't remember it well; she'd gone out there last fall with Amanda. Her boss had wanted company on the drive out to see the elderly man who lived there. Plus there'd been papers to sign and they'd needed a witness. "It's pretty rough. It might be nice for weekends, but it's going to take a lot of work to make it livable on a permanent basis."

Clint drained the rest of his root beer. "Okay, lady, you're making me pretty curious." He put the Jeep in gear and, as they left the parking lot, tossed their trash into the bin by the edge of the road, then turned right and headed toward the lake. The road was smooth and empty, with farmland stretching to the horizon on either side.

"I'm going to love this," he said. "I can feel it."

Marina's hair blew across her face and she brushed it back with her hand. "You're awfully excited about something you haven't seen yet."

"There hasn't been anything for sale out this way since I moved here," he answered. "Not anything worthwhile," he added. "I almost bought a farm, but there was so much acreage that the price—and the responsibility—was more than I could afford."

"So the next best thing is a fishing cabin. I hope you're not disappointed."

"Is it really in bad shape?"

"I think you'll have to see for yourself. I'm not sure what fishing cabins are supposed to be like."

"You don't fish?"

"No."

"Does your son?"

"No. I don't think he ever has."

"He's missing something, then. Who are his friends around here?"

Marina hesitated. "Is this a professional question or are we just making conversation?"

Clint shrugged. He took his gaze off the road to glance briefly in her direction. "A little of both, I guess."

At least the big Texan was honest, she thought. "Jon spent time with Matt Hansen last fall, but he hasn't mentioned him lately. He was also tutoring Matt's younger sister in chemistry."

"That would be Christy, right?" At Marina's nod, he added, "She's a freshman. Wonder why she's taking a science class that's usually reserved for juniors."

"According to Jon, she's taking extra science courses because she wants to be a veterinarian."

"Makes sense. The Hansens are good kids."

"Jon likes them," she agreed. "There's a sign for the lake." Marina pointed to the left side of the road. "You'd better slow down. We're supposed to turn right along here somewhere." She picked up the map from the console between the seats and unfolded it.

"Right here." Clint grinned and put on his blinker. He slowed down and left the smooth, four-lane road to turn onto a narrower one. A sign for Timberlake Lodge pointed them in the direction of the lake.

"We should look for a fork and turn left when we get to it."

"All right." He looked pleased as they headed toward a wooded area. "We must be getting close."

Marina rolled her window farther down and took a breath of pine-scented air. The road took them into the woods, and new leaves blocked part of the spring sunshine, causing a dappled effect on the road. In a matter of minutes they approached the fork and Clint turned left onto a gravel road, the opposite direction from the lodge. He slowed the Jeep to avoid stirring up dust.

"Now we have to count mailboxes," she said.

The narrow driveways disappeared into the woods and were far apart. Finally Clint turned right and drove slowly down a small lane.

"I hope this is right," Marina murmured. The lane didn't look as if it was used often, and it wound around rocks and trees until a glimmer of blue water could be seen ahead. "I don't remember it being like this."

Clint looked as if he was enjoying the adventure of it all. "We'll soon find out."

Marina wondered once again what on earth Amanda had gotten her into. Three days ago Marina had been sitting across from this man while he informed her that her son was in trouble. Now she'd eaten ice cream and driven to the lake with him. Only in a small town, she realized, could something like this occur. She'd have to get used to things like this if she stayed in Tyler.

And she definitely wanted to stay in Tyler.

Clint stopped the car at the end of the road, in a clearing beside a dark cabin. A short walk away through tall grass, the lake sparkled and a weathered dock stretched out into the water. Large trees shaded the cabin from the afternoon sun, and as Clint turned off the engine Marina heard a bird squawk overhead.

"Does this look like the place?"

Marina nodded as she set down her purse and reached for the door handle to the Jeep. Clint hurried out of the car and went around to her side. He grinned down at her. "Have I thanked you for bringing me out here?"

"It's part of my job," she answered, but she smiled to soften the words.

"And I appreciate it. Now," he said, taking her elbow

and leading her toward a rickety set of steps that led to the back door, "you get to play real-estate agent."

He unlocked the door and pushed it open to reveal a small, dark kitchen. He flipped the light switch on, but nothing happened. "Good thing we came in daylight."

Marina looked at the dark cupboards and the brown counter that divided the cooking area from the rest of the room. She didn't remember this part and realized she and Amanda must have entered through the front door. "I think there's a screened porch that faces the lake," she volunteered, as Clint strode through the kitchen and into the pine-paneled living room. A stone fireplace took up one wall. Over the mantel hung a large stuffed fish. Facing the lake was a bank of windows and a screen door that led to a wide porch, where a picnic table took up half the space.

"I'll have to cut some of that brush," Clint said, surveying the view of the lake.

"You're going to buy it?"

He turned and winked at her. "I'm going to try."

"You haven't seen the rest of the place." She waved toward a narrow hall. "I think there's a bedroom and a bathroom down there. They're probably pretty small."

"It doesn't matter." Clint disappeared down the hall and peeked into two rooms. "You're right," he called. "They're small, but they'll do." He looked pleased with himself when he returned to the main room. "This is exactly what I want."

"I guess you plan to catch a lot of fish here."

"I plan to try. Come on," he said, holding the front door open. "Let's go check out the front yard."

She followed him onto the porch and for a brief moment pictured wicker furniture and chintz cushions instead of a beat-up picnic table and a couple of metal lawn chairs.

"I like porches," he said. "Do you?"

"Yes. I'll bet there are mosquitoes out here."

"Yeah. The size of tractors." He smiled again. "Though they're bigger in Texas." He unlatched the screen door and ushered Marina outside, down three steps to a grassy path.

They walked to where the water lapped against a tiny strip of pebbly beach to the right of the wobbly-looking dock. Clint stepped onto the wooden structure, but didn't walk out to the end. "I wonder how much Amanda's client is asking for this place."

"I don't know."

"I'll call her when we get back to town. I was so anxious to get out here that I forgot to ask." He stepped off the dock and walked over to join Marina at the edge of the lake. He bent down and picked up a flat stone, then flung it out over the water, where it skipped four times before disappearing. "What do you think of Tyler?"

"It seems like a nice town."

"I like small towns," he said, picking up another stone.

"I'm still trying to get used to total strangers saying hello to me at the supermarket. It still surprises me, but I like it," she admitted. "You're from Texas, I heard." She watched as he sent another stone skipping along the water. His shoulders were wide, his forearms thick and lightly tanned. He was an attractive man, but seemed something of a loner.

Amanda had told Marina his wife had passed away a few years before. She had no intention of getting involved with any kind of man, whether he was president of the chamber of commerce or a world-class hermit. Clint Stanford seemed to be a combination of both. He was definitely a man a smart woman would back away from. And Marina was very, very smart.

"Yes, ma'am." He put his hands in his pockets and looked across the lake to the wooded shore on the opposite side. "It's peaceful here."

"No teenagers."

"No teenagers," he repeated, nodding.

"Do you miss Texas?"

"No." He didn't smile when he said the word, she noted. In fact, he looked positively grim. Marina decided to change the subject.

"Do you have a boat?"

"Not yet."

She pointed toward a small boathouse hidden in the brush nearby. "Do you think that's part of the property?"

He looked intrigued. "Could be." He eyed her flowered dress. "Why don't you wait here and I'll go see for myself? I don't think you want to be traipsing through the woods all dressed up."

"Thanks." She watched as he trudged through knee-deep brush until he found a narrow path, peered through a small window and disappeared around the corner of the building. What she could see of Timber Lake was peaceful and serene; she could understand why this little cabin would appeal to someone for a weekend getaway. You wouldn't have to fish to enjoy looking at the lake.

She glanced at her watch and figured she could be home thirty minutes after leaving the lake. And then she wondered why she was in a hurry. It wasn't as if Jon were a child who needed her there every minute between school and bedtime. He was growing up, she reminded herself. He was a young man on the verge of making decisions about college and careers. He didn't need his mother around him all the time, that was certain.

And she'd have to get used to it, whether she liked it or not.

CHAPTER THREE

CLINT CRASHED through the bushes toward her. "I think the boathouse is part of this property," he said, brushing leaves from his shirt. "There's a small boat inside, but the door was locked. I couldn't tell if the boat was any good or not."

Marina tried not to laugh. He looked like a kid on Christmas morning. But Clint Stanford was no kid. He was an attractive widower with a killer smile and an air of being in charge of every situation. A small black dog followed him, its tongue hanging out as it panted to keep up. "Who's your friend?"

Clint looked down as the dog caught up to him and sat beside him on the pebbled beach. "I don't know. I think she lives under the boathouse." The dog wagged her tail as Clint stroked her head. "She seems friendly enough, though there's no collar. I think she must be a stray."

"Or someone's pet."

He shook his head. "I doubt it. She's filthy. And way too thin." He pointed to her side. "Her ribs are sticking out."

"Looks like you've got yourself a dog *and* a fishing cabin."

Clint frowned. "I can't take her back to Tyler with me. I've rented a house that doesn't allow pets."

"She's awfully happy to see you."

He patted her again, making the wispy tail wave back and forth. "I hate to leave her to starve." He gave Marina a considering look. "What about you? Does Jon have a dog?"

"No."

"Any restrictions on your lease?"

"No. In fact I own the house."

His eyebrows rose. "But?"

"I don't know anything about dogs."

"You don't have to know much. I'll take her to the vet and make sure she's okay. And I'll supply the cans of dog food."

Marina wavered. "You'll take her back when you have a place for a dog?"

"If you want me to, but you might get attached to her by then."

"I don't think so."

"Jon's never had a dog?"

He made it sound as if her son had been deprived. "That's not so unusual. We lived in an apartment." Marina looked down at the dog, who was doing a good imitation of being in love with a Texan. "What if she doesn't like me?"

He chuckled. "She'll like anyone who feeds her," he promised. "Just wait and see."

Marina looked up at him. "Why do I feel as if I don't have a choice? I can't leave her here to starve."

Clint shook his head. "Of course you can't."

"You'll take her as soon as you can?"

"Yep."

Marina eyed the dog with some trepidation. "I don't know about this."

"Come on," he said, taking her elbow. "Let's lock up the cabin and head back to town. We can discuss the arrangements in the Jeep."

The dog followed them, as if she didn't want to let these new friends out of her sight. Her tail waved in the breeze as she trotted behind. When Clint opened the car door and whistled, she hopped in the back seat as if she'd been riding in cars all her life.

"I hope we're not stealing her." Marina waited by the car as Clint locked the doors to the cabin.

"She's skin and bones," he answered. He handed Marina the key and opened the car door for her. "I doubt she has an owner. And even if she does, he's not bothering to feed her."

"Maybe you should put an ad in the lost-and-found section of the paper."

He went around to the driver's side and got in. "Will that make you feel better?"

"Yes."

"Then I'll do it. I'll leave my office number, in case someone wants to claim her. In the meantime, she needs a name."

Marina turned and eyed the dog. "I suppose Blackie is too obvious?"

"A little," he drawled.

"Then you name her," she said. "After all, she's your dog."

He thought for a minute as he backed the car carefully around the trees and out the way they'd come in. "I'll call her Tex," he said. "People have been calling me that for years. It'd be nice for someone else to have the name."

"Tex," Marina repeated, looking at him. "It suits you."

He winced. "It suits the dog better. Right, Tex?" He looked in the rearview mirror and the dog obligingly wagged her tail.

"She looks happy about it."

"She's going to be real happy after we feed her."

"We?"

"Yeah." He guided the car out of the woods and onto the main road that led back to town.

Marina didn't want to like him. She didn't want to like the little dog, either. Hadn't she just been reminding herself that she needed to get used to being alone?

"MOM?" JON POKED his head out the front door and stared at his mother, the principal and the dog. Clint opened the Jeep's rear door and the dog hopped out of the car and hurried over to Marina's rosebush to relieve herself. Once that was done, she ran in circles around Clint's legs, her waving tail proclaiming her happiness. "What are you doing?"

Clint answered for her, sensing that Marina probably didn't have a ready answer. "Your mother is doing me a favor."

Jon stepped out onto the front porch, his expression wary. Clint tried not to smile. The boy looked as if Clint had come to haul him back into detention. "With a dog?"

Marina said, "I'll explain later. It's a long story."

"Do you have any rope?" Clint asked.

The teenager shrugged. "I don't know."

His mother gave him a look that said "mind your manners." "Check in the basement."

Jon disappeared into the house, the screen door banging shut behind him.

Clint looked down at the lovely woman standing next to him. She seemed a little uncertain, and he knew it wasn't real considerate to saddle her with a stray. He hadn't been able to help it. He had a soft spot for dogs and kids and women with great legs. "I'll be right back."

"You will?"

"I promised to buy the dog food, remember?"

"Oh." She looked down at the dog, who had settled down between them, as if awaiting further instructions.

What was the matter with him? Clint wondered. He was as tongue-tied as a junior-high kid talking to the prettiest girl in class. He cleared his throat and decided to get a grip on himself. He was sure as hell old enough not to act like an idiot over a woman. "What about you?"

She looked up at him, those hazel eyes wide. "What about me?"

Hell and damnation. "I mean, would you like to have dinner?"

"With you?"

No, he wanted to say. With St. Francis of Assisi. "Yes. As a thank-you for this afternoon."

"You don't have to do that."

"I want to." He meant it. He didn't know when he'd last taken a woman to dinner. It had been so long he didn't want to think about it.

"Thank you, but I really can't."

He had no choice but to accept the refusal with good grace. "Maybe another time, then." He moved to his car. "Stay," he told the dog, when she would have followed him. "I'll be back with the dog food."

Jon came around the house, a rope in his hand. "Am I supposed to tie up the dog?"

"Yeah. Keep her company till I get back."

Jon knelt and snapped his fingers. "Come here, girl." The animal trotted over eagerly. He turned to his mother. "Are we keeping her?"

"It's only temporary. As a favor to Mr. Stanford."

The boy grinned, a rare occurrence. "Does this mean I can skip detention to walk the dog?"

Once again Clint wondered what was bothering Jon, what made him look so serious most of the time. He wasn't a bad kid. Clint would have given a lot to know what was going on in that head. He grinned back. "Wishful thinking there, Weiss."

"I thought it was worth a shot."

Clint climbed into the Jeep and backed out of the driveway. He didn't question why he was reluctant to leave.

"YOU WERE at the Dairy King with him," Jon stated, turning to his mother after the dog was safely tied up in the backyard. Marina hesitated at the kitchen door. "Everybody saw you."

"Believe it or not, it was work. Amanda asked me if I'd show him a piece of property at Timber Lake."

"Everyone at school thinks he finally had a date."

"You mean that's rare?" She told herself it was natural to be curious.

"No one's seen him with anyone," Jon said. "I heard some of the girls talking. At first they thought he'd hook up with Sheila Lawson, but Mr. Wagner, the history teacher, beat him out. Besides, he's pretty old."

"He is not old."

"You're not going to start going out with him?"

"None of your business, kid."

"It's not my business if my mother starts dating The Cowboy, the principal of my school? The guy who's given me three weeks of detention?"

"You deserved it. A food fight, for heaven's sake," she muttered, opening the refrigerator and wondering what to fix for dinner. "How old are you?"

"Yeah, I know. Too old to throw french fries."

She took a casserole of leftover beef stew out of the refrigerator and set it on the counter. "No kidding. Can't you just stay out of trouble?"

"I'm trying."

"Excuse me if I'm not convinced."

"You don't…"

She turned. "Don't what?"

"Nothing." He sighed and turned away, a gesture she was growing accustomed to seeing.

"Jon, if you need to talk, maybe Mr. Stanford is the right person to talk to."

"About what?"

"About…anything," she said, feeling helpless. "I

thought moving here was a good thing, for both of us. I wanted you to have a real house, a place to call home, a place that was safe."

He turned, a sad expression in his eyes. "Tyler's a nice place, Mom. You did the right thing."

"You're not happy."

Jon shrugged. "You don't have to worry about me. I can take care of myself." He filled a cereal bowl with water for the dog and went out the back door, leaving Marina with a heart heavy with worry.

THE IDIOT DOG WAS GLAD to see him. Jon patted her head and set the dish of water on the grass. At least someone was glad to see him. Christy hadn't looked his way this afternoon.

That hurt.

Either she hadn't seen him or she hadn't wanted to. Matt could have told her to stay away from him. Matt could have told her a lot of things.

And none of them would be totally true.

Or totally false. Like the trick questions on Wagner's history test last week.

Now Jon was stuck with Mr. Stanford's dog, a dumb-looking mutt named Tex who wagged her tail when anyone looked at her and acted as if she hadn't seen food all winter. Looked like it, too. No wonder Stanford had peeled out of here as if he was on a mission; he was probably afraid the damn dog would die of starvation before he got back.

Jon sat on the grass beside the dog. She looked at him, waited for him to give her instructions, then lay down beside him and panted. "Idiot," he said, watching her. "You're not the brightest dog in Wisconsin, are you?"

Tex stopped panting and gave him a hopeful look.

"Then again, you're smart enough to find yourself a few friends and a new home." He patted her head once again.

"Guess you're not so dumb, after all. You might even be smarter than me, you know that?"

The dog cocked her head and stared at him. Jon threw himself backward on the grass and closed his eyes.

Life sucked.

"I WANT IT," Clint declared. He'd waited until seven to call Ethan.

"Yes, I thought you would. It's the perfect bachelor haven."

"You can come out and fish whenever you like."

"Thanks. I'll take you up on that. My in-laws live on the other side of the lake, but my brother-in-law doesn't have much time to fish since he became a father."

"Do I know him?"

"I doubt it, but I'll introduce you."

"How much is the cabin, Ethan? Any idea?"

"I don't know. Hold on." Clint heard Amanda's voice in the background before Ethan returned to the phone. "Amanda said she'd tell the owner that she has someone interested and she'll get back to you on Monday."

"Any chance he'll change his mind?"

"Not from what Amanda's said," Ethan assured him. "I think you might be the only person who knows it's for sale. I don't think it will come cheap, though," he warned. "Waterfront property never is."

"I'll manage. Tell Amanda I appreciate being able to see it."

"Wait a minute." He came back on. "My wife wants to know if you're free to come for dinner next Saturday night. Be careful how you answer. She could be matchmaking."

Clint could think of only one woman he'd like to date, and she'd made it clear she wasn't interested. "Dinner sounds good, but tell her I can find my own women."

Ethan laughed. "I'll give her the message."

Clint hung up the phone a few minutes later, after agreeing to meet Ethan at the usual time Monday morning. Marge's Diner at six-thirty had become a weekday ritual for both of them. Then Clint opened the freezer section of the refrigerator and pulled out a frozen dinner: salisbury steak and mashed potatoes with gravy. He'd rather be sitting across a table from Marina Weiss.

For the first time in years, Clint regretted not remarrying. There would have been time for children. Time for a new life, with a family. Time for a lot of things. He tossed the plastic dish into the microwave oven and waited for his dinner to heat. Tomorrow he'd go to the market and buy a side of beef and a barbecue grill.

FIRST THING ON MONDAY Clint talked to Amanda about buying the cabin. She filled him in on the asking price and details of sale. He'd have to wait for the owner to return to Wisconsin before they presented a formal offer, but Amanda assured him there wouldn't be any problems. The cabin would likely be his, for better or worse.

All he had to do was stop by with a check to make it legal. And Clint sure as hell didn't mind doing that. He planned to talk to Marina anyway, to find out how the dog liked Alpo.

And then, he promised himself, he would back off. She'd made it pretty clear that she didn't want to go out with him. She was downright skittish just being around him. He wished he wasn't so damned attracted to her.

He must be a glutton for punishment, he decided. Or a Texan who refused to quit.

"You have a minute?" Douglas Wagner hesitated at the open door to Clint's office.

"Sure." Clint waved him in and watched as Doug shut the door behind him. "What's wrong?"

Doug gave him a grim smile. "We've got more trouble than I know what to do with."

Clint leaned forward, putting thoughts of fishing and women firmly out of his mind. "I'm listening."

"It's just a rumor, but I don't like the sound of it." He pulled out a chair and sat down. "Some of the seniors are saying that Jon Weiss started the F and M fire."

"That doesn't make any sense. Why would he do that?"

Douglas shrugged. "Who knows? I told you, it's just a rumor, but considering his behavior lately…" His voice trailed off as he looked at Clint. "The kid obviously has problems. You and I have known that for a while now."

"But arson…"

"I told you, it's just a rumor."

"Brad Schmidt was in the group that worked there." Clint frowned. "This could explain a lot."

"So were Matt Hansen and Tina Mallory. Two juniors and two seniors."

"Don't Brad and Tina date each other?" He'd had to put a stop to a few of their "romantic encounters" in front of Tina's locker.

"Yeah. They've had a hot romance all through high school."

"And Matt Hansen and Weiss are friends."

Douglas shook his head. "There's been some antagonism between the two lately. I don't know why, but this could explain it. No one is going to be happy with the guy who burned down Tyler's main source of income. A lot of fathers and mothers drew their salary from the plant, including Brad's father."

"I hate to think that a kid could do something like that."

"I know what you mean. You want to talk to him?"

"I don't think it will do any good. Not right now." Clint stood up and glanced at the clock. It was almost time for the first class to begin. "I think I'll call Matt Hansen in for a little talk and see what happens."

"Matt's a good kid," Douglas said. "But I'm not sure how much he knows."

"I'll find out," Clint promised. "I was responsible for the kids being at the plant in the first place. If one of them caused the fire, then I'm the one who has to uncover that fact."

"The whole thing's a mess. There was another article in the *Tyler Citizen* last week that said the insurance company won't pay to fix the place until they're sure it's not arson."

Clint's voice was grim. "Arson with no suspects."

"The truth has to come out sooner or later," Douglas reminded him.

"I hope the truth doesn't include any Tyler High students burning down Judson Ingalls's business. There's going to be hell to pay if it does."

MARINA LOOKED UP and smiled at him when he entered the office. A good sign, Clint decided, tipping his hat and walking over to her desk, although she wouldn't be smiling at him if she knew he suspected her son of having something to do with the F and M fire.

Matt Hansen hadn't had much to say, except that he'd been sick with the flu last December and had missed the last meeting of the science group. He hadn't been much help.

"Hi, Clint," Marina said, her voice low. "Amanda's expecting you. I guess you're buying the cabin?"

"As soon as my offer is accepted." He took off his hat and ran a hand through his hair. "How's my dog?"

"Eating everything that I put in her dish. I guess you were right about her being starved. And I'm glad you're paying her food bill." She smiled.

"I'll pick her up later and take her for a run behind the school."

"Since your dog-sitter is spending the afternoon in detention, I think that's a good idea. She's very, uh, active. Jon spent the weekend feeding her and playing with her. He's even taught her how to catch a Frisbee and she comes when she's called."

"In one weekend?" He sat on the edge of her desk. "Maybe I don't have a dog anymore."

"You have a dog, all right," she assured him as she picked up the phone. "I'll tell Amanda you're here."

"You don't have to," her boss said, opening her door. "I thought I heard a Texas accent out here. Are you bothering my secretary?"

"Yes, ma'am," he said, standing up. "And I'm enjoying myself, too."

Amanda laughed and held the door open for him. "Come on into my office. We'll talk business and give Marina a break from your Texas charm."

He pretended to look hurt. "I can't tell if I've been insulted or flattered." He turned to Marina. "What do you think?"

"I guess that depends on how you feel about Texas," she said, and he laughed.

He paused as he passed her desk. "How *do* you feel about Texas?"

"I've never been there," Marina informed him.

"You're missing something," he drawled as he followed Amanda into her office.

The only thing she was missing, Marina decided, hearing her boss's door shut behind them, was the fledgling rosebush Tex had dug up yesterday afternoon. She turned back to the computer screen and tried to focus on her work for as long as she could, until the Texan would walk through the room and disrupt her concentration again.

"Can I have the car?" a familiar voice asked. Marina looked up to see her son standing near her desk.

"Don't you say hello first?"

"I did," he insisted, smiling at her with that killer smile that always melted her heart. "Twice. You must be working on something important."

"Why do you need the car?"

"To go out to the Hansens'. Christy asked me if I wanted to study for the chemistry test together. She really needs help."

Marina tried not to smile. Jon looked pretty happy about the Hansen girl's problems with science. "That's nice of you," she said.

"I thought I'd take the dog. Christy said Tex could play with her dogs and run around the farm for a while."

"I don't know if that's such a good idea. What if she runs away?"

"Yeah, Mom." He rolled his eyes. "She's going to run away from three meals a day and sleeping on a blanket beside my bed?"

"You never know."

"Mom!" His look said, *Get real.*

"All right." Marina relented. "Take the car. Take the dog. Drive carefully and be home by six."

"Thanks, Mom. You want me to pick you up?"

"I'll walk." Marina reached inside her desk drawer for the car keys and handed them to her son. "Just don't lose Mr. Stanford's dog or you could be in detention for the rest of your high-school life."

He laughed. "I won't, Mom. Don't worry."

How could she not worry? Marina watched her son leave the office and hoped that Christy Hansen would be kind.

"I DON'T GET IT," Christy moaned, pushing the papers aside. "I will never as long as I live understand these equations."

"Look," Jon said, turning the book in her direction. "It's simple. You just—"

"I'm never going to be a veterinarian. Not at this rate."

She didn't have to be anything, Jon thought, staring into those blue eyes. She could just be Christy, with the red-gold hair and the cheerful smile and the way she had of making everyone around her feel good. "Sure you will," Jon said. "And you'll be great, too. Chemistry isn't bad, once you understand it."

"It's easy for you." She smiled at him and Jon felt his heart flip over in his chest. He really wished it wouldn't do that. "You're the scientific type."

Damn. She was making him sound like a science geek.

"That's *good*," she said, watching his face. "It wasn't an insult. I just wish it came easier to me, that's all."

"Lots of things are easy for you," he said before thinking.

"What do you mean?" She rested her chin in her hand and waited for an explanation.

Jon almost groaned out loud. He'd gotten himself into this one and now he had to get himself out without sounding like a jerk. A *scientific* jerk. He waved his arm around the large family room, its windows looking out onto freshly plowed land and whitewashed buildings. "Like where you live," he said.

"What about it?"

"You're lucky, that's all."

"Maybe you're right." Her expression grew serious. "We almost lost the place after my father died. My mother did everything she could to keep the farm, which is how we ended up in the dessert business." She smiled at him. "Have you ever had Yes! Yogurt?"

He shook his head. "I think I'd remember."

Christy scooted her chair back and stood up. "Follow me."

He did. She led him through the farmhouse and into the large kitchen. He'd been over to the farm several times last fall, but he'd never done more than tutor Christy and talk to Matt. A little boy sat in a high chair and banged the tray with a metal spoon.

"Jacob," Christy said, "keep it down, will you?"

The little boy grinned and banged the spoon louder, as if to see what his older sister would do. She laughed, and he tossed the spoon onto the floor and laughed with her.

Christy's mother turned from the stove and smiled at all of them. "Hi, Jon."

"Hi, Mrs. Marshack."

"Don't mind Jacob," she said. "He just had a bath and he's feeling frisky."

Christy winked at Jon. "We all spoil him." Then she went to the refrigerator and opened the door. "Jon's never had any of our yogurt."

"Help yourself," Britt Marshack said, stirring something on the stove. "Do you have brothers or sisters?"

"No. It's just me and my mom."

"I think I met her once." The woman smiled, and looked like her daughter. "It's nice of you to help Christy with her homework."

"We've got a big test coming up on Wednesday," he told her, watching as Christy pulled three plastic containers from the refrigerator and set them on the counter. Did she really think he was going to eat all that? He wasn't even sure he *liked* yogurt.

"Here," Christy said, prying the plastic covers from the containers. "You can take your pick."

Jon approached the counter and tried to look as if he wasn't starving.

"Chocolate, vanilla-strawberry swirl or mandarin surprise?"

"Chocolate, thanks." That sounded safe. He hoped. He watched as she scooped some into a bowl and slid it toward him.

"There," she said. "Tell me what you think."

He thought he was in love, but he couldn't say that. Instead he took a spoonful of the stuff, which looked like pudding. It tasted like ice cream, only better somehow. Different. "Is this some sort of secret recipe?"

Christy grinned. "Absolutely secret. Do you like it?"

"Yeah. It's good."

Britt lifted the toddler from the high chair and swung him into her arms. "Take some home if you want, Jon," she offered. "It's the least we can do for all your help."

"Bye," the little boy said, waving his hand.

Jon waved back, then picked up the bowl. "We should get back to studying," he said. "I have to be home by six."

"Okay." Christy made a face. "I'll do my best."

The back door opened as Jon picked up the bowl and started to follow Christy out of the room.

"Weiss," Matt said, letting the door slam shut behind him. "What are you doing here?"

"Matt..." Christy's voice held a warning as she turned around to stare at her brother. "Watch it."

Matt ignored her and glared at Jon instead. "I asked what you were doing."

"Helping your sister with her chemistry."

"She doesn't need your help."

Jon smiled, but he didn't mean it and Matt knew it. "You haven't seen her chemistry grades, have you?"

"You're a real smart-ass, aren't you?"

Christy took Jon's arm and pulled him toward the family room. "Come on, Jon, let's go finish up."

Jon stood his ground. He was tired of being blamed for

everything that had gone wrong in Tyler since he moved here. He was sick of taking the blame and letting himself be pushed around by every hometown country boy who dribbled a basketball or kicked a football. They all thought brains were something you ate with eggs for breakfast. "Stick it—"

Matt stepped closer, daring him to fight. "Stick it where?"

Christy tugged on his arm again. "Come on, Jon. Ignore him. He thinks he runs my life."

"You're not worth it," Jon muttered, following Christy out of the room. He was sick of them all, the girl with the red-gold hair was still smiling at him, and she needed his help. No matter what her brother thought.

"I'm sorry," she said, once they sat down at the table again. "He's not usually like that."

"Yeah."

"What's going on with you guys? I thought you were friends."

That was what hurt the most. Jon had thought he'd found a friend in Matt. He'd thought he was a nice guy, a guy everyone respected. Jon shrugged. "I don't know."

"*I* do," Christy declared. "And I'll bet it has to do with Brad. He's a real jerk, you know."

"You don't like him, either?" His heart soared.

She shook her head. "Nope. He's a show-off and he treats Tina like—" She broke off, frowning. "He's just a jerk sometimes, that's all."

"Tell your brother that."

"They've been friends since kindergarten."

"And I'm the new guy."

"I'm sorry."

"Don't be," he said, picking up his pencil. The look in those blue eyes was going to kill him. "One more year and Tyler will never see me again."

CHAPTER FOUR

AMANDA TOOK THE CHECK and slipped it to her side of the tabletop. "My treat," she said, over Marina's protests. "It's the least I can do after you worked late to finish that contract."

"I didn't mind," Marina said, embarrassed. The diner was crowded with people at twelve-thirty. Amanda had insisted they put the answering machine on, lock the door and walk down the street to Marge's for hamburgers and french fries. So far she'd met the police chief, the librarian and Anna Kelsey, a friend of Amanda's mother. Mrs. Kelsey was also the mother of Patrick Kelsey, Jon's gym teacher, a name Marina recognized from open house at the high school. By the time she'd finished her hamburger and the last of the fries, Marina felt as if she'd chatted with half of Tyler.

"We should do this every Wednesday," Amanda said, wiping her mouth with a paper napkin. "It sure beats yogurt and tuna fish sandwiches."

"Only if we take turns with the check," Marina said, still uncertain about letting Amanda pay for lunch.

Amanda nodded. "Fair enough." She looked around the crowded restaurant and waved to the waitress. "Let's get more coffee and pretend we don't have to go back to work. I loved this place when I was a teenager. We used to come here after school to hang out."

"A lot of teenagers were at the Dairy King Friday." *Including my son*, she added silently.

"That was the day you took Clint out to the lake?"

"Yes. We stopped for ice cream."

Amanda leaned forward. "Ice cream? How…fun."

The waitress hurried up with the coffee carafe and hovered over the table. "More coffee, ladies?"

"Please," Marina said, moving her cup forward.

Amanda smiled at the young woman in turn. "And thank you. How's your mother doing?"

"Much better. She got out of the hospital yesterday."

"Tell her I said hello," Amanda said. The young woman promised to do that and hurried off to the next table of customers.

"You know everyone in town," Marina said. "I'm constantly amazed. And envious, too."

"I grew up here. It's my home and I've never wanted to live anywhere else."

"That's very special," Marina said. "And unusual."

Amanda took a sip of her coffee. "I know. I'm a weird duck. Except for the years at college and law school, I've lived the same place all my life. I *like* my family and I'm a happy person. Not exactly someone who could appear on a television talk show, am I?"

"No." Marina laughed. "I don't think they do 'Truly Happy People in Wisconsin' shows. But they should," she added. "Just for a little variety."

Amanda made a face. "I've had enough publicity to last a lifetime."

"What do you mean?" Her boss looked like the last person in the world who would attract attention.

"Three years ago my grandfather was accused of murder."

Marina tried not to let her mouth hang open, but it wasn't easy to hide her surprise. "Your grandfather?"

"You didn't hear about it in Chicago, I guess."

"No. And you don't have to talk about it. I didn't mean to pry."

"That's okay. It's how I met Ethan, and everything worked out all right. I had to represent my grandfather, only I was never so scared in my entire life."

Marina couldn't picture her boss scared. But she could picture Amanda winning whatever case she set her mind to. "But you won."

"Yes. With a lot of luck." Amanda finished her coffee and looked at her watch. "I guess we'd better get back to the office." She made a face. "I have such a case of spring fever!"

"Take the afternoon off," Marina offered. "You don't have any appointments, do you?"

"No, but—"

"Take off," Marina insisted. "You've been working long hours lately."

Amanda put some bills on the table and stood up, hoisting her purse strap over her shoulder. "You might be right," she said. "Ethan's said the same thing, only he doesn't slow down, either."

"What about going on vacation?"

"I'd be happy just to stay home and not do anything," the other woman admitted. Marina followed her out the door and into the bright sunshine. Amanda paused on the sidewalk. "What are you doing this weekend?"

"Planting more flowers. Painting the bathroom. Spring cleaning." *Walking the dog. Renting old movies. Feeling a little bit more lonely than I want to.*

They walked down the shaded street, around the town square. "Would you like to come for dinner Saturday? I'm having a small party and I would love it if you joined us."

Marina's first impulse was to refuse. Politely, of course, but refuse all the same. She hated cocktail parties; it was so awkward to make conversation with strangers, especially in a town where everyone knew everyone else. "I don't—"

"Please don't say no," Amanda urged. "It'll just be the six of us for an informal dinner. I'm not much of a cook, but I keep practicing on my friends. I bought a new cookbook last week."

It was hard to refuse her. And if there were just five other people it wouldn't be so bad. "All right. What can I bring?"

Amanda laughed. "That's what everyone in Tyler always says when they're invited anywhere. This time I'm not letting anyone bring anything. I'm doing the whole dinner myself, straight from the book."

"Are you sure?"

"Positive. Are you on any special diet or do you have any food allergies that I should know about?"

"I just ate a zillion grams of fat at lunch." Marina made a face and chuckled. "And I loved every bite, so I don't think you need to worry about what I eat."

"Good," Amanda said, satisfaction in her voice as they approached the office. "I can't guarantee fat-free *anything*." She pulled out her keys and unlocked the door. "But come hungry and don't expect anything gourmet."

MARINA SHOULD HAVE expected Clint Stanford. The rest of the week had been so busy she hadn't given much thought to Amanda's dinner or the other guests. Somehow she assumed it would be Amanda's family; her boss had plenty of relations in town. But the large Texan was standing in Amanda's comfortable living room when Marina arrived. Of course her boss couldn't resist throwing them together. Amanda wasn't shy about matchmaking.

Clint wore shiny black boots, dark slacks and a pale blue denim shirt. He held a drink in his hand and he was in profile, facing Ethan in front of a bank of windows. He turned as Marina entered the room, Amanda beside her.

"Hello," he drawled. "I've missed seeing you this week."

Marina saw Ethan's eyebrows rise. Clint didn't have to make it sound so intimate, damn him. "Your dog seems to be thriving," she said as calmly as she could.

Ethan took her hand. "I'm so glad you could come. You're very brave, you know. My wife has recently decided to learn how to cook."

"She warned me." She smiled at her host. "I thought it was kind of you to include me."

Amanda waved toward the couch. "You'd better make yourselves comfortable. My gravy won't thicken."

"Can I help?" Marina would be more at home in the kitchen than she would in this luxurious living room with these two men. One looked pleased, the other intrigued, and neither made her feel the least bit relaxed.

"Nope," Amanda said, moving out of the room. "Have Ethan fix you a drink. The others will be here in a little while. They called to say they were running late."

"Amanda talks about you often," her husband said. "And since I've never talked to you more than three minutes at a time, I'm looking forward to visiting with you. What's this about a dog?"

Clint chuckled. "I hoodwinked Marina into taking care of a stray we found out at the lake."

"Temporarily," Marina interjected, taking a seat on a comfortable cream sofa. It was the kind of sofa someone with children would never own. "Clint's going to take her back when he has a place for her."

"You're not a dog lover, Marina?" Ethan asked, stepping over to an oak sideboard set up as a bar.

"Not exactly," she admitted, thinking of her uprooted rosebush. "My son is the one who takes care of her."

"What would you like to drink? I think we have just about everything," her host said. "Including beer." He gestured toward Clint, who took a seat near Marina on the couch.

"Just a little white wine, please."

Clint set his beer on the glass-topped coffee table. "Tex has gained weight."

"That's an understatement, don't you think?" The dog had doubled in size. Tripled, maybe. She took the glass Ethan handed her and thanked him.

"I have another week's supply of dog food in the Jeep. I'll bring it by tomorrow."

"All right." He'd stopped by to see the dog every afternoon, according to Jon. Marina had told herself she wasn't disappointed to have missed seeing him.

Ethan sat down in a sleek chair across from them. "I think we'd better make ourselves comfortable. Amanda's not going to come out of the kitchen until she's satisfied that everything is perfect."

"I wish she wouldn't go to all this trouble."

"Amanda loves a challenge," her husband said, a bemused expression on his face. Clearly he was a man in love with his wife, Marina realized. Suddenly the judge didn't seem quite so intimidating. She took another sip of her wine and started to relax.

"Don't most women?" Clint asked, his eyes twinkling as he looked at Marina.

She didn't try to hide her smile. "What is that supposed to mean?"

He shrugged. "Just an observation."

"From a bachelor," Ethan interjected. "Who should know better than to say things like 'most women.'" The doorbell rang, and Ethan excused himself. "Try not to get into any more trouble until I get back," he told Clint. "You may need a lawyer."

"What did I say?" Clint asked, pretending ignorance.

"Nothing," Marina assured him, as Ethan left the room. "I'm sure you know a lot about women."

He grinned. "Is that good or bad?"

Marina chuckled. "I suppose that depends on whether you're right or wrong."

Amanda hurried into the living room, a wooden spoon in her hand. "Did I hear the doorbell?" Clint stood as Ethan ushered a man and woman into the living room. "Oh, good," she said, spotting the rest of her guests. "I'm so glad you could make it!"

As Amanda made the introductions, Marina shook hands with Glenna Kelsey McRoberts and her fiancé, Lee Nielsen. Glenna was about Amanda's age, with dark hair and blue eyes and a slightly shy manner. Lee was tall, a good-looking man with a steady gaze and firm handshake. He and Clint appeared to know each other.

"We had a problem at the last minute getting a baby-sitter," Lee explained. "And Megan wouldn't settle down."

"She wanted to try on the dress Grandma made her for the wedding—yet again. I swear, Amanda, that dress is going to be ruined before we even get married," Glenna declared with a laugh.

"Glenna has two small children," Amanda explained to Marina while Ethan took drink orders.

"Which means we're always late," Glenna interjected. "It's always something."

"I have a teenage son," Marina said. "I know what you mean."

Lee shot her an interested look. "Really? So do I. How old is yours?"

"Sixteen. He's a junior at the high school."

"Jon Weiss," Clint explained, giving Lee a warning look. "One of my science-team members. You probably met him during the investigation."

"Yes," Lee said, turning to Marina. "I'd give a lot to be able to solve that particular mystery."

Ethan handed him a glass of wine. "So would most everyone in town."

"Thanks. I have a funny feeling about that case," he continued. "It's as if the answer is right under my nose and I can't see it."

"You're the arson investigator?" Marina asked.

"Yes. And not a very popular man in town."

"Don't say that," Glenna murmured, taking a seat on the couch beside Marina. She gave Marina and Clint an apologetic look. "It hasn't been easy since the F and M was shut down. Until someone can prove that it wasn't arson, the insurance won't pay the claim."

"There isn't anyone in town who isn't affected in some way," Amanda added. "My grandfather is determined to rebuild, no matter what."

"If anyone can, it's Judson," Ethan agreed, smiling at his wife. "How's dinner coming?"

"I've conquered the gravy," she announced proudly. "So all of you *will* be getting dinner tonight."

"We never doubted it," Marina said.

"Spoken like a true friend," Ethan declared. He turned to the new arrivals. "Marina is Amanda's legal secretary at the office now."

Lee leaned forward. "Where are you from?"

"Chicago."

"What brought you to Tyler?"

"I was tired of city living."

"And what about your son? Does he like it here?"

Marina paused. "He's having trouble getting used to it, but I hope he'll grow to like Tyler eventually. It's not easy moving to a new town when you're a teenager."

Lee nodded. "I know just what you mean."

"Oops, I forgot the appetizers." Amanda hurried off

again. Marina and Glenna looked at each other and, smiling in sudden understanding, left the couch and followed her.

"We'll help you," Glenna called. "Come on," she said to Marina. "There's no telling what she's doing in there. She might never come out again."

Marina decided she liked the younger woman. The two of them made their way through a wide dining room and into the bright kitchen, which was filled with delicious smells. Pale oak cupboards hung above white countertops. Hunter-green accents dotted the room, which had a butcher-block table at its center. The counter was covered with dishes, the sink filled with pots soaking in soapy water.

"We're having roast beef and whipped potatoes." Amanda pointed to a large pot on the stove. "I already fixed them. The vegetables are in the microwave and dessert is in the freezer. I hope that's enough."

"It sounds wonderful," Marina assured her.

Amanda dipped a spoon into a pot on the stove and frowned. "Maybe it isn't so thick after all," she said.

"Here," Marina said, going to the stove. "Let me make myself useful."

"All right," she said, giving her the spoon. "I'm close to giving up."

"What can I do?" Glenna asked. "Do you want me to take the appetizers out to the men?"

"Sure. Let me put them on a plate." Amanda unwrapped a block of cheese and set it on a plate.

Marina stirred the gravy and lifted the spoon to check the consistency. "Would you mind if I put a little more flour in this?"

"Not at all," Amanda said. "Do you mind that I invited Clint to join us?"

"Well, it's a little awkward. If you're matchmaking, you've picked the wrong two people."

Glenna grinned. "'The Cowboy' is quite gorgeous. I like his boots."

Amanda's eyebrows rose. "The Cowboy?"

"That's what the kids call him, or so Pat tells me," Glenna explained. They soon established the fact that her brother, Patrick Kelsey, taught Jon's gym class.

Amanda stepped closer to the stove and watched as Marina scooped flour into a small bowl. "I didn't know you could add more flour."

"As long as it's mixed with liquid. If you just shake it in, the gravy will have lumps." Marina added a little water and stirred the mixture.

Glenna opened a box of crackers and spread them out on a pottery dish. "I still say that Clint is an interesting man."

"He's interesting all right, if you like the type."

"The type?"

"You know. With all that supermasculine self-confidence."

Amanda and Glenna exchanged amused looks, then Amanda laughed. "He talked you into taking care of his dog?"

Marina shook her head and stirred the flour mixture into the gravy. "Yes. In a moment of weakness."

"I've had a few of those," Glenna said, trying to keep a straight face. "And now I'm getting married again."

"Laugh all you want," Marina told the laughing women. "But I intend to stay single for the rest of my life. It's easier that way."

"But not as much fun," Amanda added, peering into the pan. "Do you really think that's going to thicken?"

"I promise."

The rest of the evening went smoothly. The gravy thickened, the dinner was delicious and the company entertaining. Marina realized she'd forgotten how much fun it could be to spend an evening with adults. Clint sat to her left, with

Glenna across from her. Ethan, on her right, kept a steady conversation going among the six of them, and the laughter and good spirits were genuine. The evening passed quickly. Over Amanda's protests, Marina and Glenna helped Amanda clean up the kitchen. The three men joined them; Ethan made coffee and cut the black-bottom pie into six thick wedges. They ate dessert in the living room, and finally Lee and Glenna rose to leave. Marina looked at her watch and was surprised to see that it was almost midnight. She rose in turn.

"I'd better say good-night, too," she said. "It was a wonderful evening. And a delicious dinner," she added, turning to her hostess.

"I'm glad you came," Amanda said.

"I'll be leaving as well," Clint said, standing next to Marina. "Thanks for having me. I get tired of eating alone."

Ethan draped his arm over Amanda's shoulders as they walked their guests to the front door. "We're glad you came. We're glad *all* of you did."

"You don't all have to leave at once," Amanda protested. "I can make another pot of coffee."

Marina smiled. "Thanks, Amanda, for everything. I enjoyed it."

Clint shook hands with Ethan, then leaned over and kissed his hostess's cheek. "My compliments," he said. "And my gratitude."

He guided Marina out the door behind Glenna and Lee and into the cool spring air. A sliver of moon hung above them in a star-studded sky as they walked down the path to the driveway. As the other couple pulled away, he turned to her. "Do you need a ride home?"

"I have my car, thanks."

He nodded. "That's what I thought. I'll follow you home, just to make sure."

"You really don't have to do that."

"Humor me. It will make me feel better."

She knew she might as well save her breath. The man would do exactly what he wanted to no matter what she said.

Tex barked once when Marina drove up. Clint paused at the end of the driveway and rolled down his window to call a quiet good-night. Marina waved at him, shut her car door and made her way to the back door. Not until she'd turned off the outside light did she hear the Jeep pull away. Jon had left the kitchen light on for her, but the house was quiet. He'd probably spent the evening at his computer.

Marina greeted Tex, who came padding into the kitchen. She patted her on the head and told her she was a good dog. Satisfied, the animal returned to her bed upstairs. Marina followed her and watched as the dog went into Jon's room and took her place on the rug beside his bed.

"Mom?"

"Yes," she answered, pausing in the doorway. "Did I wake you?"

"No. I was just lying here thinking."

"About what?"

"Nothing much. Did you have a good time?"

"Yes." She decided it would be best if Jon didn't know that his school principal had been part of her evening.

"What was Stanford doing in front of the house?"

So much for discretion. "Making sure I got home safely. He was one of the dinner guests tonight."

Silence. Then Jon said, "Jeez, Mom, you're not *dating* him, are you?"

Her first inclination was to deny any chance of that happening, but Marina hesitated. She liked the man. She liked him despite his lady-killer eyes and Texas charm. Or maybe because of them. She was only human.

And only thirty-nine.

"No, but would that be so awful?"

She heard her son sigh. "I just don't want him hanging around here, that's all."

"I wouldn't worry about that if I were you," she assured him. "Good night."

"Night," he said. Marina walked down the hall to her own room and switched on the light. Was it wrong to feel lonely?

"Jon!" Clint caught up with the boy outside of Room 21 as Jon was about to enter detention. The boy's shoulders were rounded, as if he had the weight of the world piled on him. He turned, fear flashing in his eyes before he hid it.

"Yeah?"

"I have an offer for you. Alternative detention." Clint clasped Jon's shoulder and turned him around in the opposite direction, then walked him down the hall.

"What's that?"

"A new idea in education," Clint drawled, heading toward the double doors that led to the faculty parking area at the back of the school. "It beats sitting in detention for an hour, I promise you."

"Yeah, well, a lot of things are better than that." The boy stopped at the door and faced him, waiting for an explanation.

"I bought a computer system this weekend. Haven't taken it out of the box. You want to put it together for me?"

"It won't take an hour."

"Then you'll have to show me how it works."

He grinned. "That'll take *more* than an hour."

Clint opened the door and ushered Jon outside. "I might be smarter than I look." Jon's grin widened, as if he was thinking of a retort he didn't dare say out loud. "So? You coming with me?"

"I guess it beats sitting in detention. Should I tell Mr. Wagner why I won't be in there?"

"I already did." Clint watched as Jon looked around. The boy was afraid that someone was going to see him leaving the school with the principal. Why? Something was going on here, Clint could feel it in his gut. The kid was hiding something. Something serious, too.

And the kid needed a friend. Despite what his mother thought, Clint knew that Jon was in trouble. Marina would need to face up to that reality sooner or later.

Clint kept up a casual conversation during the short distance between his house and the high school. He had to drive past the town square. "Do you want to stop and tell your mother where you are?"

"I'm not ten years old."

"Guess that's a no, then."

"Sorry," Jon muttered, surprising him. "I didn't mean to sound like a jerk."

"No problem," Clint said easily, turning down the street toward his house. He wanted to befriend the kid, not alienate him. "How's Tex doing?"

"She's still eating a lot. She dug up another one of Mom's plants."

"How many do I have to replace now?"

"Two rosebushes and now some yellow thing."

"Is your mother angry?"

Jon shrugged. "Not really. She just gets a weird look on her face, but she doesn't say anything."

"I guess that's good?"

"If you ever saw her mad, you'd know that not saying anything is okay."

"I'll take your word for it." He drove into the driveway and parked in front of a small white bungalow.

"What kind of computer?"

Clint shrugged and got out of the Jeep. "Something that's supposed to have everything."

"What about a CD-ROM? I don't think you can buy a computer without it now."

"Yeah. I think so."

"Pentium?"

"What?"

"Never mind," Jon said, following him into the house. "I'll check it out for myself. Uh, why did you buy a computer?"

"I thought it was time I joined the twentieth century. Want a Coke?"

"Sure."

Clint opened the refrigerator and took out two cans of soda. He handed one to Jon. "Come on. I left the boxes in the dining room." He led him into the front room, where three boxes sat on a thick beige rug. Clint pointed to a wide oak desk in the corner of the room. "I thought I'd put it there."

"This is the dining room?"

"I use it for a study." He pointed to another door. "That goes to the living room and the stairs."

"You have an electrical outlet somewhere close?"

"Yeah. And I bought a power bar."

"Good." Jon bent over the biggest box. Clint handed him a jackknife and Jon proceeded to slit the cardboard and lift out the contents of the box. It looked pretty damn complicated to Clint, but the teenager didn't seem the least bit concerned.

"Cool," he muttered a couple of times, to Clint's relief.

"Do you need help with anything?"

"Just a Phillips screwdriver, I think."

Clint found one in the kitchen drawer and brought it to him. The boy looked relaxed sitting there at the desk attaching cords to various parts of the computer, monitor and keyboard. He looked confident, something that didn't show in school. Clint was determined to know more about this teenager. Despite the mystery, Clint liked him. And not just because he was Marina's son.

"How's it going?"

"Great," Jon replied, connecting something on the back of the monitor. "It'll be ready to turn on in a minute. I'll connect the printer first, though."

"I appreciate this."

"No problem," the boy said. "Like you said, it beats sitting in detention."

"How are things between you and Schmidt lately?"

Jon avoided his gaze. "I try to stay out of his way."

"Any idea why he's doing this to you?"

"Not really." Jon bent over the last box, the one that held the printer, and slit open the flaps. "He's an idiot, but he's a hometown boy, so that makes it all right."

"For everyone but you," Clint added, carefully keeping any hint of sympathy out of his voice. "Must be tough."

"I'll be out of here in one more year. I can take it till then." He lifted the printer out of the box. "You want this on the desk, too?"

"Sure."

"Left or right?"

"Left. There's more room."

Jon hooked up cables, plugged everything into the power bar and plugged it into the wall. "You're all set," he said. "You want to sit down and see if it works?"

"Sure," he said, pulling out a chair. Jon took the other chair and scooted it next to him. He showed Clint how to turn the computer on, then gave him a brief explanation of the operating system and how it worked. He ran the machine through its paces, giving Clint an overview of the system and what it was capable of.

"There's lot of stuff you can buy, especially on CD-ROM," Jon said.

"Do you have that on yours?"

"Yeah. I added it last year, but it's not as fast as this one."

Clint looked at his watch. "It's after four. Don't you think we'd better tell your mother you're over here?"

"It's that late? Okay. I'll call her." He reached for the portable phone that lay on the other corner of the desk.

"I'll start dinner. Don't look so surprised. I cook."

Jon grinned. "Yeah, sure you do, Mr. Stanford."

"You like chili?"

"Yeah. Who doesn't?"

"Ask your mother if she wants to come over for dinner."

"No way," Jon said, punching the numbers in. "No way will she say yes."

"Tell her you're doing me a favor, but don't mention the chili, and I'll bet she'll agree."

"Okay." Jon gave him a doubtful look, but his eyes glinted with amusement. And, to Clint's relief, he didn't look like a haunted kid any longer. "Hey, Mom. No, not yet. I'm at Mr. Stanford's house." He paused. "Putting together his new computer. Yeah, it's neat. He wants to know if I can stay for dinner. You, too. Wait a minute." He turned to Clint and handed him the phone. "She wants to talk to you."

"Hi," Clint said, trying not to smile as he heard her voice. She was hesitant at first, until he explained that Jon was helping him. "What time do you get out of work?"

"Five-thirty."

"I'm in the white house on the corner of Third and Morgan. Opposite a church. You'll see the Jeep."

"What are you up to, Clint?"

"Nothing," he replied blandly, and she laughed. He smiled into the phone, forgetting Jon was in the room. "Come hungry."

CHAPTER FIVE

"Is this the way they make it in Texas?"

"Yes, ma'am."

Marina scooped a cautious amount of chili and lifted the steaming food to her mouth. She hesitated. "I have a feeling I'm going to regret this."

"I didn't make it as hot as I normally would." Clint pointed to the bottle of hot sauce on the table. "You can add as much of that as you want."

She took a bite and swallowed. The chili was spicy and hot, hotter than she had ever tasted in her whole life. "Good heavens," she managed to croak, catching her breath.

Clint pushed her glass of beer closer. "That's what beer is made for."

She took it and drank half the glass. Her son watched her in fascination. "What are you staring at?" she asked him.

He hid his grin. "I've never seen you drink beer before."

"You've never seen me eat Texas chili, either," she countered, her eyes stinging. The beer, bitter and icy cold, cooled her burning mouth. She turned to Clint. "How much beer do you have?"

"Enough," he said. "What do you think?"

"It's, uh, good," she said.

Jon took a spoonful and coughed. "Why aren't there any beans in it, Mr. Stanford?"

"We don't put beans in our chili in Texas. We don't use ground beef, either. This is real shredded beef."

"It's very...unusual," Marina said, taking a smaller

spoonful this time. "But I think a whole bowl of this would kill me." In fact, the whole evening was rather strange, she decided. Sitting in Clint Stanford's kitchen was the last thing she'd expected to be doing tonight. And she wouldn't be doing it, either, if it wasn't for Jon. Clint could be right; the boy might need a man to talk to, after all. He certainly seemed happy enough. "How did everything go with the computer?"

"Fine," they both said at once. Then Clint chuckled.

"I'm learning the basics," he said. "And Jon has a lot of patience."

The boy smiled. "You've got a long way to go," he said, "but you're doin' okay."

"I guess that's a compliment," Marina murmured.

"I'll take it," Clint said. They ate in silence for another few minutes until he turned to Jon. "Got a date for the prom yet?"

Jon kept his eyes on his bowl. "Not yet."

"When is it?" Marina asked.

Clint answered. "Four weeks from Saturday. If you're going you'd better ask someone fast."

"I don't know."

"I hate to see you miss your own prom," Marina said, feeling bad for him.

He shrugged. "It's not that big a deal, Mom."

"It's going to be out at Timberlake Lodge this year," Clint told them. "Dinner and dancing from seven to twelve, then a postprom party back at the high school gym until four in the morning."

"And I'll bet you're a chaperon," Marina said, reaching for her beer. Her throat still burned, but the cold liquid helped, just as Clint said it would.

"Just for the twelve-to-four shift. I'll skip the first half and rest up."

"Can I be excused?" Jon stood up, his empty bowl in his hand. "I've got a lot of homework."

"Of course," Marina said, realizing Jon didn't want to discuss the prom. Being a teenager wasn't easy.

"Thanks for dinner," Jon said, setting his dirty dishes in the sink.

"Thanks for the computer lesson," Clint replied.

"You want me to take the car or should I walk?" he asked his mother.

"I'll drive you home," Clint said to her.

"You don't have to do that," Marina said. She watched her son pick up his books and head toward the kitchen door. She wondered if she should go with him, but she hadn't finished her dinner yet and she didn't want to hurt Clint's feelings by running off.

"See you later," Jon called on his way out the door.

"The keys are in the car," she called, hoping he heard her. If not, he'd find out soon enough. "Drive carefully."

"I'll put some coffee on," Clint said, going to the counter. He switched on the radio and country music played softly in the background. "Do you want any more chili?"

"No, this will be plenty," she said. He turned off the burner under the pot and then assembled the coffeepot. He lifted two brown mugs from the cupboard and set them on the counter before returning to the table. It was very much a bachelor kitchen. In fact, the other two rooms she'd seen had looked sparse, too. Neat, but a little too empty, as if the person who lived here could move out with three hours' notice.

"I hear you're finalizing the deal on the cabin," she said, as he sat down in the chair across from her.

"Yes. Amanda's doing the title search and drawing up the preliminary papers...." He stopped. "I guess you already know that."

"I typed them up this afternoon. I'm sure she'll be calling you. Congratulations."

"Thanks."

"Are you moving out there right away?"

"No. I'm going to stay here while I do the repair work. As soon as it's livable, though, I'll move out to the lake. I never did like renting."

"Have you lived in a lot of places?"

"When I was in the Air Force, yes. I grew up in a small town in western Texas called Crystal Creek that would make Tyler look like New York City, so I don't mind putting down roots and living in one place now. What about you?"

"I'm trying to get used to someplace so small that everyone knows my business before I do." She laughed. "I know I've been referred to as 'that new woman from Chicago' all year."

"I know what you mean," he said.

"Why did you move to Wisconsin? Why don't you live in Texas?"

"Too many memories," he said, the smile disappearing. "There was no sense going back, so I took this job and decided to become a fisherman in my spare time." He got up and poured the coffee. "Want to sit out on the front porch and drink this?"

"All right." And everyone in town would think they were seeing each other. Amanda would hear and would be chirping with joy at the thought.

He led her through the dining room and out onto the narrow porch that faced the street. Two wicker chairs took up most of the space. The air was perfect, not too hot or cold, and Marina smelled hamburgers cooking nearby. Someone was taking advantage of the beautiful weather and grilling their dinner.

"Thanks for having Jon over today," she said.

"He needs a friend."

"Maybe you're right. He does seem so...lonely lately. I keep thinking that once he gets used to Tyler he'll be all right."

"Maybe," Clint said, not sounding convinced.

"No matter what you think," she said, "he's not a troublemaker."

"I don't know what to think, Marina. All my instincts are telling me there's something going on with that kid." He paused, then added, "Do you date anyone around here?"

"What?"

He smiled. "I thought I'd change the subject before we got into an argument. I don't want to argue about Jon, and I *do* want to ask you out on Saturday night. Would you like to go to the movies?"

"I don't date," she said slowly, then took a sip of her coffee.

"Never?"

"Never," she replied, feeling a little ridiculous. Now she was stuck giving him an explanation about things that were none of his business.

"Is there a reason or is it just me?"

"I just don't date anymore," she replied. "It became too complicated."

"Complicated? In what way?" He leaned forward, his coffee forgotten in his hand, an interested expression on his face. As if he'd encountered a new specimen of fish bait.

She sighed. She'd gotten herself into this one, all right. "I don't want another husband," she said. "And Jon doesn't need a father. We do fine by ourselves. I support myself, which is enough as long as I'm careful. So why date?"

He looked surprised. "I guess you have a point. But don't you get lonely?"

"No," she lied. "I don't."

"You didn't explain why dating was complicated. You don't have to marry anyone you go out with."

"No, of course not, it's just that, uh, I don't want any romantic involvements in my life." He still looked as if he couldn't figure out what she was talking about. "You know, one date leads to another and then pretty soon the man figures we should go away for the weekend and…"

"Sex," he supplied.

"Well, yes."

"You have something against it?"

"No, of—of course not," she sputtered. "I just don't need the aggravation."

Clint laughed. And laughed some more. When he was finished, he asked, "If I promise not to, um, aggravate you, would you go to the movies with me?"

"No."

"Strictly platonic," he assured her. "As two new people in Tyler who don't have three hundred relatives in town and don't have the same best friend since fourth grade."

"It's not that bad."

"Yes, it is. I bought the damn computer for something to do. Jon showed me how to play solitaire on it."

"That's a pretty expensive deck of cards."

"Damn right."

"You're not going to make me feel sorry for you. I'm sure there are lots of women who would love to go out with you."

"Maybe I don't want the complications, either," he murmured. "Go out with me. Forget the movies. Let's go out to dinner instead."

"No."

Again that interested look crossed his face. "I thought we could be friends."

"We can, I guess," she assured him, and realized that she liked the idea.

"And friends have dinner together. We just did, as a matter of fact."

"Are all cowboys this persistent?"

He crossed his booted feet at the ankles and leaned back in the chair. "Of course. That's how we won the West."

"All right," Marina agreed. "I'll think about it."

"I'll pick you up at seven, Saturday night. We'll drive out to the lodge and eat something fancy for dinner." As she was about to protest, he added, "As friends, of course."

Then he winked at her, and Marina knew she'd lost. Still, she could do worse than have Clint Stanford as her friend. Whether she'd go to dinner with him or not was another story.

IF SHE SAID NO, he'd have to make sure he didn't sound disappointed. Jon cleared his throat and said, "Hey. No big deal."

He tried three more times until he was sure he got it right. "Hey, no big deal," was harder to say than he thought it would be. But then again, everything was. He'd been trying for days to find the courage and the privacy to make this call, and now there was no turning back. His mother would be home anytime now—he knew she wasn't going to hang out with Mr. Stanford for the rest of the evening—and then he wouldn't have a chance. He wrote the Hansen phone number in big letters, brought the phone into his room, closed the door and sat on the bed. Tex whined on the other side of the door, but he didn't let her in. He didn't want her making any embarrassing noises while he was on the phone.

"Hey, no big deal," he said once again, liking the sound of the words. Now all he had to do was dial the phone and ask her. He punched the numbers, then the phone rang twice before someone—a woman—said hello. Thank God. If Matt had answered, he'd be dead meat.

"Hello," Jon said. "May I speak to Christy, please?"

"Sure. Just a sec."

He heard the phone being set down, then heard Christy's name being called. In a few seconds the phone was picked up and Christy herself said, "Hello?"

Jon took a deep breath. "Hi, Christy. It's me, Jon Weiss."

"Hi!" She sounded happy. But she always sounded happy, he thought. He didn't know how she did it, but it was this major part of her personality that really made him want to be around her. "I wanted to call you tonight to tell you that I got a B minus on my test," she said. "Can you believe it? That's the highest grade I've ever gotten in chemistry."

"Hey, that's great."

"It's all because of you. So thanks a lot. You've saved my life this year."

"Hey, no problem." Now he was starting to sound like a geek. *Now or never, Weiss.* "I called to see if you wanted to go to the prom with me." He said it faster than he wanted to, but at least he got the words out coherently.

"Really?" she asked. "The junior prom?"

"Yes. To both questions."

She laughed, a little soft laugh that made him smile into the receiver. "I guess that sounded dumb, didn't it?"

"No," he said, his confidence increasing. "Do you want to go?"

"I want to," Christy said, "but I'm not sure I can. Can I call you back?"

"Sure." *You can call me fifty times a day. You can call me at midnight, you can call me at dawn. You can—*

"Can I let you know tomorrow?"

"Sure."

"Okay. Bye."

"Bye." He hung up very carefully and wiped his palms

on his jeans. He really hoped he lived through being a teen-ager. This crap was killing him.

"HI." AMANDA handed her a cup of coffee the minute Marina approached her desk. Marina took the mug, sipped and and set it on her desk, then sat down.

"Thanks," she said, giving her boss a questioning look. Amanda had never before met her at the door with coffee. "And good morning."

Amanda sat down in the extra chair and scooted it closer. "I can't wait to ask you. How was dinner last night?"

"Hot," Marina replied, thinking of the Texas version of chili. "You wouldn't believe how hot."

Her boss stared at her. *"Hot?"*

She slipped her purse in the desk drawer, then removed the plastic cover from her computer monitor. "I didn't know if I would live through it, but the beer helped."

"The beer," Amanda repeated, her eyes wide.

Marina glanced over and saw the incredulous expression on her boss's face. "We ate chili," she explained. "It was hot. As in spicy. He said that's the way they make it in Texas."

Relief and disappointment crossed Amanda's face, then she chuckled. "You can't imagine what I was thinking."

"I thought lawyers didn't jump to conclusions."

"This one does. And shouldn't have," she said, taking her coffee and standing up. "But it was an interesting thought while it lasted."

"There's nothing the least bit hot going on," Marina assured her. "I told him I'm not interested in dating anyone."

"Did he ask you out?"

"Yes. To dinner on Saturday."

"That means he's interested."

"That means he's lonely," Marina countered. "He's offered his friendship to me and to Jon, which I appreciate, but that's it.''

"Why?"

"I don't need a husband and Jon certainly doesn't need another father.''

"Jon will be in college, with his own life, in another year,'' Amanda remarked gently. ''You'll be free. Free to do anything you like.''

"I was married once,'' Marina said, turning to her computer to flick the switch to the On position. ''After that, I swore never again.''

"It was bad?''

"It was hell.'' She turned to Amanda, who still hesitated by her desk. ''Once you've been through something like that, you learn that living by yourself is a pleasure.''

"So you're not going out to dinner with him?''

"I said I'd think about it,'' she admitted, much to Amanda's amusement. ''Just as friends,'' she added. ''Nothing more.''

Amanda looked as if she was trying not to laugh. ''Of course,'' she agreed, her eyes sparkling. ''Just friends.''

JON WAS STANDING in front of his locker, after spending another hour in detention, when he felt a hand on his back, fingers tightening on his shirt collar, and suddenly he was hauled into the nearby janitor's closet. ''What—''

"Shut up, asshole,'' Brad hissed, loosening his grip, ''or I'll shove one of these mops down your skinny throat faster than you can yell help.''

Jon turned around and faced his attacker. ''Don't you get tired of this crap?''

The blond boy didn't blink. ''You don't take warnings very well.''

"I've kept my mouth shut,'' Jon insisted. ''You're the one getting us both in trouble.''

"Stanford followed your mother home Saturday night. You were at his house yesterday."

"What are you, Schmidt, the FBI?"

"Stanford's at your house checking on that dog all the time, too. I *don't* want any trouble."

"Then why the hell am I in a closet?" Jon asked, wishing he could hit Brad Schmidt in his big square face and knowing he'd be dead if he tried it. The larger boy's eyes narrowed and he looked nervous.

"I told you to stay away from Tina, and you didn't. And look what happened."

Jon's stomach rolled in fear, but he lifted his chin. "I didn't do it."

"No one will believe you. Especially after I tell *my* side of the story. I'm warning you, Weiss. One word to Stanford and someone's gonna get hurt. Maybe the Hansen girl, huh?"

"Don't you lay a finger on her," Jon growled. "She doesn't have anything to do with this."

"She might," Brad warned, sticking his face close to Jon's. "Unless you keep your mouth shut."

The door opened and a surprised janitor glared at them. "What are you boys doing in here?"

"Just talking, Mr. Ferris," Brad said, smiling for the man's benefit. "We didn't want anyone to hear what we have planned for Jessie Camden's birthday."

The man relaxed. "No one's out here, son. You get out of there so I can get my good mop."

"Yes, sir."

Jon hadn't uttered a word, but he nodded toward Mr. Ferris as they stepped out of the large closet. The man muttered something about foolish kids and bent over his equipment as soon as they were out of his way. Jon stopped at his open locker and Brad continued on down the empty hall as if nothing had happened. Jon wondered if he would be waiting in the parking lot to beat the crap out of him.

Just for fun, of course.

Jon got out the books he needed, cursed the fact that he didn't have a car and began to worry. All the way home he worried. He worried about his mother and Mr. Stanford. He worried that Christy might say she wouldn't go to the prom with him. He worried about Brad killing him, and Matt and everyone else in school who looked at him as if he was something they'd scrape off their shoes.

By the time he saw Tex all he wanted to do was go upstairs to his room and throw up.

CLINT DELIVERED two rosebushes and a forsythia bush to the Weiss front yard the next evening. He'd timed it perfectly, after dinner and before sunset, the calmest part of the day. Hopefully Marina would be too tired to protest, either his gifts or his presence. Call him crazy, but he was determined to do his best to convince the little lady that she liked cowboys.

Or would, if she gave one particular cowboy a chance.

The dog ran around the corner and barked at him, but the sound held little danger. "Hey there, girl," Clint said as the animal approached, her tail wagging. "Remember me? I'm the guy with the Alpo."

Tex sniffed his feet and trotted around him as he headed toward the front door. Marina came from the backyard, a trowel in her gloved hand. She wore worn denim shorts and a Grateful Dead T-shirt that looked as if it had once belonged to her son. It was a nice combination: shapely legs and denim. She didn't seem aware of how damned appealing she looked, though, as she approached him. Clint lifted one of the rosebushes. "Where would you like this?"

"What are you doing?"

"Making up for Tex's destruction."

Marina smiled. "You don't have to do that."

"I did already. Just tell me where you want them."

"In the back," she said. "But—"

"Show me," he said, eyeing those legs through the branches after she turned to lead him to the other side of the house. *Stanford, you are a brilliant man,* he told himself, following her.

Jon stopped the lawn mower when he saw the principal coming toward him. The boy looked a little pale, despite the sweat on his forehead. He didn't meet Clint's gaze, either, something that made Clint frown. This kid was one moody guy. He hoped he didn't get that particular trait from his mother.

"Hello," he called to the boy. "I remembered what you told me."

"Yeah. I can see that." He grabbed the dog by the collar and tied her to a length of rope attached to the one tree in the yard.

"There are more out front," Clint said.

"I'll get them," Jon offered, looking anxious to get away from him.

"Thanks." What the hell had changed since yesterday?

"Don't mind him," Marina said. "He's been a little...jumpy this afternoon. I think he's expecting a phone call."

"Must be a girl," Clint said, hoping it was nothing more than that. As much as he wanted to like Jon, the boy made it difficult. "They can do strange things to a guy."

"I'm beginning to realize that," she said, as Jon came into the yard with two bushes squashed in his arms. "He could have made two trips."

"No one under eighteen does anything the easy way," Clint murmured.

The boy dumped the bushes at his mother's feet. "There," he said. "Anything else?"

"Just the mulch. If you open the—" The sound of a phone ringing interrupted her words, and Jon pelted across the lawn, up the steps and into the back of the house.

Clint watched the door slam shut, then a second later the phone's third ring was cut off. "I guess he was expecting a call."

"I guess so." They shared an amused glance, then Marina turned away as if she was uncomfortable with the sudden intimacy.

Clint cleared his throat and looked around. A wooden fence separated her small yard from the neighbors on the sides, and a thick hedge guaranteed her privacy along the back. A wheelbarrow stood beside a wide strip of bare earth that ran the length of one fence. "I'll dig the holes if you tell me where."

"I guess I'd better take you up on that. Jon doesn't have his mind on landscaping tonight."

"It won't take long," Clint assured her, but he intended to stretch it out for as long as he could. Tex had provided him with the perfect excuse for dropping by and he intended to make the most of it. He would dig slowly, and then he would accept her offer of a cold drink. And if she smiled at him with any kind of encouragement he would approach the subject of dinner again. Clint picked up the shovel that lay on the ground by a bag of mulch. "Just tell me where," he said.

She showed him the spot where Tex had managed to destroy the last landscaping attempts, and Clint began to dig. They'd planted the two rosebushes before Jon appeared again.

"Looks nice," he said, jamming his hands into the pockets of his jeans. "Can I have the car?"

Marina glanced at her watch. "Isn't it getting late?"

"It's only seven-thirty."

"Where are you going?"

He darted a look at Clint, then looked back at his mother. "A bunch of us are getting ice cream at the Dairy King. I'll be back by nine, promise."

"What about your homework?"

"I can finish it later, no problem." He grinned at her and held up the car keys. "Come on, Mom. You know you're gonna say yes."

She couldn't help returning his smile. "All right. Just be home by nine, no later."

"Thanks." Then, remembering his manners, he turned to Clint. "Bye, Mr. Stanford."

"See you later, Jon."

"Be careful," Marina called as Jon hurried across the yard. She looked back at Clint. "What's the matter?"

He didn't realize he was frowning. "I was just trying to remember what it was like to be that young."

"Me, too. Sometimes I can't believe I was." She swept a lock of hair behind her ear and left a trail of dirt on her cheek. "The Dairy King and a clean shirt. There must be a girl involved."

Clint hated to break her bubble of young love, spring nights and ice cream, but she really needed to have a better grip on reality. "There's a kegger—a beer party—out by Timber Lake tonight. Brick Bauer already knows about it, so anyone there will be arrested."

"And you're assuming that's where Jon went?"

"I'm not assuming anything," he said, meeting her gaze. "I'm just telling you what's going on tonight. The seniors are feeling their oats, and I'm sure a lot of underclassmen will be involved, too. There usually are."

"Not Jon," Marina said, lifting her chin. "He doesn't lie."

"I hope so, for your sake. Because they're going to get caught."

"You're ready to think the worst of him, aren't you?"

Clint paused, the shovel poised to dig a third hole. He turned to look down at her. "Jon might be a good kid, but even good kids make bad decisions. And I think there are a lot of things that he keeps secret. I don't know what they are, but I'm sure as hell going to find out."

"He's not the troublemaker you think he is and he's not heading to a drinking party," she insisted.

"Good. I'd hate to have you get that particular phone call tonight." He took the shovel and pointed to an empty area next to the roses. "Is this where you want the forsythia?"

She ignored his question. "Is that why you came over here? To see if Jon was home?"

"Dammit." He pushed the shovel in the ground so it stood up, then he turned to look down into her angry hazel eyes. Or were they green? He'd like to take his time and find out. "I came to see *you*. Haven't you caught on to that yet?"

"I told you, I'm not—"

"Interested," he finished for her. "I remember." He lifted her chin with one finger and bent down to touch those soft lips with his own. She didn't resist, but she didn't respond, either. It was as if she was waiting to make up her mind. Or was simply curious. He lifted his head and took her shoulders in a gentle clasp. Now he would do it right. After all, she wasn't running out of the yard, just gazing up at him with a surprised look on her face.

He kissed her again, only this time he lingered longer, tasting, absorbing the soft texture of her lips. She didn't touch him.

He wished she would.

But she returned the kiss slowly, as if it had taken seconds to overcome her surprise. Or to thaw. She kissed him back, and heat hit him with a swift sweep through his body. Visions of dropping down on the carpet of grass and making love to Marina filled him, but Clint didn't move his hands from her shoulders, as much as he wanted to. He resisted the urge to deepen the kiss. Instead he enjoyed the feel of her lips, the heady scent of flowers and the smooth shoulders under his palms.

When he lifted his mouth from hers, he didn't move away. He stood there, waiting for her to send him away. Daring her to. But Marina simply looked up at him, the surprised expression still on her pretty face.

Dammit. Didn't she think he could kiss? "I'm not going to apologize," he growled.

Those green-gray eyes stared up at him and the woman had the guts to look amused. "I didn't expect you to."

"I've wanted to do that since I first saw you."

Her eyebrows rose slightly. "That sounds like a load of Texas…baloney. Aren't you known for exaggerating?"

Clint chuckled. "I wouldn't call it that."

"No?"

"No." He eyed those lips again, then decided he'd better quit while he was ahead. He reluctantly dropped his hands from her shoulders and took a step back. He wouldn't be exaggerating his need for her, but he didn't want to scare her off, either.

Tex barked, a "remember me" sound that caused them both to look over to her. She'd wrapped her rope around the tree trunk and couldn't move.

"Dumb dog," Clint muttered. "I'd better rescue her."

"You'll have to do more that that," Marina said, following him across the yard to the panting dog. "Tex is going to have puppies." He shot a surprised look over his shoulder. "What does that make you?" she drawled. "A father? A grandfather?"

"An idiot," he muttered. "In more ways than one."

CHAPTER SIX

JON WAS HOME at 8:55, a smear of hot fudge on his shirt and a smile on his face.

He didn't look like a kid who'd been drinking beer out at the lake. He didn't look like a kid who would lie to his mother, Marina decided with relief. He looked like a kid who'd eaten ice cream and had some fun with his friends.

"Did you have a good time?" she asked, hoping her position on the couch looked casual. She'd been trying to read a magazine; she'd been trying to listen to "Prime Time Live," but neither had held her interest. She kept wondering if Clint was right about the drinking party. She kept remembering the way his lips had felt. She kept reminding herself that she was happy being alone in her bed at night.

"Yeah." He flopped into a chair and stretched his legs out. "It was pretty cool."

"Who was there?"

Jon shrugged. "The Hansen kids and some other people." He paused, then reached down to pet the dog at his feet. "I got a date for the prom." He grinned at his mother. "Drumroll, please."

"Congratulations. Who's the lucky girl?"

"Mom," he groaned. "Cut it out."

"Who are you taking?" She couldn't help smiling. Thank goodness he wasn't going to let the fun parts of high school pass him by.

"Christy."

"Hansen?"

"Yeah." He couldn't help another smile. "Pretty cool, huh?"

"Yes."

"Come on, Tex," the boy said, getting to his feet. "Time for bed."

"So early?"

"I'm gonna read my English in bed," he explained. "Night, Mom."

"Good night, honey." She watched him saunter out of the room, the dog trailing happily behind him. She'd given up trying to confine Tex to one part of the house. The dog went where Jon went, period. To keep her downstairs would be cruel and unusual punishment. Marina didn't know what either one of them was going to do when Clint moved into his cabin and took the dog with him.

But she hoped he'd hurry up and take his dog. Before Jon grew any more attached to the animal and before the puppies arrived. And before Clint spent so much time over here that she became accustomed to having him around.

"HOW BAD IS IT?" Clint shoved his hands in his pockets as he stood beside Brick in the parking lot of the police station. He'd gotten the call from the police chief and, as he'd expected, a large group of high-school students had been caught drinking illegally.

"Last count seventeen," Brick said. "There are still a few hiding in the woods, but we towed their cars. We brought in anyone who flunked our little sobriety test."

Clint nodded his approval. "Good. Have all the parents been informed?"

"Everyone is on their way," the police chief assured him. "We've been trying to curb these parties, but it looks like this one got out of hand."

"I don't mind the kids having fun," Brick said. "But the alcohol part worries me."

"They picked the wrong place to party." Clint didn't bother to hide his irritation. The ink had barely dried on the purchase-agreement papers and a bunch of teenagers had picked his cabin for a drunken gathering. "I'm going to put a chain across the driveway."

"I don't think you'll have to," the policeman said. "As soon as word gets out that you own the cabin, the kids won't go within five miles of there."

"You sure there wasn't much damage done?"

Brick shrugged. "It didn't look like they broke in. They gathered on the beach and the dock. I bet there's some garbage around, but I don't think any of the property was harmed. We'll check it again in the morning."

"Thanks. I appreciate that. Damn kids."

Brick handed Clint a piece of paper. "Here are the names so far. I'll give you an update in the morning."

"Thanks." Clint turned on the car's interior light as Brick was called back inside the station. He ran through the names quickly. Most of them were no surprise, except for Brad Schmidt and Tina Mallory. He wouldn't have expected either one of them to be partying on a school night. They must have been caught consuming alcohol or they wouldn't have been brought in. No Jon Weiss, which meant the boy was home tucked in his bed or hiding in the woods. Clint's woods.

He turned off the light and switched on the ignition. He was done here; the rest he could take care of at school in the morning. But there was one more thing he had to do before going home.

A few minutes later he slowed his car as he approached Marina's house. Her car was in the driveway and the bottom half of the house was dark. Lights shone from the upstairs rooms and the porch light was switched off, which meant that Jon and Marina were safe and sound at home. The pregnant dog didn't bark, either.

Clint stepped on the gas and headed home before he was tempted to stop and kiss Marina good-night one more time.

"DO YOU WANT to talk about it?" Ethan thanked the waitress who refilled his coffee, then turned back to Clint.

"You're the juvenile judge." Clint hesitated. "I'm not sure I wouldn't be compromising your integrity."

"Let me worry about that." Ethan looked over at the piece of paper Brick Bauer had handed his friend. "Is that the list?"

"Yes," he said, folding the paper and putting it into his shirt pocket. "These are the names of the kids who were caught on my property last night."

"You signed the contract already?"

Clint nodded. "Your wife works fast. She pushed everything through for me."

"And I'm sure Marina helped."

"Amanda made certain of that."

"She's a hopeless romantic," Ethan warned, trying to hide a smile. His friend looked miserable, and he didn't think it was because a bunch of teenagers had thrown beer cans under his pine trees. "I'll suggest she back off if you want."

"No. I could use all the help I can get."

"The lady isn't interested?" Ethan didn't bother to hide his surprise. He'd overheard remarks about Clint's appeal to the ladies in town. There was something about cowboy boots that attracted women, though Ethan couldn't figure out precisely what the appeal was. Right now the Texan looked like he was attracting trouble and nothing more enjoyable.

"I can't tell."

"Women are tough to figure out," Ethan agreed. "Have you asked her out?"

"Yes."

"And?"

"She hasn't given me an answer."

"What's the problem?"

"Her son, I think. Jon. He's a junior and he's been in some trouble at school. I'm even wondering…" He stopped before he mentioned the fire. "He seems like a nice enough kid, but there's something going on underneath. I've stuck him in detention for three weeks."

"And Marina won't go out with you because of that?"

"I'm not sure. She seems leery of letting a man into her life."

Both men picked up their coffee cups and drank in silence, considering the problem.

"We need a fishing trip," Ethan declared, setting his cup down as the waitress dropped the check on the Formica table. "Men only."

"When?"

"Tomorrow night. Your cabin. We'll get up early Saturday and fish for our breakfast."

"Sounds good," Clint said. "I'll make chili."

"Mind if I bring a friend?"

"Of course not."

"Have you met Jake Marshack? He married a friend of Amanda's. A widow with four kids. His oldest stepson is Matt Hansen."

"I think I've seen him at some of the basketball games. Is his wife a redhead?"

"That's the one. I'll call him when I get to the office. Does Jon fish?"

"I doubt it."

"Maybe it's time he learned," Ethan suggested. "Maybe his mother would appreciate your taking an interest."

"You're a smart man, Trask." Clint reached for the check. "It's on me."

THE WORD WAS ALL OVER the school. The senior beer blast had taken place at Mr. Stanford's cabin. The isolated place that had seemed like a good choice for a private gathering had turned out to belong to the principal.

An announcement over the loudspeakers had informed students that underage drinking was illegal and would not be tolerated at the upcoming prom festivities.

One by one those students who had been taken to the police station were called into Stanford's office. Clint was pleased to see that Jon Weiss was not on the updated list Brick had given him at the diner this morning. Brad Schmidt was the final name, and the large teenager strolled into the office as if he didn't have a care in the world.

Clint didn't offer him a seat. He let the boy stand while he sat behind his desk and leaned forward. Technically there wasn't much he could do about after-school parties. He couldn't tell parents what to do about their own children, after all. But he felt strongly that a warning to each student involved in last night's escapade would be advisable.

Especially since the principal's property was involved.

"I hear you were one of last night's organizers," Clint drawled. "What made you pick that particular cabin?"

The boy shrugged. "You have the wrong guy, Mr. Stanford. I was there, sure, but I didn't have anything to do with setting it up."

"Then who did?"

"I wouldn't know that, sir." Brad's face softened into a friendly smile.

Sir. Nice touch. Clint eyed the kid with interest. It wasn't the first time the football player had stood in this office professing his innocence. "Try again," Clint said, this time with an edge in his voice that both of them heard. Brad's smile faded.

"I don't know, Mr. Stanford. Someone heard that it was empty, that the old guy who lived there had it up for sale."

"It's still private property."

"Yeah. It was a dumb thing to do."

"I was out there this morning. Luckily for all of you, there was no damage to the cabin."

Brad shoved his hands into the pockets of his jeans and waited for Clint to continue.

"I would be a lot happier if the mess that was left behind gets cleaned up before this weekend," Clint mentioned, the same thing he'd said to all the others. "Otherwise I might get cranky. I don't think anyone would like that. Especially you seniors. You have the most to lose."

"You don't have to worry, sir."

Clint didn't believe him for a minute. "Get back to class," he told him. "And stay out of my way."

Brad turned and sauntered out the door, as if to prove he wasn't intimidated by a mere high-school principal. Clint watched him go. There was something about the boy that was beginning to annoy him. He almost felt sorry for Jonathan Weiss, after all.

MAYBE THERE WAS a God, Jon thought. The same God that had stuck him in this town had also arranged for Schmidt to get his butt fried in Stanford's office this morning. A lot of kids had made that trip, and none of them had looked too happy for the rest of the day.

The word was that several people were going to be cleaning up Stanford's property this afternoon. He'd even heard that the senior prom could be canceled. As long as it wasn't the junior prom, Jon didn't care.

She'd said yes. Life was looking up. He dumped his books in his backpack and, preparing to head for the detention room, shut his locker.

"Weiss," a low voice behind him called. "Wait up."

Jon turned to see Matt approach. He didn't look too happy. "Yeah?"

"I hear you asked my sister to the prom."

"Yeah." He waited. Christy's brother looked as if he'd like to hit him. "You have a problem with that?"

"It's a problem, all right," Matt hissed, stepping closer. "I don't like my sister dating an arsonist."

Jon's stomach tightened. "I didn't do it."

"They're saying you did."

"They're wrong."

"Your word against theirs, Weiss."

"You weren't there."

"If I had been maybe I could've stopped it."

"There was nothing to stop. Everyone knows it had to be some kind of accident," he lied.

"Yeah?" Matt frowned at him. "Then why hasn't the investigator said so? Most of the town is out of work."

"I told you," Jon repeated, edging away from the boy he'd thought was his friend. "I don't know what happened."

"Christy likes you, so there's not much I can do about it. I'll keep my eye on you, though. We'll go out to the lodge in one car."

"Fine," Jon said. "Do what you want." He turned around and headed towards Room 21 before he was late. Let Matt think he was bothering him by driving. Jon would go to the prom with a troop of gorillas as long as Christy was by his side.

Stanford was waiting for him inside the door. *Speaking of gorillas.*

"Hello, Jon. Do you like to fish?"

"Never have." Jon didn't attempt to push past the man. He didn't want to antagonize him, either. He was having too good a day. *She'd said yes.*

"Then it's about time you learned. I'm inviting a few people out to my cabin for an overnight camping trip. Matt

Hansen is a friend of yours, right?'' Jon gave a faint nod. ''He'll be there.''

''I don't have any fishing gear.'' *And if Schmidt finds out I'm hanging out with Stanford, he'll shove me into another closet and beat the living crap out of me.*

''Just pick up a license and be at my house at five tomorrow. I'll clear it with your mother.''

''Thanks.'' Or at least that was what he thought he should say. A fishing trip sounded pretty cool. And maybe Matt would calm down and stop acting as if Jon was the spawn of the devil, out to burn down his precious town.

He liked Matt. That was what hurt. And he didn't blame him for wanting to protect Christy.

He was just protecting her from the wrong guy, that's all.

THAT WAS GOING TO BE the end of that, Marina decided. She pushed the grocery cart past the canned vegetables and headed toward the salad dressings. She wasn't going to go out with The Cowboy.

She wouldn't mind having him for a friend, but even that seemed a little too dangerous. Like befriending an elephant. You couldn't trust anything that big.

And you couldn't trust a man who kissed like that. My God, she'd been rattled for hours after he'd finally driven away last night. She'd told herself it was because she was worried about Jon, but even after the boy was safely in his room for the night, she'd still felt a little shaky inside.

Kissing and weak knees and invitations to dinner were not part of what she'd expected when she'd moved to Tyler. She was going to join a garden club and learn to quilt. She was going to drift slowly into old age and tend her flowers and sit on her front porch swing. She wasn't going to start acting like a teenager with a crush on a guy with interesting footwear.

Marina studied the selection of dressings and tossed three

bottles of Lite Ranch into the cart beside the two heads of lettuce. Jon didn't eat enough leafy green vegetables. She'd bet that Clint was a steak-and-potatoes man. And chili, of course.

She'd have to tell him she couldn't go out with him Saturday night. She shouldn't go out with him, of course. Not if he was going to lean down and kiss her every once in a while. He wasn't the kind of man who would be satisfied with "once in a while," either. She'd be deluding herself if she thought that was the case. He was obviously a virile man, and the look in his eyes had been anything but platonic.

Amanda wasn't helping any. She'd had Marina call Clint's office twice to relay messages about the sales contract on the lake property. Both times he'd sounded pleased to hear her voice. Neither time had he asked her to go out with him. She got the definite feeling he was waiting for an answer. It had been a very long Thursday.

Her answer would be no, of course. That would be the most sensible decision. And she was nothing if not sensible.

"Marina," said a man's voice—a voice with a Texas accent. And there was Clint, looking up from the meat display. He held a package of beef in his large hand and smiled at her. "Just the person I wanted to see."

Just her luck to run into him next to the ground beef. She wished she'd thought to put on lipstick before she went grocery shopping after work. "Hi, Clint," she managed to say. "Making more chili?"

"As a matter of fact, I am," he said, tossing the package into his cart on top of a plastic bag full of green peppers. Tomato juice, onions and five bags of taco chips filled the cart.

"It looks like you're having a party."

He nodded. "Out at the lake tomorrow night. I suppose

you heard that the kids' beer party took place out at my cabin last night?''

"No, I didn't know that." She gave him a worried look. "Is the place harmed?''

"No. They left a mess. Jon wasn't involved.''

"I know. He came home by nine, with ice cream on his shirt.''

"I'm glad.''

"Me, too." *Glad that I didn't have to eat my words last night.*

Clint cleared his throat. "Anyway, Ethan and I are going to christen the cabin with a fishing party." He moved his cart so he was standing beside her. "That's what I wanted to talk to you about.''

She waited, not believing that he wanted to invite her to go fishing.

"Matt Hansen and his stepfather are going, too. I asked Jon if he wanted to join us, and he did, so I told him I'd talk to you about it.''

"You already asked him?''

"A couple of hours ago," he admitted.

"Why Jon?''

Clint shrugged. "Do I need a reason?''

"Yes," she said. "I think you do.''

"He looks like he could use a break," Clint said. "Call it a way to repay him for the computer lessons.''

"You're certainly going out of your way for a 'trouble-maker,'" she said, remembering the man's words during that first meeting at the school.

"I like the kid's mother. And I'm starting to like the kid." He smiled down at her, willing her to smile back. "Give me a break. I'm doing my best.''

Marina considered the request as she moved her cart forward slightly to allow an older gentleman to pass. "Does he need to bring anything special?''

"No. I told him I'd supply the gear."

"This is nice of you." Jon needed a friend. He needed someone on his side, and who better than the principal of Tyler High?

"It should be a good time for everyone. I'll bring him home on Saturday afternoon. Are we on for dinner?"

"I don't know, Clint. I really shouldn't—"

"You can tell me Saturday," he interrupted, cutting off her refusal. He maneuvered his cart around hers and went up an aisle lined with soda pop. Marina stared after him, wondering how she could stop this very handsome freight train from mowing her down.

MARINA RENTED *Dr. Zhivago* and *Same Time Next Year,* splurged on microwave popcorn and a bottle of white wine and got ready for a cozy, solitary evening.

"This is weird," Jon muttered, tossing his backpack onto the table.

"What is?" She rummaged through a kitchen drawer. There had to be a corkscrew in here somewhere.

"I'm going out with The Cowboy and you're the one staying home."

She found the simple device and set it on the counter next to the wine. She'd have a drink while she soaked in a bath-tub full of bubbles. "So?"

"Shouldn't it be the opposite?" He grinned at her. "He's always looking at you and smiling."

"I don't go out with every man who smiles at me."

"It's not that I *want* you to go out with him," Jon said, pretending to shudder. "I'm just saying it's weird."

"I'm sure you'll have a good time."

"Maybe."

Marina looked up from trying to uncork the wine. "It was nice of him to include you in the invitation."

"Yeah, well…" He joined her at the counter. "You want help with that?"

She handed him the corkscrew. "Be my guest."

"It's a simple principle of physics," he said, taking the bottle. "Why are you drinking wine? Diet soda is more your speed."

"I don't know. I just felt like it." She watched him ease the cork from the neck of the bottle. "It seemed to go with the movies."

He made a face. "Pretty bad stuff."

"You've never seen those movies, kid. They're classics."

"Old-lady stuff, Mom. I thought you had better taste."

"Just because I don't feel like watching *Lethal Weapon* again?" The front doorbell rang and Tex, trotting across the hall from her favorite spot on the living-room rug, barked a greeting. "Never mind. The old lady will get it," Marina said.

"Sure I can't change my mind and stay home?" Jon called after her.

"No," she said, not bothering to turn around to see if he was serious about backing out of the fishing trip. She opened the door and Clint smiled down at her. He wore jeans and a navy windbreaker, and when he stepped inside he hesitated. "Hi," he said. "I'm wet. It just started raining."

"Come on in anyway," Marina said, waving him toward the kitchen.

He greeted the dog with a gentle pat on the head. "You can go next time," he promised her.

"Are you still going fishing in this rain?"

"Yes, ma'am," he replied, exaggerating his drawl to make her smile. "Those gol-dang fish ain't gonna be safe no-how no-where." He turned to Jon. "Hi. You ready?"

"Yeah." He set the cork on the counter and picked up his backpack.

"You have a jacket?"

"In the bag."

"Well, okay, then. Let's go."

Marina resisted the urge to kiss her son goodbye. He'd never forgive her if she embarrassed him. She wished he'd show a little more enthusiasm for the fishing trip, though. She wished he was five and she could take him into the other room and remind him of his manners. "Have a good time," she said, catching his eye and giving him a watch-your-mouth look. "I'm sure you will."

"Yeah, Mom. We'll bring back dinner tomorrow."

She'd take that as an attempt at humor.

"That's what I like," Clint said. "An optimist."

As soon as they were out the door, Marina poured herself a glass of wine and said a silent prayer that all would go well.

"IT'S LADIES' NIGHT at the farm," Amanda said. "Britt thought we should drive over there and have dinner with her. I said yes for both of us."

"What?" Marina glanced toward the television. Alan Alda was looking romantic. Too bad he wasn't wearing cowboy boots. "I'm, um, pretty well settled in for the night, Amanda."

"I don't want you to be alone," her boss said. "And it's about time you met Britt. Come on, it'll be fun."

"I don't—"

"Pick you up in fifteen minutes," Amanda said, and hung up the phone.

Marina looked down at her rumpled jeans. At least she was dressed, having decided to have her bath in between movies. She took a last sip of her wine and ran her fingers through her hair. The movies could wait, and so could the bubble bath. Jon had talked about the farm for months now. Maybe it was time she met Christy and learned what the attraction was. Maybe Amanda was right: it would be fun.

Marina couldn't remember the last time she'd done something fun with a group of women. She'd been by herself for so long now, she'd forgotten what it was like to have a good time.

"WHO WANTS MORE?"

Matt and Jon spoke at once. "I do," they said.

Clint dipped a ladle into the pot and refilled their bowls with chili. He was amazed at how much they could eat and not seem to get full. Like two ticks on a heifer's ear, the boys were. And about as communicative. Ethan's idea might not have been the best he'd ever had.

The boys clearly didn't have much to say to each other. Which was odd, because Jake spoke as though Jon had been a frequent visitor out to the farm. Could the Hansen girl need *that* much help with her chemistry assignments? And Marshack spoke as if Jon had been Matt's friend.

Ethan and Jake leaned on the Formica table and debated what kind of bait should be used in the morning. Clint had bought the contents of the boathouse, too, so the men were hoping to get the motor on the boat up and running. If not, there were oars and two teenage boys who needed exercise.

When everyone was through eating, Clint told the boys they could unroll their sleeping bags on the front porch. When they disappeared onto the porch, Clint shut the door behind them and returned to the kitchen.

"Maybe this wasn't such a good idea," he said to Ethan. "I can't get anywhere with that kid."

"It takes time," Jake assured him. "It wasn't easy for me to be accepted as a stepfather, but we worked it out. And Matt was the toughest one."

"I've no intention of being a stepfather," Clint said, keeping his voice low and accepting the glass of whiskey a sympathetic Ethan pushed toward him. "I can't even get that woman to go out with me."

"Jon's mother?" Jake asked, looking at both men. "You matchmaking?"

The judge winced. "No, but my wife is."

"I could use all the help I can get," Clint admitted. "Marina isn't interested."

"And the kid?"

"Is hard to figure out. One day he acts like any normal teenager, then the next minute he's in trouble, sitting in my office and telling me it won't happen again. Then he acts like he's scared spitless to talk to me."

Jake chuckled. "Having any better luck with the mother?"

"Not really."

"There are a lot of women in Tyler," Jake suggested. "You can cut your losses and move on."

Clint took a deep swallow of the whiskey, letting the liquid slide down his throat in a smooth burn. It settled in his stomach and warmed him. Maybe Jake was right. There were other women in town. He didn't have to keep being rejected by Marina Weiss. Surely there were other women with a good pair of legs and a pleasant smile and green-hazel eyes that melted a man's heart just to look at them. There would be other women with lips that drove him crazy and an I'm-happy-by-myself-leave-me-alone attitude that made him want to prove her wrong by taking her to bed and showing her that being alone couldn't give her the pleasure that he could.

Jake and Ethan exchanged a quick glance as Clint swore under his breath.

Ethan broke the silence. "Anyone up for a game of cards?"

"Sounds good to me," Jake replied. "Nickel poker?"

"Sure," Clint said, more than willing to get his mind off Marina. "I'll get the cards."

He stepped outside into the darkness and walked to the

Jeep to retrieve the last cardboard box of supplies. He shut the car door quietly, unwilling to disturb the quiet of the night. On the way back he moved down the dirt path toward the lake, trying to get a better glimpse of the moon. The trees, beginning to leaf out, blocked his view. He heard one of the boys say, "Jeez, man. You're the one who wasn't there."

Then silence for a long moment. Matt's voice, deeper and slower, came out of the darkness. "Why'd you do it?"

Clint couldn't hear the response, though he would have given a day's pay to know what they were talking about.

"—Off my tail," Jon said. There was more Clint couldn't hear, and he didn't try. Whatever was going on between them, the kids would have to make their own peace. He turned to go back to the cabin, but Jon's voice stopped him.

"...Right about one thing, Hansen," the boy said, his words clear in the stillness. "The fire was no accident."

CHAPTER SEVEN

"CHRISTY LIKES your son. A lot," Britt confided. "She's so excited about the prom that she's driving me crazy."

"She's a sweet girl." Christy had served coffee and yogurt cheesecake to her mother's company, all the while chatting about nothing in particular. Which was the difference between girls and boys, Marina realized. Girls chatted; boys didn't. It was that simple. Boys didn't open their mouths unless they had something to say or needed to put food inside.

"I like her," Britt said, chuckling. "She's growing up fast, though. I wish I could keep her little. And instead she's dreaming of proms."

Marina watched as the redheaded woman lifted her little boy from his high chair and into her arms. Jon had been little like that once, with sticky fingers that wrapped around her neck and tousled curls that tangled with her own. "Jon's looking forward to it, too."

"It was nice of him to ask her. He's been a godsend for Christy and this chemistry class she insisted on taking. She got special permission to take advanced science classes, so she'd have a better chance of getting into veterinary medicine. I don't know how she does it."

"Jon's enjoyed helping her." Of course, that was an understatement of gigantic proportions. Her son had practically run to the car to go to the farm every time Christy Hansen called him for help.

Amanda passed the bowl of popcorn to Marina. "Have you bought the dress yet?"

"No." She rolled her eyes and adjusted her grip on the little boy. "We're still shopping for the *perfect* dress."

"What's the perfect dress supposed to look like?"

"Short, black and sophisticated," Britt said.

Amanda nodded. "With that red-gold hair, I'll bet she's stunning in black."

"Just let Jon know, so he can get flowers the right color," Marina added.

Britt laughed. "It gets complicated, doesn't it?" She pushed the high chair from the table. "Let me put this guy to bed. I'll be back in about five minutes."

"Need help?" Amanda asked.

"No, thanks. It won't take long." She disappeared around the corner, Jacob waving goodbye with a pudgy hand.

"I remember when Jon was that age. I don't think I could go through that again."

Amanda looked thoughtful. "I'm not sure I can go through it at all."

"Having babies, you mean?" Marina wasn't sure what to say. "Do you mean you can't have children or you don't want to?"

Amanda gave her a bemused smile. "I'm not sure I want to, and Ethan isn't either."

"If you're not sure—"

"Then we shouldn't," Amanda finished for her. "I know. I feel guilty sometimes because I think I *should,* you know? But I love my job and I love my husband and I love my nieces and nephews, and somehow that seems like enough."

"What matters is that you be happy with your own decision, whether it's to have six kids or none at all."

Amanda smiled. "Would you have more children, if you married again?"

"No way. I'll be forty this year."

"Lots of women in their forties are having children."

"I've no intention of marrying again, either," Marina insisted. "No matter how hard you try to fix me up with that Texas cowboy you like so much."

"What am I missing?" Britt asked, coming into the room. "It sounds interesting."

"That was fast," Amanda said.

"Christy took over for me." Britt sat down at the table and leaned back in her chair. "Boy, am I glad to sit down." She looked at both of them. "Did I hear the words 'Texas cowboy'?"

"Amanda wants to know if I would have more children," Marina said. "And I told her absolutely not."

Britt grinned. "What does that have to do with our handsome principal?"

"He has the hots for Marina," Amanda explained. "And she's not making it easy for him."

"I didn't know I was supposed to make anything easy for him."

Britt looked at her with sympathy. "He's not your type?"

"Well…" Marina hesitated, remembering the kiss. He'd been very much her type that evening, when he'd kissed her and she'd kissed him right back. Eventually.

The other women waited for an answer.

"You're blushing," Amanda said with her customary frankness. She turned to Britt. "I guess that answers your question."

Marina opened her mouth to protest. "I don't want to get involved with anyone," she insisted.

"He's a good-looking man," Britt said. "I can't blame you for being interested."

"She's not interested." Amanda picked up her coffee cup and grinned. "Can't you tell? She's keeping his dog at her house, and she's been to his house for dinner."

"Friendship," Marina said. "That's all it is."

"Friendship," Amanda echoed, rolling her eyes toward Britt. "If I was a betting woman, I'd put my money on The Cowboy."

"You'd lose."

They both turned to Britt, who threw her hands in the air. "Don't look at me! I've got enough problems around here with two teenagers."

Marina silently agreed.

"HE'S A NATURAL." Clint tossed the cleaned fish into Marina's sink. "The kid picked it up real easy."

Jon grinned at his mother and tipped his baseball cap off his forehead. "I caught most of 'em," he announced, bending down to scratch Tex behind the ear. The dog went to each person, hoping for a little attention, but stopped beside Jon and panted with joy.

Marina eyed the pile of fish in her sink. A distinctly fishy odor wafted from them, mingling with the smell of rain and mud on Clint and Jon's clothing. "What do I do with them?"

"Fry them. Or bake them," Clint said. He wore tight jeans and a battered pair of boots that looked as if they'd traveled across the entire state of Texas. His flannel shirt was clean, though, and the brown plaid material made his eyes look darker.

"How? I've never cooked anything with…eyes before."

"I'll cut the heads off," he offered. "If you just want fillets."

"Thank you. I'd like that." She turned to her son. "You had a good time?"

"Yeah," Jon said, unzipping his jacket. "We've been up since five. It was pretty cool."

High praise. Marina glanced over to Clint, who removed his denim jacket and leaned against the counter. "You have a sharp knife?" he asked. "If not, I've got one in the car."

"Behind you," she said, indicating the wooden knife holder in the corner.

Jon tossed his jacket over a chair. "Did you watch your movies, Mom?"

"No." She grabbed the cutting board and set it near the sink. Clint looked determined to decapitate the fish right this minute. "I went to a party." Two heads swiveled in her direction. "Amanda and I went to Britt Marshack's house last night."

"Did you, uh, see Christy?"

"Yes. She seems like a nice girl."

"Yeah," her son said, smiling at nothing. "She's okay."

Which was definitely an understatement, Marina thought, hiding a smile. "Why don't you take Tex out for a walk? I took her this morning, but she likes the rain a lot more than I do."

"Yeah, sure." He put his jacket on, all the while asking the dog if she wanted to go out. Tex ran around in circles, wagging her tail, her toenails clicking on the linoleum floor, until Jon hooked her up to the leash. She waited impatiently for him to open the back door, then led him outside.

"I'll put these in a garbage bag if you have one."

Marina turned, the smile still on her face, as she faced The Cowboy. She wished he wasn't quite so good-looking, in that earthy Western way. He caught her smile and the corners of his eyes tilted. "Are we having dinner together tonight?"

"Tonight?"

"Yes," he said. "I remember asking you. Saturday. To dinner."

She had to stand next to him to get the garbage bags from the cupboard under the sink. "Isn't it getting late?"

"It's only four o'clock. I could pick you up at seven."

"I don't think that's such a good idea." She handed him

the plastic bag and watched as he cleaned up the mess from the fish.

"We've been through this before, Marina," he said, turning on the water and washing his very large hands.

She wanted to go out with him, she wanted to say yes, but there were other things to consider. Like the complications that could develop from dating anyone. Not that Clint Stanford was just "anyone." He was a special man. And then there was the problem of what Jon would say. So far he'd accepted Clint as a family acquaintance, a necessary evil. Lord only knew what her son would say if he knew she'd kissed The Cowboy. In the backyard, no less.

She didn't want to hurt Clint's feelings, so she thought quickly. "What if we cook the fish? I'll put some potatoes in to bake and make a salad."

He looked amused, which surprised her. "Just the three of us, huh?" Marina handed him the towel that hung by the sink and he dried himself off. "That's not exactly the romantic dinner I had planned."

"Whatever happened to going out as friends?"

"I lied," he said, stepping closer. He put those large hands on her shoulders and looked down into her face. "I want to do this," he whispered, touching his lips to hers for a brief, enticing second. "And this," he added, pulling her closer to him so that her breasts touched his chest. He kissed her again, this time lingering long enough to send frissons of sensation throughout her spine.

"Nice," he murmured, lifting his head slightly.

"Jon—"

"Is walking the dog," he finished for her, nuzzling her lips with his, dropping his hands to her waist. "I knew that animal would come in handy."

She couldn't help it. She twined her arms around his neck and slanted her mouth for his kiss. Crazy, she knew, but she was unable to resist the solid warmth of his body against hers.

It had been a long time. She'd forgotten how hard a man's chest could be. He urged her lips apart, taking the kiss to a new level of sensation.

SHE SEEMED TO MELT into him, Marina thought later, after the kiss was over. Jon's voice, talking to the dog in the yard, had stopped what had been an earthshaking embrace. Maybe it was the day. Maybe it was the Texan. Maybe it was her own silly, empty heart. Whatever had caused her to dissolve into Clint's embrace wouldn't happen again.

He'd gone home to change. He would be returning for dinner, a little family dinner for three, which was better than going out alone with him.

At least she hoped so.

Tonight she would cook fish and bake potatoes and microwave a couple of boxes of broccoli. She would offer the Texan a glass of wine and a cup of decaffeinated coffee and, as the evening darkened, she would stay out of his arms.

THE RAIN CONTINUED, matching Clint's mood. The fishing party had gone well, from a fish-catching standpoint. Ethan and Jake had been good company, and Matt and Jon had formed some kind of uneasy truce. It had been hard for the kid to remain distant when he was the one catching most of the fish.

But the conversation Clint had overheard last night continued to haunt him. *The fire was no accident.* What in hell was that supposed to mean?

It meant that Jon Weiss knew a lot more than he was saying, that's what it meant.

Clint parked in front of Marina's house and hurried through the rain to her front door. He would have preferred a quiet, intimate evening in a candlelit restaurant, so he could pretend that she didn't have a son. But he was going to sit at her kitchen table instead. He would eat his fish and sit across the table from a kid who could have set the F and M on fire. He would have to pretend nothing was wrong. Just the way he'd been pretending since last night.

She opened the door as he approached the narrow front porch. Her dark hair was soft and fluffy against her shoulders and she wore wheat-colored jeans and a pale green silk shirt. And she smiled at him as he handed her the bottle of wine he'd stopped to buy on the way over.

Clint's resolution to make it a short evening faded as he caught a whiff of perfume.

"Hi," she said, setting the bottle on a little table by the door. "I hope you're hungry."

He knew he should back up and run out into the dreary night, but he stood his ground. The smiling woman had made him dinner. He'd been trying to figure out how to get a date with her for several weeks now, and here was his big chance. Or close to it.

He could walk out now, and leave Marina and her son alone. Or he could stay, figuring his attraction to the woman would wear off.

Clint stepped inside the door and removed his Stetson. "Good evening," he said, pausing to wipe his feet on the mat inside the door. "Sure smells good in here."

"I made dessert," she said.

"It smells like chocolate cake." He took off his jacket and she hung it in the hall closet.

"Yes," she said, turning around and collecting the wine. "Come on into the kitchen and tell me how I should cook this fish."

"Where's Jon?"

"Upstairs doing homework, he said. I think he's playing games on his computer instead."

"You don't have to worry about his grades, do you?"

"No. It's always come easy to him."

Clint attempted a casual-sounding query. "Was Jon's father that way, too?"

"No."

So much for that question. He tried again. "So he gets his scientific genes from his mother?"

She considered the question as she handed him the corkscrew. "Possibly. I have a logical mind. I was better at math than science in school, though."

"Where did you go to college?" He made short work of opening the wine and filled the two glasses she'd set on the counter.

"I didn't. I went to a secretarial school and then got married and had Jon." She handed him a glass of wine. "Cheers."

He touched his glass to hers. "To successful fishing trips."

"Jon had a good time." She led him over to the kitchen table and sat down. "He wants to buy a fishing pole now."

"And that surprises you?"

"It's a little out of character," she admitted. "He's never been much of an outdoors kind of kid."

Clint pushed his glass aside and leaned forward. "How did Jon meet Matt Hansen?"

"On the science team last fall. That was a great experience for Jon."

"Yeah. Until the place burned down." Suddenly Clint didn't want to talk about the fire anymore. He would rather talk about wine, fish or pregnant dogs. He had the uncomfortable and growing feeling that high-school students had been involved in the biggest disaster the town had faced in years. Marina would be dealing with the problem soon enough.

"So," he said, "how's Tex?"

"Your dog is as cheerful as ever. She follows Jon around when he's home."

"I'll take her to the vet this week, make sure she's okay."

"What am I going to do with puppies?"

"I can build a pen in the backyard," he offered. "The weather's nice enough, and if I build a house and room to run, they should be safe."

"Well…"

"I can't take them out to the lake when no one is living there. At least, not yet."

"Are you moving out there for the summer?"

"Definitely. As soon as school is out."

She took another sip of wine. "And you'll take Tex and her family with you?"

"Promise." He grinned. "Unless you decide you want to keep her."

"No way, cowboy. You conned me once. You won't do it again." Her green eyes sparkled at him.

He grinned. He couldn't help it. "I probably could."

Marina shook her head. "You caught me in a weak moment. The hot fudge sundae had lulled me into stupidity."

"You just have a soft heart. I can tell."

Her smile dimmed. "No. I'm a lot tougher than I look."

Clint studied her for a moment. "Where's Jon's father?"

"I have no idea. Roasting in hell, maybe, if we're very, very lucky."

He cleared his throat. "It was that bad?"

"Marriage to James Weiss was worse than you could imagine. I thought I was marrying the boy next door. Instead he was an angry man who couldn't control his temper. Or his fists."

"He hurt you?"

"He certainly did." She stood up and went over to the stove. "I got out my biggest frying pan," she said, effectively changing the subject. "Is this what you need?"

"And Jon? Did he hurt him, too?"

"No. I left him before he could, when Jon was only two."
Marina picked up a spatula. "The cookbook said something
about dredging the fillets in flour before frying. Is that what
you want to do?"

It didn't make sense. She'd been on her own for fifteen
years, then. And she liked it that way. Which, of course, he
didn't blame her for. If she'd been married to some son of
a bitch who hurt her, then she wouldn't be too thrilled to
get involved again. But hell, most men weren't bastards.
Most men would cherish a woman like Marina.

He would, if he was interested in marrying again. Which
he wasn't. He couldn't resist one more question, though. He
went over to the stove and looked at the pan. "That's fine,"
he assured her. "I can fry up a mess of fish in that, no
problem.... So, you never married again?"

"I came close. After that I decided to be on my own."
She looked up at him, her expression serene. "And it's
worked out quite well."

He thought of the past three winters he'd spent sleeping
alone. "You don't get lonely?"

She shrugged. "I get over it."

"We'll need salt and pepper." Clint rolled up the sleeves
of his denim shirt and prepared to fry some fish.

HE WAS OVERWHELMING, Marina decided. That was the
problem. The Cowboy was too big, too strong, too curious
and took up too much space in her small kitchen. Even after
they'd moved to the dining room to eat dinner, he still
seemed too large for the oak, pressed-back chair.

And he asked too many questions. He'd kept Jon talking
about the science team for the past ten minutes.

"Did you notice anything strange that Saturday?" Clint
asked.

Jon took his time answering, Marina noted. "Strange like what?"

"The four of you were there the day before the fire. Did you notice anything at all different from the other Saturdays?"

"Not really. Matt Hansen wasn't there. He was sick. Tina was upset about that because Matt was the one who was supposed to type up the notes that day, and she got stuck with it."

Marina passed the bowl of baked potatoes to Clint. "Would you like another?"

"Sure," he said, forking one onto his plate. "They're real good."

"Thank you. So was the fish."

Her son smiled. "Yeah. Real fresh, don't you think?"

"Absolutely," his mother agreed.

"Then nothing strange happened while you were there?" Jon blinked. "No."

"It was just a typical Saturday then," Clint said, reaching for the butter dish. "Everyone got along just fine."

"No one ever got along 'just fine,' Mr. Stanford. Tina was whining and Brad was in one of his moods. Typical stuff." He took a long swallow of water and avoided Clint's gaze from across the table.

Marina stared at her dinner guest. "Clint..."

He shook his head and flashed her his charming smile. "Sorry, darlin'. I keep thinking I can figure out what happened that weekend, you know? I was responsible for those kids being there."

"The science team didn't burn the building down," Marina said. "It didn't happen until the next day. I don't know why Lee—the investigator—hasn't figured out what happened yet." She glanced at Jon, who had turned pale. He set his fork down, next to a half-eaten potato and a pile of fish bones.

"May I be excused? I've got an English essay to write."

"Sure," she said, hiding her worry.

"He thinks it's arson," Clint said when Jon had left.

"Who?"

"Lee. He thinks it was done on purpose."

"Why are you asking so many questions?" Marina pushed her plate away and wiped her lips with her napkin. "You can't possibly think that the kids had anything to do with the fire."

"I don't know." He leaned back in his chair. "I just don't know." He didn't want to tell her what he'd overheard. He couldn't try to explain that Jon himself had said the fire wasn't an accident. All he could do would be to contact Lee and then hope the boy would come forward and tell what he knew. Clint couldn't hurt Marina, not until he knew the truth. For now, he'd keep his mouth shut.

He drank his coffee and ate the most delicious chocolate cake he'd ever tasted in his entire life. After cleaning up the kitchen together, they took their coffee into the living room and made small talk into the evening. He told her about Crystal Creek, true Texas tales that made her smile.

He said good-night long before he wanted to. He would have stayed for hours, telling her stories and making her smile, but he knew he couldn't do that. Instead he reminded her of his dinner invitation.

"Next Saturday," he said, putting on his jacket when she walked him to the door.

"I don't know if that's such a good idea."

"Why not?" He looked down into those hazel eyes and waited for an explanation that he could argue with. Dammit, she wasn't making this easy. "We both have to eat."

She smiled. "You make everything so simple."

"Isn't it?"

"No."

"We'll have dinner. Just like tonight, only you won't

have to cook it.'' He took advantage of her hesitation and said, ''I'll pick you up at seven. We'll go out to the lodge.'' He bent down and kissed her cheek. He forced himself not to move to her lips. He'd never get out of here if he did that, and he might scare her off. He sensed it wouldn't take much. ''Good night,'' he said, and opened the front door. The night was thick with rain, but he grinned to himself as he crossed the lawn.

She hadn't said no.

''IT WAS LEFT on my desk,'' Doug said, handing Clint the sheet of white paper. ''I thought you should see it.''

Clint took the paper and read the neat print, then looked back at Douglas. ''When?''

''Somewhere between first period and third period.''

''I want a list of the students in those classes.''

Doug handed him another piece of paper. ''I thought you would,'' he said. ''But anyone could have ducked into the classroom in between classes and left it. Kids are in and out of there all the time.''

Clint looked back down at the paper with the mysterious words. ''Who do you think wrote this?''

''Someone who knows something and doesn't want to get in trouble.''

''The Weiss kid?'' Clint suggested.

''Possibly.'' Doug sat down. ''I've got him in my class.''

''Him and eighty-four other kids.''

''He'd still be my first guess,'' the history teacher said. ''He's too smart for his own good.''

''Goddammit,'' Clint muttered, going over to the window. It was a clear day, and the daffodils were blooming on the west side of the parking lot. ''Damn it all to hell.''

''What are you going to do?''

''I'll have to make a decision soon.'' He'd have to call Lee. Or the police. He couldn't sit on this and wait for something else to happen. He turned away from the sunshine and returned to his desk. "You don't think it's a prank?"

Douglas frowned. "I wouldn't be here if I did, but you never know. Someone could have gotten it into his head that he would complicate your life."

Clint picked up the paper again. "With this?"

"Why not?"

Doug glanced at the large clock above Clint's head. "I've got to get back. Call me if you need me."

"Sure. And let me know if anything else turns up." Doug nodded and left the room, shutting the door quietly behind him. Clint sank down into his chair and eyed the mysterious message. *The answers to the fire are here at the school,* it said.

It could be a prank. Or someone was trying to tell him something.

"DO YOU THINK he's still mad about the beer party?" Christy leaned forward as she whispered, and her red-gold hair spilled across a page of *Understanding Chemistry.* They both watched the principal walk through the library and speak to Mr. Wagner. Neither man looked very happy.

"Could be," Jon said. "But he seemed all right this weekend. He didn't act upset about anything, and the place was cleaned up."

"I heard you caught all the fish."

"Yeah." He leaned his head on his hand and studied her. She was easily the prettiest girl in the school. And she'd said she'd go to the prom with him. He still couldn't believe his luck. "Matt wasn't too happy."

"Matt's not happy about anything," his sister said. "He's taking Tina Mallory to the prom now that she and Brad broke up, but he doesn't seem real excited about it."

"How'd he get himself into that?"

"I don't know. He doesn't date much."

"How's, uh, Brad taking that?"

Christy shrugged. "I don't know. He's just…Brad. You know."

Yeah, he knew all right. He'd bet a hundred bucks that Schmidt was going ballistic over this. "What kind of flowers do you want?"

"I don't care." She smiled. "I like everything."

Damn. That wasn't exactly the answer he needed. His mother had been on his case to find out the color of her dress so the flowers wouldn't clash. He thought his mom was taking this too seriously, but he didn't dare tell her so. "Well," he said, hoping he sounded as if he asked this question all the time, "what color is your dress?"

"I don't have it yet," she admitted. "But it will probably be black."

"Black," he repeated. What flowers went with black?

Her blue eyes looked worried. "Do you hate black?"

"No. You'd look good in that color." Red, he decided. Red roses would be safe. But he didn't want to be safe. He wanted a color that would go with her hair.

"Thanks." They watched Mr. Stanford leave the library. He glanced in their direction, but he didn't wave or smile. He looked like a man who had a lot on his mind. "He doesn't look happy, either." She turned back to Jon. "Your mother is nice. She was at my house on Friday. Is it true she's going out with Mr. Stanford?"

"No. I mean, not really. I think they're just friends."

Christy didn't look as though she believed him. "Your mother is really pretty."

"Yeah, I guess so."

"How long has she been divorced?"

"Since I was a little kid."

"Does she date a lot?"

Jon laughed. "My mother? No way."

"Well," Christy said, pushing her hair behind her ears, "I think Mr. Stanford's a really nice guy."

"Yeah. For a principal, not a father."

"I like *my* stepfather."

"You're the exception," he told her. Then, hoping to change the subject, he pointed to the complicated diagram on page 143. "Did you understand this today?"

She smiled, and his heart turned over in his chest. "Of course not."

"It's not that bad," he began, directing her to his notebook. He pretended to be serious, when he really wanted to tug on that strand of hair that had escaped to trail over her arm. He wanted to see if it was as soft as it looked.

CHAPTER EIGHT

"THIS IS LIKE, an official date?"

"Yes." Marina peered into the mirror and wondered if her earrings were too big. Maybe she should wear the more delicate drops. "What do you think about these earrings?"

Her son looked at her as if she was insane. "Why are you going out with him? I thought you said it was just, uh, a friend thing."

"It is a 'friend thing.'"

"You don't get that dressed up for a friend," he said with a snort, crossing his arms over his chest. He leaned in her bedroom doorway and continued to frown as she replaced the gold button earring with the pearls. "This is so weird."

"Why wasn't it weird when he was over here for dinner? Or when we ate chili at his house?" The pearls were definitely the better choice.

"It *was* weird," he agreed. "But I thought it was temporary."

"I'm not marrying him, for heaven's sake." Marina picked up her favorite lipstick and put it on in careful strokes. Satisfied, she stood up from the dressing table and smoothed the front of her ivory dress. It was a sleek, short-sleeved gown with buttons down the center. She'd seen it in Gates Department Store and knew it was the perfect spring dress. She hadn't bought it just for a dinner date, of course. She intended to wear it many times. "How do I look?"

"Like you're going on a date."

"Good." She smiled at her son, unperturbed by the scowl on his face. "You should go on dates, too," she told him. "It might put you in a better mood."

"Very funny." He stepped aside to let her pass him. She patted his cheek and went into the hall and down the stairs.

"What are you going to do tonight?"

He followed her downstairs, his large feet heavy on the wooden treads. "Call 900 numbers. Watch X-rated movies and eat candy that will rot my teeth."

"Well, have a good time," she said, pausing at the hall table to collect her purse. Headlights swept across the front of the house. "Looks like my date is here."

"Oh, boy," Jon muttered. "The Cowboy has arrived. You gonna let him come to the door or are you going to run out and meet him in the driveway?"

Marina gave him a stern look. She was growing a little tired of his attitude tonight. "If your manners don't improve, I'll have to send you to bed without your supper."

"I already ate," he said, but he grinned sheepishly. "I'll behave, I promise."

"Where's the dog?"

"I shut her in my room so she wouldn't jump on you."

"You're a good kid," she told him. "When you're not being a pain in the—"

"Watch it, Mom," he said. "Your date is about to ring the doorbell."

Sure enough, the bell sounded. Marina opened the door and saw a Clint Stanford she'd never seen before. He wore black dress slacks and a tan sport jacket. A white dress shirt and a black-and-tan print tie completed the outfit, making him look more handsome than he had a right to. Of course, she noticed as she looked down, he wore cowboy boots. This time they were black, polished to a shine.

"My dress boots," he explained, noting the direction of her gaze.

"How many pairs of boots do you own?"

He shook his head. "That's privileged information, darlin'." He turned to Jon. "Hi, Jon. How's it going?"

"Fine," the boy said. When Clint turned back to Marina, Jon made a face at his mother and mouthed "darlin'" behind the cowboy's back. Marina hid a smile and concentrated on listening to her date.

"...Reservations at eight," he said. "We'll have time for a drink before dinner."

"I'm ready whenever you are."

"You look beautiful," he said, and the appreciative gleam in his eye convinced her he meant the compliment.

"Thank you." She turned to her son. "Behave yourself," she warned.

"You, too," he said.

Clint opened the door for Marina, but stopped before following her. "Good night, Jon."

"Yeah. See ya."

Marina hesitated on the doorstep. Maybe she was being ridiculous. Maybe she shouldn't be dating the man at all. Maybe she should forget the whole thing. But it was hard to forget it, when it was a gorgeous spring night and she had a new dress and she'd never had dinner out at Timberlake Lodge before. And she was surprisingly attracted to the man beside her.

That didn't mean anything, she told herself, stepping onto the sidewalk that led to the driveway. It was just a date, after all, and she'd been on dates before.

She just couldn't remember when.

CLINT WAS GRATEFUL for having had a quiet week. There'd been no more beer parties and the band's spring concert on Tuesday night had had a record attendance. He'd told Lee about the anonymous letter, but the investigator had warned him that it was most likely a prank.

Clint hoped the man was right. He didn't want to believe one of his kids had set the fire. He didn't want that kid to be Marina's son. Especially now, when Clint had finally accomplished what he'd thought was impossible. Marina sat across from him at an intimate table for two in the middle of the rustic Timberlake Lodge dining room. He had her all to himself, which was an accomplishment in itself. She was a beautiful woman, and yet she didn't seem to realize it. She made him feel awkward and protective at the same time.

The waitress brought their menus and told them what the chef's specials were, then Sheila Lawson made her way among the tables toward them.

Clint stood to greet her, then turned to his date. Marina had a decidedly curious look on her face. "Sheila, I'd like you to meet a friend of mine, Marina Weiss. Marina, this is Sheila Lawson."

The young blond woman shook her hand. "I'm glad to meet you. Please, let me know if there's anything special you need, all right?"

"Thank you," Marina said.

"Sheila is the manager here," Clint explained. "She's going to marry Doug Wagner, one of the teachers at the high school. And a good friend." He turned back to Sheila. "When's the wedding?"

"We're still deciding," she said, smiling brightly. "I'm sure Doug will let you know."

"Congratulations," Marina said.

"Thank you." A waitress came over and whispered something, and Sheila excused herself. "Don't forget to let me know if you need anything. I guess I'd better get back to work."

Clint took his seat again. "I didn't think it would be this crowded."

The waitress overheard him as she stepped closer to take their order. "We have a convention here this weekend. Have you decided on dinner or would you like a few more minutes?"

Clint looked at Marina. "I'm ready," she said, her voice low. He liked that voice.

She ordered baked stuffed shrimp and Clint decided on a steak. He ordered a bottle of wine and talked her into sharing an appetizer of marinated mushrooms with him. They discussed the weather and his plans for the fishing cabin as the wine was delivered and tasted. It was going well, he thought, pleased that he'd thought of the lodge for tonight.

The waitress delivered the mushrooms. "Be careful," she said, setting the plate between them on the linen tablecloth. "It's very hot." She put small plates in front of them and hurried off.

Marina took one. "This is—"

"Toilet paper!" a man shouted. "Try *that!*"

Clint turned to his left to see a paunchy man burst into laughter. His companions, two other elderly men, shook their heads.

"Too easy," one said.

Marina looked at Clint and smiled. "I wonder what's going on," she said. "Maybe—"

"It's soft on your bottom, it's kind to your skin, if you buy Little Softeez, your rashes will end," the bald man announced.

"'Skin' and 'end' don't rhyme."

The "poet" shrugged and took another forkful of his salad. "Close enough," he muttered.

A woman's voice came from behind Clint. "That's the worst I have ever heard, Frank. You've outdone yourself this time."

"I can do worse." The bald man gave her a wink. "And I can do better. After I eat."

Clint looked at Marina. "I'm sorry," he said, whispering. "I'm not sure what's going on here."

She didn't seem upset. In fact, she looked as if she was trying not to laugh. "That's okay. Maybe they're visiting poets."

"Squeeze me, squeeze me," another man sang, "I don't mind. I'm soft as cotton on your behind." Several people around them laughed.

"Bill, for heaven's sake! Toilet paper is overdone," the woman said, sniffing. Her voice was high and just a little too loud for comfort. Clint winced and fought the urge to turn around and see what she looked like. He took another sip of wine.

"Soap is still big, though," someone announced.

"I prefer cleaning products," another woman said. "A lot of things rhyme with 'shine.'"

"Yes, Betty," someone else said. "Like fine, mine and line."

"And dine," Clint muttered, spearing a mushroom. "Which I'd like to do in peace."

"Divine," Marina said, holding up her glass. "And wine."

Clint glanced around him. "Who the hell are these people?"

"They're having a good time," Marina said placatingly.

"They're singing about toilet paper," Clint muttered. "It sounds like a damned television commercial around here."

Marina laughed. "That's it! Maybe they write television commercials."

Clint looked at the men at the next table. They didn't look like New York advertising executives to him, but then again, he'd never met a New York advertising executive.

"Does anything rhyme with zucchini?" the man with the original toilet paper question asked.

"Bikini?" Marina whispered to Clint. He couldn't believe she was having a good time.

"You meanie," Betty said, giggling.

"Too teeny," Marina offered, this time a little louder.

Clint stared at her. The three men at the table next to them smiled appreciatively.

"Sorry," she whispered, taking another sip of wine. "Maybe I've had too much wine. I'll be, uh, fine." She smiled at him and he smiled back. He couldn't help it. "I couldn't resist," she confessed, her lovely hazel eyes twinkling at him.

"As long as you're having a good time," he drawled. He was sitting in the middle of a group of people who were a few sandwiches shy of a picnic. And now his beautiful, sophisticated, elegant date was joining them.

"I am," she said. "Aren't you?"

He leaned forward. "It wasn't exactly what I had in mind."

"And what was that?"

"Something romantic," he said, figuring he might as well be honest.

"Something romantic," she repeated, looking at him with an odd expression on her face.

"I wanted to please you."

Marina's lips curved into a smile. "You are. Even if you're not a poet."

"Who said I'm not?"

"A Texas cowboy poet? I've never heard of such a thing."

She was flirting with him. He liked that. The boisterous sounds of the people around them faded. He couldn't rhyme his way out of a canyon, but she didn't have to know that. "I could surprise you."

"Go ahead."

Damn. He should have known she wouldn't let him get

away with it. "I will when the spirit moves me," he said, stalling.

"All right. I can wait."

The waitress cleared their plates and delivered bowls of salad and a container that held three kinds of dressing. "Enjoy!"

"Just a minute," Clint said. "Exactly what kind of group is staying at the lodge this weekend?"

"Jingle writers. They're really a fun bunch. We've enjoyed them."

Why? he wanted to ask, but he didn't say a word. He thanked her for the salad and turned to the beautiful woman seated across from him.

"I'm waiting," she said.

"Waiting?"

"For a poem."

The woman behind him screeched with laughter. "I *love* the singing doughnuts! I just knew Fred had to be part of that one!"

Clint shuddered. "You want a poem about singing pastry?"

"Sure."

"I was kidding."

"I know," she said. "I wanted to see how far you'd go."

"I thought it would be quiet here."

"It's fine," she assured him, but he could tell she was listening to the conversation about the doughnut commercial while she tasted her salad.

"—Sprinkle, sprinkle everywhere!" the man named Fred finished to a round of applause.

Clint speared a chunk of iceberg lettuce. "I'm going to slit my wrists."

"Before or after you use your fists?" Marina giggled. "Sorry. It's contagious."

"No, it's not."

She tilted her head and studied him. "Unless, of course, you have no heart."

The man beside them leaned toward Marina. "It's true, my dear, you'll have to part."

Marina laughed in surprise. "This date, you see, is just a start."

"A first date?" another woman asked. "How lovely."

"I thought so," Clint said, forgetting for a minute that the people who surrounded him were strangers.

"Like that mouthwash commercial, Betty. Remember?"

The elderly man flirting with Marina looked as if he was just getting warmed up. He gave her an admiring look and said, "There was a young lady from Munich—"

"That's enough," Clint declared, giving the man a warning look.

"We haven't ordered dessert yet," the old man said. He looked at Marina. "My apologies, my dear, if we are too noisy. We tend to enjoy ourselves, you see."

"It's not a problem." Marina assured him. "We're enjoying ourselves, too." She turned to Clint. "Aren't we enjoying ourselves?"

"Oh, yeah. Enjoying ourselves." He never wanted to hear a rhyme again. "Marina, would you like more wine?"

"Yes, thank you."

He refilled her glass and wondered if he should ask Sheila to move them. Halfway through dinner was a little late for that, though. And the place looked filled, too. They were trapped, surrounded by people who created bad poems about toilet paper.

It was either fight 'em or join 'em. He just had to come up with something that rhymed with lettuce or salad or dressing. He glanced over at Marina, who had obviously asked him a question he hadn't heard. "I'm sorry," he said. "What did you say?"

She shook her head. "It's not important. I just asked if everything was all set here for the prom."

"Yes. Two weeks from tonight the lodge will be filled with teenagers. Dinner and dancing in the ballroom."

"It's a great idea."

"Keeps them from driving all over the county," he said. "And the lodge doesn't rent rooms to any of them."

"There are kids who do that?"

"A few. Some have more money than sense."

"Sounds more sophisticated than my proms, which were in the high-school gym."

"Mine, too." He smiled. "Things have changed."

"Were you a wild kid?"

"Why do you ask?"

"Just a hunch."

"Yeah. I was a wild kid. I got in so much trouble I took my father's advice and went into the Air Force before I could get into any serious trouble."

"And you were there for a long time?"

"Twenty years. I got an education and a whole world of experience. When I came out I wanted to work with kids. So here I am."

"Do you like it?" She seemed interested in the answer.

"Yes. I do."

"You don't miss the traveling?"

"No. My wife and I enjoyed it, but I'm ready to settle down and live in one place after all those years of moving around." He didn't usually talk about Judy, but it seemed natural to do it now. "Judy was the daughter of one of my commanding officers, so she knew what military life was like and never seemed to mind living in different parts of the world."

"It sounds like you had a good marriage," Marina said, as the waitress delivered their dinner. The jingle writers had quieted down a little, though an occasional eruption of laughter covered the sound of piano music coming from the lobby.

"Yes." He didn't feel comfortable saying any more, so he looked down at his steak. "Dinner looks delicious," he said, hoping to change the subject.

She took the hint and picked up her fork. "It smells wonderful."

Clint breathed an inner sigh of relief. So far so good.

THIS WAS definitely more fun than she'd thought it would be. The shrimp was tender, the stuffing spicy and hot. The jingle writers surrounding them were funny and totally oblivious of the non-jinglers in the dining room. She and Clint might be the only non-poets in the entire lodge.

She'd thought it was going to be awkward to make conversation with him, but he was an easy man to talk to, although he shied away from personal subjects. Like his wife. She didn't mind; she didn't like personal subjects herself.

Marina looked over at her date, who cut a piece of meat and smiled at her. "No poems about shrimp?" he asked.

She considered his question, and the bald man next to her said, "Excuse me, but *pimp*, *blimp* and *limp* come to mind."

"Thank you." She hid a smile at the expression on Clint's face. "Are you sure you want a jingle about dinner?"

"Not now."

"I could come up with something," she offered, wiping her lips with her napkin. "Maybe about the steak."

A wary expression clouded his eyes. "You really don't have to."

The men at the next table gave her encouraging nods. "You can do it, miss," one said. "Take your time. No need to rush."

The gray-haired woman behind Clint peered over his shoulder. "We could all help."

Marina didn't want to hurt their feelings, but she didn't know how to get out of this without sounding ungrateful. And besides, her big mouth had trapped her. "Well, give me a minute," she said.

Clint looked relieved. "Would you like coffee?"

"I'd love it."

He caught the waitress's attention and she came over. "How was your dinner?" she asked.

"Excellent, thanks," he said. "We'll have coffee and the dessert menu, please."

"Of course."

Marina finished the last of her wine and thought hard while the woman cleared their table. Ache, break, make…

"Marina?"

She looked back at her date. "I'm trying to come up with words that rhyme with steak."

"Partake," a man beside her said loudly. "It's a natural."

"For poetry, maybe," Betty said with a sniff, "but not for a jingle. You have to keep it *simple* for a jingle. How many commercials use the word *partake?*"

"I'm just trying to be different," the man said. He smiled at Marina and stuck out his hand. "The name's Howard. Howard Levinson."

She took his hand and shook it. "Marina Weiss. It's nice to meet you."

Clint cleared his throat and, when he had their attention, nodded toward the elderly man. "Clint Stanford."

"Ah, a Texas accent," the man said, standing to shake Clint's hand. "You don't often hear one of those in these parts."

"Fake, take, bake, cake, lake," Betty announced. "You ought to be able to do something with that."

"Thank you," Marina said and asked the waitress for a piece of chocolate chip cheesecake. Clint ordered apple pie.

"I'll bring your coffee in just a sec," the woman promised.

"Could you bring it in plastic foam cups?" Clint asked. "We're going to take it with us." He turned to Marina. "I hope you don't mind."

"Uh, no." She didn't have any idea if she minded or not. "But where…"

The waitress hesitated. "The desserts, too?"

"Yes. We'll take the desserts 'to go,' too. We're, uh, running late."

Marina raised her eyebrows, but didn't say a word. It was kind of interesting to see what Clint would do next. The man wasn't boring, she'd give him that much.

"I'll be right back," the waitress said, as if "to go" was a typical phrase in the elegant lodge.

"Do you mind if I ask where we're going?"

He leaned forward. "Someplace without jingles."

She pretended disappointment. "You mean you don't want to hear my poem about steak?"

He smiled, a gleam in his dark eyes. "No way in hell, lady, do I want to talk about food."

He was too attractive for his own good, of course. And she shouldn't blame herself for being attracted to him. She hadn't had much exposure to the long, lean cowboy type, so maybe it was just the boots.

He paid the bill, left a hefty tip, nodded toward the jinglers and guided Marina through the dining room. He said good-night to Sheila, picked up a large paper bag and winked at Marina.

Fifteen minutes later they were at the other side of the lake, driving down the narrow road to the cabin.

"Those people were driving me crazy," he said, giving her a sheepish look as he parked the car and turned off the ignition.

"They meant well."

"I wanted an evening that wasn't quite so...public. Do you mind?"

She should say yes, but she couldn't. The quiet cabin, with its view of the dark bay, was much more appealing than the lodge and its quirky inhabitants. On the other hand, being alone with the cowboy was dangerous. "No."

He looked relieved as he picked up the bag and got out of the car. Marina followed him to the back door. He unlocked it and switched on the kitchen light. The place looked much as it had a few weeks ago when she'd accompanied him the first time. Except it was cleaner, and there were signs that someone was using it.

She smelled furniture polish and noticed that the counters had been cleared of the jumble that had covered them. Leave it to a military man to get everything shipshape. "Do you spend a lot of time here?"

"No. I'm just using it as a place to get away for a few hours once in a while." He set the coffee and dessert boxes on the counter. "Want to sit out on the porch?"

"Okay."

He pried off the plastic lids and poured the coffee into white mugs with colored fish stenciled on them, then handed her one. "Nothing fancy, I'm afraid."

"It's fine," she assured him. He rummaged through a drawer and found forks while she went into the living room.

"I haven't changed anything yet," Clint said, stepping through the doorway. "I think I might have to buy a new rug, but I'm not going to do any remodeling for a while."

"Are you still going to live out here all the time?"

"Eventually," he said. "Can you open the door? I have my hands full."

Marina found the latch and opened the door. The pine-scented air was cool, but not chilly. The rhythmical calling of toads was the only thing to disturb the silence. "The kids didn't hurt the cabin when they came out here?"

He put the food on the metal table. "No. There would have been hell to pay if they had."

She sat in a metal lawn chair and took a sip of the coffee. It was still hot and she was careful not to spill it on her dress. "I was pretty relieved to see Jon come home that night."

"I didn't mean to scare you, but…" Clint hesitated as he sat down in the chair beside hers and moved the table in front of them.

"But you thought he was up to something," she finished for him, setting down her coffee.

"Yes." He handed her the plate containing the wedge of cheesecake. "I was glad to see he wasn't at that particular party."

"What happened to the kids who were out here?"

"That's up to the police and their parents. I had a talk with each one and made sure they came out here and cleaned up the beer cans."

She wouldn't have liked to be one of those kids facing Mr. Stanford about that topic. She took a bite of the cheesecake. "This is so good. I enjoyed dinner."

"So did I. We should do it again."

Marina looked at him. "I don't know. I told you, I don't usually date."

"And I told you," he said, a quick smile crossing his face, "I'm a persistent man."

"I figured that out."

"Good." He put his coffee cup on the table beside his untouched pie. "That's a start."

"A start to what?"

"To this." He took the plate from her and set it down beside his, then cupped the back of her neck with his hand. "I've always wanted to kiss a woman with cheesecake on her lips."

"I guess this is your big chance," she whispered, knowing kissing him was as inevitable as the trilling of toads. It was crazy. And against her better judgment, but she leaned toward him and met his mouth with hers. He tasted faintly of coffee, and his lips moved over hers with a tempting pressure. The metal chairs creaked as they leaned closer to each other. She liked the taste of him, liked the way he cupped her head and held her to him. Her hands went to his shoulders and stayed there. She was afraid she'd fall out of the rickety chair and land on the floor.

The skin above his collar was warm to the touch as her hand crept higher. Her fingertips brushed his soft dark hair as Clint slanted his mouth over hers and took possession of her mouth. It was as if he couldn't get enough her, she thought, wondering at the quick, hot passion that flared between them. She could kiss him for hours. She could lose track of time while he held her.

He lifted his mouth from hers a scant inch. "I couldn't do this in the dining room."

"Not without shocking the jingle writers," she murmured, unwilling to move out of his arms. She felt safe and very, very female.

Clint gazed down at her with dark eyes and touched her cheek with one finger. "It was worth the wait," he said, and bent to kiss her again.

It was as if she hadn't been kissed for years. She met him with her own need, not realizing until long afterward that she had missed that part of her life, that sexual part that she'd ignored for so long.

He didn't demand more than her kisses. They stayed in their chairs, as if that would keep them from taking a step neither was ready for. And when they paused, Marina took a shaky breath and tried to smile. "I think you owe me a poem," she said, hoping to lighten what had become an incredibly hot night.

"Be prepared to sit here all night then. I can't rhyme my

way out of a feed bag.'' He swept her hair from her cheek. ''I've wanted to kiss you like this since the first time I saw you.''

''In your office?'' She couldn't imagine the intimidating principal having those thoughts while he was telling her about a fight at school.

''Yes, ma'am.'' He kissed her again, and Marina realized she could imagine him doing just about anything he put his mind to. It was much later when she unwound her arms from his neck, later still when he kissed her as they sat in his car in front of her house.

And it was much, much later when Marina finally drifted off to sleep.

CHAPTER NINE

"WELL?" AMANDA PAUSED by Marina's desk. "Are you going to tell me or keep me in suspense all morning?"

Marina knew what her friend was asking, but couldn't resist teasing. "Tell you what?"

Amanda sighed. "You know exactly what I'm talking about. The date. With Clint. How was it?"

Marina recalled that heart-stopping kissing session at the cabin and lost her train of thought for a minute. "Um, it was very...nice."

"You're hopeless," Amanda muttered. The phone rang and Marina laughed before she picked up the receiver.

"Baron-Trask Law Office," she said. Then she turned to her boss. "It's for you. A man who wants to know if you're coming into Sugar Creek today and will join him for lunch."

A look of delight crossed Amanda's face as she leaned over and took the receiver from Marina's hand. "Ethan? Hi. I didn't expect you to call this...okay, I'm dropping off those papers in a little while. One. Fine. Bye."

She hung up the phone and grinned. "Guess I have a lunch date."

"I gathered." It must be wonderful to be in love with your husband, Marina thought. Had she ever been that starry-eyed? Once, many years ago, until reality had set in. "I'll have the papers finished by ten."

"No hurry." Amanda plopped down in a chair. "I must

have a big case of spring fever. I'd like to get in my car and drive for hours."

"That sounds like spring fever, all right."

"Haven't you ever wanted to do that?"

Marina didn't have to think twice. "Not really."

"Aren't you going to tell me about your date? Did you wear the new dress?"

"Yes," Marina said, pushing away from her computer screen. "It was perfect."

"I knew it! Did you go out to the lodge?"

"Yes. I loved it."

A wistful expression crossed Amanda's face. "It used to belong to my grandfather. I'm so glad people are enjoying it again."

"It's a busy place." She smiled, thinking of the jingle writers. "And the food was wonderful."

"Ethan and I need to go out there more often." Amanda leaned forward and put her elbows on the desk. "Tell me it was a romantic evening."

"It was a romantic evening."

"Really?"

"Really," Marina admitted with some reluctance. "He's a very attractive man and I'm only human."

"He likes you."

She liked him, too. More than a lot. More than she wanted to think about. If she could do whatever she wanted in this crazy life, she'd still be on that porch kissing The Cowboy. "Do you want to go over the Mason contracts?"

Amanda didn't budge. "You don't have to look depressed about the fact that he likes you. Unless you're really not interested in him."

"It's not that. It's just that I'm not ready for a relationship right now. I have Jon to think of, and…" She stopped, not coming up with any other reason for avoiding dating Clint.

"Jon doesn't like him?"

"They…clash sometimes. And other times they get along really well. Like the fishing trip."

"Ethan had a great time out there. He almost wishes he'd bought the place himself."

"Jon liked it, too." She paused, trying to explain her dilemma to the woman across the desk. "When he and Clint aren't in school, everything's okay."

"There's still trouble there?"

"I think it may have stopped. Jon won't talk about it. And Clint thinks Jon knows something he's not saying about the fire."

"The *fire?* He thinks the kids are somehow involved?"

"I don't know, but he's worried."

"The whole town is, Marina. If Jon knows anything, he should talk to the police or anyone who can help."

"I can't even get him to talk to me," Marina said.

"You're going to have to," her boss said, looking more serious than Marina had ever seen her do before. "The future of the entire town could be at stake."

"We're going to River Falls next weekend to look at the university. That might be a good time to talk, when he's stuck in the car with me."

"Whatever it takes," Amanda said. "I'm certainly no expert on children or teenagers, but I know what the closing of the plant has done to my family, especially my grandfather. One way or another, we have to have some answers."

"WHEN DOES the college tour start?" Jon dumped his duffel bag on the kitchen floor while Marina peered into the refrigerator.

"As soon as I get organized," she promised. "Did you eat the last of the roast beef?"

"Yeah. I had a sandwich for breakfast and took one for lunch. Is that a problem?"

"No." She shut the refrigerator and turned around. Tex wagged her tail as if she thought Marina had selected something special for her to eat for dinner. "No. We can eat out. I just thought we wouldn't take the time."

"I can go to the store."

"Okay. Take some money from my purse and get a couple of ready-made sandwiches from the deli section. I have potato chips and soda already packed in the car." She looked at her watch. "Clint should be here in about ten minutes, so hurry."

"What kind?"

"Roast beef or turkey. No onions or pickles." She scooped dry dog food into a plastic storage container. Clint was taking the animal out to the lake for the weekend, which worked out just fine. This was an important trip for her son; he was going to visit colleges and have a preliminary interview with one, with early acceptance depending on the outcome.

She was more nervous than Jon, Marina thought, going upstairs to finish packing. It didn't take long. She was driving in jeans, but included a casual summer dress for walking around the campuses tomorrow. Jon had decided to major in premed instead of chemistry, at least for a couple of years until he decided what he wanted to do. Research would be his field, though. That much was clear. She finished collecting her makeup and tossed in a paperback historical romance for the quiet evenings in the motels, then carried her belongings downstairs to the foyer.

Tex ran to the front door and barked her usual greeting. Marina looked out the window and saw Clint parking in front of the house. She opened the door and let the black dog run across the lawn to meet him.

He spent some time petting the excited dog before he noticed that Marina stood in the doorway watching him. A pleased smile crossed his face, making her glad she'd taken the time to put on lipstick and brush her hair.

Not that it mattered, she reminded herself. She wasn't trying to impress him. She wasn't interested. She certainly didn't plan to continue this dating thing.

"Hey," he called, his handsome face smiling at her. He looked Friday-afternoon casual, wearing a dark green T-shirt and jeans, and a pair of sneakers. Sneakers?

"Sneakers?" she blurted.

He glanced down at his feet as if to see what she was talking about, then looked at her as he crossed the lawn. "Yeah, that's what they are, all right. I'm taking Tex for a run."

Marina stepped onto the porch to greet him. For one crazy, scary minute she thought he was going to kiss her, right there in the middle of the afternoon with half of her neighbors weeding and planting nearby.

He did step closer. Too close, Marina thought, but didn't move. She lifted her face to tease him about his pregnant dog, but the expression in his brown eyes stopped her. He looked...happy. Happy to see her? Amazing.

"Marina," he began, stopping before he came indecently close. The sound of a car slowing down made both of them look toward the road. Jon honked the Oldsmobile's horn and turned into the driveway, the car making a flapping sound as he turned.

"That noise," Clint said, frowning as Jon pulled the car to a stop and turned off the engine. "Have you had it checked?"

"No." Marina waved to Jon, noticing his smile didn't fade when he started toward her and the principal. That was an improvement. "It's been doing it for weeks, but only when I make a turn. After a while it stops."

Clint's frown deepened. "That's not good."

"Why?" She hated car trouble. She preferred to ignore it whenever she could.

"It sounds like it's in the axle. Have you run into anything lately?"

Marina thought for a second. "No, I don't think so. Jon," she said, as he approached, Tex at his heels, "how long has the car been making that noise?"

"A few weeks, I guess. It's getting worse, Mom."

"What about potholes? Hit any of those lately?"

Jon looked sheepish. "Yeah. There's a wicked one by the Hansen farm. I only hit it once. After that I knew where it was."

"That'd do it. It happened to me a few years ago," Clint said. "Not with this car, but with an old truck I had. Can you postpone your trip until you have it fixed?"

"You don't think it's safe to drive?"

"You can take it to a garage and get an expert's opinion, but I think they'll tell you the same thing."

They did. The mechanic took three minutes, no more, to explain to Marina what the problem was. They would order the part. It might take a few days or maybe a week to get and yes, it was pretty expensive, but what could you do? She shouldn't drive it over thirty miles per hour because the wheel could damn near fall right off.

"This really sucks," Jon muttered.

"Jon," she warned, hating that particular teenage phrase. They were following Clint the five blocks back to the house. He'd gone with them, just in case they had to leave the car. "We'll figure something out."

"Take my car," Clint said, when they arrived.

"I can't do that."

"Sure you can. It has about half a tank of gas and is almost brand-new. You shouldn't have any trouble with it. Tex and I will catch a ride out to the lake with Ethan and you can pick us up Sunday night."

"I don't think that's such a good idea."

"Mom!" Jon gave her a stricken look. "You know how long I've waited for this interview. I can't cancel."

"I can't be responsible for driving someone else's car. It's across the state, not across town, Jon."

"I don't mind," Clint said. "I offered."

"I just don't think it's right."

He took her arm and led her over to his car. "See? Nothing scary."

"Except the shift."

Clint looked surprised. "I'd forgotten about that. I've driven standard transmissions for so long I'd forgotten how unusual they are."

She tried to smile. There really was no way out of this mess. "Unusual for a city girl, anyway."

Jon edged closer. "Can we rent a car?"

"Not in Tyler. Madison, we could."

"I'll drive you to Madison," Clint offered. "I'll drop you at the nearest rental agency and you'll be on your way."

And it would cost quite a bit, too, on an already tight budget. And now Marina faced an expensive car-repair bill, too. But she didn't want Clint to know that money was an issue, so she said, "Thanks. I'll give that some thought."

He was silent for a minute. He leaned against the car and absently patted Tex's head. "Of course, there's an even better idea."

Jon looked up from staring at the ground. He was clearly trying not to panic. "What? I'll listen to anything, Mr. Stanford."

"Let me take you." He raised his hand to still Marina's instant protest. "The Jeep is big enough to take all three of us in comfort, and I enjoy driving."

"I couldn't," Marina began. There were so many objections she couldn't even list them.

"Why not? You two get a driver and a car and I get a

trip across the state *and* the pleasure of your company." He smiled down into her eyes. "It sounds fair to me."

"We're not coming back until Sunday. We're visiting two colleges. You can't possibly—"

"Sure, I can," he insisted. "Look at it this way, anything's better than having Jon miss out on his interview at...where?"

"Macalester College in St. Paul."

"And U of W, in River Falls," Jon added. "If I major in chemistry instead of premed."

"I still don't—"

"Mom." Jon put his hand on her arm. "This is a big deal, okay? If Mr. Stanford wants to go with us it's fine with me. If I cancel the interview they might think I'm some sort of freak who can't even get to St. Paul."

"Everyone understands car trouble, Jon."

He shook his head. "It sounds like a bogus excuse, Mom. Come on." He looked over at Clint and grinned. "Besides, you're outnumbered."

"What about Tex?"

Jon took the dog by the collar. "I'll call Christy. Maybe she would keep her out at the farm while we're gone."

Marina eyed the dog's growing belly. "She's not going to have her puppies this weekend, is she?"

"No," Clint said. "I think we have a couple of weeks yet, according to the vet. Look at it this way. I should know more about the colleges my students go to. I'll get a lot out of the trip, too."

"Mom? Okay?"

She couldn't refuse him, especially since it involved his dreams coming true. Not after how hard he'd worked for his grades and to get this interview with Macalester and the tour of the University of Wisconsin, too. She just hadn't intended to spend the weekend with Clint Stanford.

But she was grown-up. A big girl.

"Let a friend help you out," Clint said. "I think it sounds like an interesting weekend. I have students going to River Falls, but I've never seen the place."

"Next thing I know you'll be telling me I'm doing you a favor."

He grinned and patted her on the shoulder. "Let's unpack your car and get rid of that dog."

There was no use fighting the inevitable. "Okay."

Jon let out a whoop of joy. "I'll call Christy. She's always saying she owes me a favor for her chemistry grade."

"All right," Marina said, knowing it made sense in one respect. "Go ahead."

"Wise move," Clint said. "Now I have a date for the whole weekend."

"This isn't a date. In fact, I'll make sure to pay for your motel rooms." Hopefully there was a little more life left in her credit card. Maybe she should rent that car instead. "This is getting so complicated," she said.

He frowned. "You're not paying for my rooms. Not when I invited myself along."

"Invited yourself? You're saving my rear and you know it."

He shook his head. "No. This sounds better than talking to Tex all weekend."

"I thought you were going fishing."

"The fish will wait." He put his arm around her and walked her to the Oldsmobile. "I'm not playing fair, am I?"

"You're being very nice," she countered, trying very hard to remember why she shouldn't like this man so much. "And I'm not interested in a serious relationship, remember?"

"Yeah." He slowly dropped his arm from her shoulder, but he still looked as if he'd like to kiss her. Instead he winked. "You can't blame a guy for trying."

SHE'D EXPLAINED her plan to him. It was to get across as much of Wisconsin as possible before stopping for the night, in order to be close to the university at River Falls, in the northwest part of the state. They would tour the campus in the morning, then drive the short distance across the state line to St. Paul.

"First thing in the morning," she said, folding the map to show the area in which they were traveling, "we'll be ready to see the college."

"What time is the interview at Macalester?"

"Four o'clock." She peered at the map again. "If we can get as far as Eau Claire tonight, we'll be in good shape. According to the map, it's 260 miles from Madison to St. Paul and should take about five hours."

"No problem. It's all interstate."

"Do you want another sandwich?"

"No, thanks. I'll wait until we find a motel and get something there if I'm hungry." Clint looked at his watch. It was after nine; they hadn't left Tyler until five, since he'd had to pack and take the dog to the Hansen farm. He'd watched Christy greet Jon with genuine enthusiasm. He'd thanked Britt, smiled at the toddler that followed Britt to the car, and then he and Jon had left the dog. Tex didn't even look as if she noticed or cared that she was somewhere else for the weekend.

The weekend. Clint liked that. He and "his" little family were off doing a very ordinary thing, setting off in the car to scout colleges. Jon had been quiet for the past hour; Clint assumed the boy had fallen asleep. Driving along Interstate 94 was better than fishing, surprisingly. This was better than being alone and wondering if Marina would continue to go out with him.

It hadn't been easy to stop kissing her Saturday night. He had silently cursed the lawn chairs for keeping their bodies from touching. He wanted to touch her, wanted to fit himself inside of her and make her his. Wanted to make love to her for hours, then start all over again.

Clint was glad the inside of the car was dark.

It hadn't been easy to stay away from her all week. He'd almost wished Jon would get into trouble so he'd have an excuse to call her. Which was ridiculous. He certainly could have called her if he wanted to. He didn't want to think about why he felt so uncertain doing such a simple thing. And when she'd called him to make arrangements for the dog's care this weekend, he'd smiled just to hear her voice on the other end of the phone. Crazy, sure. Clint glanced over at the woman beside him in the darkness. If he could ever figure out how to get her alone for more than an hour, he might be able to convince her to give him a chance.

"We should start seeing signs for Eau Claire soon," he said. "Just tell me where you want to stop."

"All right."

It didn't take long to reach the outskirts of the city and see signs that advertised convenient places to stop for the night. Marina pulled an AAA guidebook from her bag, then directed him to the motel she selected for the night. There was a brief discussion about who was paying for his room, but Clint stood firm. Marina finally gave up, muttering something about stubborn Texans and breakfast. He'd tried not to laugh when he'd said good-night.

"TELL YOU WHAT," Clint said, shoving his hands in the pockets of his slacks. "I'll let you buy me dinner."

Marina shook her head. "Tonight I'm paying for your room *and* dinner." And hoping her Visa card didn't explode when it went through the cash register. She had some backup cash, though. And the restaurants they'd passed on the outskirts of St. Paul hadn't looked outrageously expensive.

"No."

The clerk stared at them and cleared his throat. "I'll be happy to take a credit card from either of you."

They both slapped plastic on the counter at the same time. Clint stared the man down. "Put both rooms on mine," he said, in a voice that sounded as if he wasn't used to being argued with.

"Now that's too much!" Marina protested.

Clint didn't look over at her. "I'm tired of arguing about this. We'll settle it later."

"You're darn right we will," she muttered, watching the desk clerk process the motel bill. He placed two keys on the counter.

"You're in 202 and 204," he said. "There's an ice machine at the west end of the hall and the stairs are to your left." He put a registration form in front of Clint. "If you'll sign this, we're all set."

Clint scrawled his name, picked up the keys and turned to Marina. He handed her a key. "If you want to go up to your room, I'll bring the bags."

"I can help you."

He shook his head. Of course. "Go on up. I don't need any help."

Marina thanked him, but she wasn't used to having someone else do her work for her or drive for her or pay her motel room for her. This was a strange weekend. They'd toured parts of the University of Wisconsin, then traveled on to Minnesota and the smaller, more expensive Macalester College. They'd met more deans than she could keep track of; they'd waited nervously in a reception room while Jon had his interview with the admissions board. Marina had a discussion with a woman in the financial aid and scholarships department. Clint had somehow located two students from Tyler who were more than happy to talk to Jon about the school.

So happy that one of them—a sophomore—had invited

Jon to spend the night at the dorm and attend a barbecue and a local jazz concert. Jon had looked as if he'd landed in the best place in the world and, anxious to let off steam after the pressure of the interview, was pleased to accept the invitation.

Leaving his mother with The Cowboy two miles away in the Sunset Motel.

Marina looked at the number on her key and went upstairs. The motel was a three-story brick structure that looked clean and, according to her AAA book, was reasonably priced. She unlocked the door to Room 202 and stepped inside. Double beds lined one wall, with a dresser and television opposite. It looked like any other motel room in the country. She crossed the room and pulled back the drapes to reveal an expansive view of the parking lot and the interstate beyond, but Marina didn't mind. She was too tired to care about the view, so she shut the drapes and switched on the bedside light. The blue-and-rose-striped bedspreads were attractive, blending with the blue carpet and matching drapes.

She peered into the bathroom, switched on the television to see if it worked and opened the door when she heard Clint's knock. She stood back to let him enter.

"Not bad," he said, looking around the room. He placed her small suitcase on the floor beside the nearest bed. "Looks comfortable."

Marina went over to her purse and unzipped the pocket with her emergency cash inside. She handed Clint several bills. "Here," she said, trying for the no-nonsense tone she'd heard him use often enough.

He looked confused and didn't take the money. "What's that for?"

"The room."

"I thought we'd settled all that," he said, ignoring the money and backing toward the door.

"You *thought* you settled it." She followed him, but he'd already opened the door and was halfway out.

"How about if we discuss it over dinner? The clerk said there's a decent steak house about three blocks away. I'll be back in an hour." With that, he closed the door and left her alone in the room.

She could never win, Marina decided, tucking the money back into her purse. If she could figure out how to pay for dinner, though, she'd be closer to even. Marina looked at her watch. She had time for a relaxing soak in the tub before changing into tomorrow's outfit. After walking across miles and miles of campus, her feet were tired. And her head was spinning with information about college loans and scholarship programs. Everything sounded complicated and very, very expensive.

Marina went into the bathroom and turned on the faucet in the tub. She'd try to soak her concerns away. Then she'd figure out how to pay for dinner.

SHE DIDN'T, much to her exasperation. Clint excused himself during dessert, and she assumed he was going to the men's room, not quietly paying the check. He'd said it was a date, and she could owe him a home-cooked meal back in Tyler.

It was like fighting the wind.

Back at the motel, Clint led her to his door, and Marina stopped.

"I'd better say good-night," she said.

"I thought we were going to have a glass of wine and look over the college information."

"It's awfully late," she hedged.

"Are you sure?"

She wished he didn't look so disappointed. The truth was she didn't want to be alone in that room. "Well…"

"Come on," he said, opening his door. "Don't tell me I bought a bottle of wine for nothing."

She relented, knowing she'd just worry about her son and watch television if she went back to her room. "Maybe one glass."

His room was the mirror image of hers: double beds against the wall, a small table and two chairs in front of the window. Clint took two glasses from the tray on the table and opened the wine with a corkscrew on his Swiss army knife.

Marina sat in one of the chairs. "Do you think Jon should go here to school?"

"If they offer him a good enough financial-aid package. It looks like a fine school. I guess you have to know your child. Would he do better in a small college or a big one?"

"I guess that's up to him." She sighed. "Do you think Jon's all right at the dorm? Maybe I shouldn't have let him stay all night."

"It's too late now, Marina. It's almost midnight." He handed her the drink.

"Thanks. I guess I got caught up in the moment. He's only a junior, but he looked so old today. He looked like he belonged on a college campus. I couldn't believe how young the other kids looked."

"He's growing up. He's going to be going off on his own after next year."

He sat down on the edge of the bed and touched his glass to hers. "Here's to kids growing up."

She made a face. "You wouldn't feel that way if you had some of your own." Then she thought about it and said, "Or maybe you would. There are days…"

"Yeah," he said. "I know. I would have liked a few kids, but it just never happened and I got used to it. Now it's too late."

"Not if you marry someone who wants a family."

"No, thanks. I think I'm beyond changing diapers and driving to preschool."

He looked so serious she couldn't resist teasing. "Some sweet young woman might make you change your mind."

"I don't think so." Clint's eyes twinkled. "How old are you?"

The blunt question didn't bother her. "Forty. Almost."

"I'm fifty. Almost. And I'm not interested in sweet young women. I'm interested in an almost-forty legal secretary who likes my chili and lets me spoil her in restaurants."

Marina couldn't help smiling at him. "I don't let you spoil me."

"You will. It'll get easier. Trust me."

"My mother said to never trust a man who says, 'Trust me.'"

He grinned. "You're right. I have ulterior motives."

"Which are?"

"To kiss you, for one thing. Now that we're alone, I think that's an excellent way to end the day. Put your glass down."

"You're so used to giving orders."

He looked genuinely apologetic. "Sorry. It's an old habit. Put your glass down, please. How's that?"

She set her glass on the table and let him take her hands in his. He leaned forward so their knees were touching and tugged her gently toward him. He didn't kiss her, simply trailed his lips along her jaw, sending sweet shivers down her spine. He tasted her earlobe and moved down the column of her neck.

"Nice," he murmured, returning to her mouth to touch the corner of her lips. "No kids, no toads."

It was crazy to move her head a fraction of an inch and find his lips. Madness to kiss him first, but she couldn't help it. It felt so damn good to move her lips against his. They kissed for long, excruciatingly wonderful minutes and Marina didn't think about anything but how good he tasted and how good the warmth felt. He dropped her hands, encircled her waist and lifted her onto his lap in one smooth motion. Their lips never separated, and Marina slid her hands around his neck.

Passion, pure and simple, had taken over. The kiss continued; they fell over backward on the bed. Somehow Marina was partially on top of Clint's broad chest, her hair falling against his cheek. His hands had tugged her blouse clear of her waistband and his fingers swept along her back, igniting the skin under his touch.

She lifted her mouth and looked down into those dark eyes. He unhooked the back of her bra and moved her to her side in a tangle of limbs.

"This is crazy," Marina said, panting. "This was supposed to be a good-night kiss."

"Who said?" He slid his hand under her blouse and touched her breast, making Marina close her eyes and pray for control. How long had it been since anyone had touched her like this? His hand felt so good she couldn't think.

"I think, uh, you did," she managed to say. "Now I'm on your bed in a motel room and you have half my underwear off me. I can't believe this."

"Me, either," he said, against the corner of her mouth. "Damn fool luck if you ask me."

"Damn fool luck," she repeated. "Is that a Texas expression?" If she could keep talking maybe she wouldn't start taking her clothes off and jumping on top of him.

"Hell," Clint said, fumbling with her blouse. "These buttons are too damn small."

"Do you always swear when you undress women?"

He lifted his head and gave her a level look. "Women?"

"Well, uh, you must have a lot…" She stopped, not really wanting to know how many women he'd slept with in Tyler. He was a virile man who could certainly take advantage of those cowboy boots of his.

"A lot of *what*, Marina?"

"Sex," she whispered. "You must get a lot of it. Anytime you want, I mean."

He flopped on his back and started to laugh. She felt his chest rumble under her hand. "What's so funny?" she asked.

Clint took a deep breath and chuckled again. Then, propping his head on his elbow, he turned to face her. "Lady, you have a lot to learn about me."

"Meaning?"

"Meaning I don't have sex with every woman I date, and I prefer celibacy to making love to someone I don't care about. And since my wife died I haven't cared about anyone enough to make the effort to go to bed with them and do a decent job of it." He smoothed the hair from her face with his free hand. "Until now," he added. "And I won't be able to make love to you tonight, either, because I don't even have a condom with me." He grimaced. "I thought I'd be spending the weekend with Tex, you see."

She ignored the surprising flash of disappointment. Her traitorous body wanted nothing more than to make love until dawn. "I thought you dated a lot of women in Tyler."

"Dated a few, I guess, but that doesn't mean I went to bed with any of them. Surprised?"

"Yes."

He leaned over and kissed her again. "I could find a drugstore," he said.

"Maybe it's better to leave it this way. I haven't exactly done this in a while, either."

Clint looked fascinated. "How long?"

She blushed. She felt the heat rise to her face and struggled to sit up. "A long while," she said, struggling to hook her bra with trembling fingers.

"Let me," Clint said, pushing her hands away and fastening the hook with ease.

"It never seemed worth the risk," she added. "At first it

was being afraid of being hurt again, and then, well, it seemed risky with all the talk of disease, so I just decided it wasn't worth it.''

His eyes sparkled, but he said, "I know what you mean."

Marina smoothed her blouse, but the wrinkles looked back at her. "I'd better go." She stood up on shaky legs and picked up her purse.

"Take your wine," Clint said. "You might need it to sleep tonight."

He was right, darn him. She picked up the glass and followed him to the door. He watched as she opened the door to her room, but before she disappeared inside she turned to look at him once more. "Thanks again for dinner."

"You don't have to go," he said.

"I think it's better if I do," Marina said, and went into her room. She shut the door behind her and leaned against it, closing her eyes. She'd come close to making love to a man who promised to turn her life upside down. Clint Stanford wouldn't be content with one night and she wasn't ready, willing or able to let a man into her life.

But still, lying beside him had felt so damn good.

CHAPTER TEN

MOM GAZED at Stanford when she didn't think he was looking. And The Cowboy checked out his mother whenever she was looking the other way. At this rate, Jon figured, it was a miracle they were getting across Wisconsin without crashing into something.

He watched from the back seat and tried to figure out what was going on. His mother had gone out on a date with the guy last week, which was probably pretty harmless, considering the principal's age. Stanford had to be at least forty-five, and Mom was heading toward forty really fast. They were a little old for anything fancy, Jon decided.

But, then again, you never knew. There were eighty-year-old guys who became fathers. Jon studied the back of The Cowboy's head. He didn't think Stanford would like being an eighty-year-old father.

They'd been alone together last night, Jon realized. In a motel, too. He almost laughed out loud. His mother wasn't exactly a quickie-in-the-motel type. In seventeen years Jon couldn't even remember her going out with a guy more than twice. If she was going to have sex with anyone, she would have done it before this. When she was young.

The Cowboy didn't have a chance if he thought he'd get anywhere with Mom. She liked living alone and she liked being in charge of her own life. She'd said it often enough. Still, she peeked at Stanford again and then turned away when he caught her looking and smiled.

Now they were discussing the music on the radio, so Jon

went back to reading college catalogues and daydreaming about living in a dorm. He would hate to leave his mother alone, of course, but he figured she'd be fine. He wasn't going far.

And he'd be home for holidays. The guys had told him that after the first year it was as if you'd been on your own forever. If you could survive being a freshman, you could make it. Unless you got addicted to partying, that is. Jon didn't think he was the partying kind, although the beer blast on the fourth floor Saturday night had been a pretty good time. He'd only had two beers because he didn't want to puke and make an ass of himself in front of the college kids.

There'd been pretty girls, too, to talk to, though none of them had been as pretty as Christy Hansen. Christy Hansen, who was his date for the prom next week. Talk about luck.

He tossed the brochures aside and looked out the window. He'd be lucky if he could get into Macalester. He'd be lucky to get into college anywhere if they found out about the fire.

He had to keep it quiet, at least until he'd been accepted somewhere. Both schools had early placement; both admissions directors had encouraged him to apply. With a 4.0 average and high SAT scores, he knew he was a prime candidate for acceptance. But would an arrest screw it all up?

He didn't know how much longer he could go on like this. He'd tell Stanford everything, though, if it weren't for Christy. No way was she going to get hurt by all this garbage. If he blabbed now, he could lose her.

Jon stared at farmland, rolling green to a blue horizon, and fought down the sudden wave of carsickness. He didn't know how much longer he could go on hiding the truth.

MARINA SAT DOWN on the swivel chair and took off her sneakers and socks, then slipped on a pair of leather, open-toed sandals. She'd stopped at Carl's Garage before she'd come to work, but there was no word on her car. They were still trying to locate an axle and assured her that they should have her car fixed within the week. With luck, the mechanic had added.

Amanda opened her office door and peered out. "Hi! I thought I heard someone out here." Her gaze fell to the sneakers. "Are you on an exercise program?"

"No. My car is broken."

"I would've picked you up. Why didn't you call?"

"It's not that far to walk. And it's a beautiful day."

Amanda crossed the room and opened the blinds. "Yes, it sure is. If I didn't have so much work…" She stopped. "We should eat out today."

Marina lifted her lunch bag. "I brought my lunch."

"Then we'll eat on the square. I have an old blanket in the trunk of my car. We'll have a picnic."

Marina chuckled. "You are an amazing boss."

The younger woman shrugged. "Tessie, my first secretary, used to boss me around something awful. It's kind of fun to be on the other end of that for a change." She headed back to her office. "After you get settled, come on into my office and we'll go over this week's schedule, okay?"

"I'll be right in." The phone rang. "After I answer this. Are you taking calls?"

"If it's not an emergency say I'm in a meeting." She looked at her watch. "Which isn't exactly a fib. I have to be at my mother's in an hour."

Marina answered the phone, took a message from a new client and then made a fresh pot of coffee. Then she picked up her notepad, stepped inside Amanda's open door and sat down across the desk. She and Amanda organized the week, including a court appearance and a meeting with a family concerned about their father's will. Marina looked over her notes and calendar. It promised to be a busy week.

"How was your weekend? Did Jon find any colleges he liked?"

Marina leaned back in her chair. "It started out with the car making a strange noise and ended up with Clint driving us to St. Paul."

"Clint?" Amanda's face lit up with delight. "You spent the weekend together?"

"Not the way you mean," she said, hoping her face wasn't growing red. It was all too easy to remember lying on top of him in that motel room. "It was nice of him to take us."

"*Nice?* He must think a lot of you to do something like that."

"He was supposed to take the dog and—" The phone rang again, so Marina leaned across the desk and answered it. "Baron-Trask Law Office. Good morning," she said. "Just a moment, please." She pushed a button and looked at Amanda. "Your mother is on the phone."

"I'll take it." She took the receiver and punched the button to open the line. "Hi, Mom. Yes, I'm still coming." She paused. "All right." She hung up the phone and frowned. "The meeting's been changed to ten-thirty."

"Is something wrong?"

Amanda shook her head, but she didn't look too happy. "It's a family meeting, and Lee is going to be there to explain what's going on with the investigation so far." She gazed at Marina. "Has Jon said anything else?"

"I don't think he knows anything," she assured her friend. "No matter what anyone thinks, those kids couldn't have had anything to do with the fire."

"MAYBE I CAN HAVE one of the puppies," Christy said.

Jon leaned against the row of lockers and waited for her to finish taking her stuff out for the night. He'd hung around long after most everyone had left, just so he could talk to

Christy after she made up an English quiz. "Sure. Stanford hasn't said what he's gonna do about the puppies."

"Maybe you should keep one, too."

He shrugged. "Mom won't want a dog when I'm away at school."

"That's a year away," she reminded him, shutting her locker and spinning the combination. "Maybe she'll change her mind."

"I'd rather keep Tex," he admitted, falling into step beside her. "She's pretty cool."

Christy smiled over at him, making Jon's heart pound faster. "She was very well behaved. She didn't bother the other animals and she let Jacob pet her. She can come visit anytime."

"Thanks, but I don't think I'll be visiting any more colleges."

"You decided, then?"

"Well, that's up to the schools. And whether or not I get any scholarships next year."

"You will," Christy said, heading toward the back door to the parking lot. "You're smarter than anyone else in the school."

"Yeah," a low voice said behind them. "Weiss is a regular Einstein, aren't you, Weiss?"

Jon turned to face Brad Schmidt. "Don't you ever quit?"

"No." The senior's gaze slid to Christy. "Hi, kid. Why don't you go on to wherever you were going?"

"No," the girl said. "I'm staying right here."

"Christy—" Jon began, but she stopped him.

"I've known you since you were six years old." She lifted her chin and stared at the taller boy. "So don't pull your scare tactics on me."

"You're hanging out with the wrong kind of people, Christy. It might get you into trouble."

Jon decided it was time to shut the jerk up. "We'll see

you around, Schmidt,'' he said, and turned away. Christy went to follow him, but Brad grabbed her by the arm.

''I hear you're all going to the prom together. Christy and Jon, Matt and Tina. Sounds real cozy. Tell Matt to cancel the date. She's going out with me, not with anyone else.''

Christy pulled her arm away. ''Stop it, Brad. You don't scare me. And Tina can go out with anyone she wants.''

Brad acted as if he didn't hear her. ''Remember,'' he said, looking at Jon. ''I warned you. It's all your fault any—''

''Is there a problem here?'' Mr. Stanford asked. No one had heard him round the corner. He didn't look too happy as he stared at them and waited for an answer.

Brad smiled. ''Hi, Mr. Stanford. We were just talking about the prom.''

''What does that have to do with you, Brad? You're a senior.''

''Giving advice,'' he said, acting as if he was the nicest guy in the world. Jon didn't smile and Christy looked angry.

''I thought you had baseball practice, Brad,'' Mr. Stanford reminded him. ''You're late.''

''Yeah.'' He smiled again and backed up a couple of steps. ''Thanks for reminding me. See you guys later.'' Brad turned around and headed for the stairs, then Stanford fixed his gaze on Jon.

''Anything you want to talk to me about?''

''Uh, no. I was just walking Christy to the parking lot. Matt's probably wondering what happened to her.''

''I'm late,'' Christy added. ''He's going to have a fit.''

''Go on then.'' Stanford relented, but he looked as if he'd give a fifty-dollar bill to know what was going on. ''I'll see you later, Jon.''

Jon almost groaned out loud. He'd promised The Cowboy he'd help him figure out the Internet this afternoon. Jon ignored Christy's curious look. ''Yeah,'' he said, moving toward the exit. Christy followed him, thank God. Within minutes they were out in the bright sunshine. A horn honked from the other side of the lot, meaning Matt wanted his sister to hurry.

"What was that all about?" Christy asked, stopping at the edge of the cement.

"Oh, I'm teaching Stanford how to use his computer."

"Not that. With Brad. He looks at you like he wants to beat you up."

He does. "I made the mistake of talking to Tina last fall."

"He's really jealous. Tina said that's why she broke up with him," Christy said.

Jon knew exactly how jealous Brad Schmidt really was. "She was smart."

Christy glanced at the truck, then back to Jon. "Matt doesn't want me going out with you. What's going on between the two of you?"

He took a deep breath. "He thinks I burned down the factory. Haven't you heard that rumor around school?"

Her eyes were wide as she looked up at him. "Why would my brother think that?"

Jon shrugged. "He's friends with Schmidt, that's why."

"Not anymore," Christy said. "Not since he asked Tina to the prom."

Jon was happy to change the subject. "Hey, what time should I pick you up Saturday?"

"Matt's getting Tina, then coming back home so Mom can take pictures. He can pick you up after he gets Tina, probably around quarter of six, okay? That should give us time for enough pictures to make our mothers happy, and then we can leave. I think we're supposed to be there around six-thirty or so for dinner." She smiled up at him and Jon felt warm all the way to his size-ten feet.

"I'll tell my mother," he said, smiling back. "She's been wondering how she'd get to take pictures."

"She's really nice. Tell her to come to the farm around six-fifteen."

"I will." He wanted to kiss Christy, but he never had before. And her brother was glaring at them through the windshield of the truck. So his timing would be pretty rotten if he leaned over and kissed her on the lips as he really wanted to. "See ya," he said, wishing they were alone someplace dark and quiet.

She smiled, and those blue eyes sparkled at him. "Bye, Jon," she said, moving away with a little wave. "I'll see you tomorrow. Can I call you if I have trouble with my chemistry homework?"

"Sure. I'll be home all evening." *As if I would go anywhere if you told me there was a chance you'd call.*

"Thanks!" With that, she was gone. He watched as she crossed the parking lot. Matt leaned over and opened the passenger door and Christy climbed inside. They were out of the parking lot in two minutes, and Jon turned and headed to Stanford's house. With any luck, the principal would catch on fast.

MARINA COULDN'T refuse his offer this time, Clint knew. She would have to accept a ride out to the farm so she could see Jon and his date all dressed up and ready to go. She'd managed to avoid seeing him all week, except for waving once when he'd come to take the dog out for a run. Not that Tex was much into running. She didn't mind a little exercise, but a Frisbee game left her panting and lying down on the grass a lot sooner than she used to.

While the dog panted and watched a nearby squirrel scamper down a tree, Clint had flopped on the grass beside her and pondered the mysteries of women. He wanted Marina; she wanted him. It should be easy.

But it wasn't. In fact, it was damn difficult and growing more difficult by the minute. Marina didn't trust him; a son of a bitch husband had left her with a definite mistrust of men in general. Which was ridiculous. Clint had never laid a hand on a woman in his entire life. Marina had nothing to fear from him, if she'd only open her eyes and face the truth.

And then there was the boy. Jon was hiding something, but unless he'd single-handedly burned down the F and M, there wasn't much that could get him into trouble. Lee's investigation of the mystery note hadn't turned up anything, except everyone wished the author hadn't used an ink-jet printer to do it. A typewriter would have been easier to trace, and handwriting would have been a gift.

But Clint didn't want to believe that any of his kids had anything to do with the fire, and until there was something more to go on, he refused to believe they could have. The fire had taken place the day after the science team had met. Clint himself had let them into the plant; Brad's father had locked up behind them when they left. Everything had been just as it should be.

Until the place exploded into flames.

A forty-percent chance it had been an accident, Lee Nielsen had said in Clint's office this afternoon. He'd told Judson Ingalls and his family the same thing this week, at one of their family meetings. A decision would be made soon, but Lee and Brick Bauer still suspected that someone had deliberately set the fire.

But none of that should affect the way Clint and Marina felt about each other. He smiled, remembering the shape of her breast under his hand. A surprisingly strong and sudden passion had flared between them, and it wasn't going to go away. No matter how much Marina chose to ignore it.

CLINT BROUGHT the dog back and refilled her water dish, then repeated his offer to drive out to the farm for the picture session. Amanda had offered, too, but Marina had hesitated to take her up on it. Her boss naturally preferred spending Saturday nights with her husband.

"Call me if you need me," Amanda had said.

Now Clint stood in her kitchen, taking up more space than he should in the small room, offering once again to drive her to the farm. He leaned against the kitchen counter as if he belonged there. He looked casual and sexy and very, very good. She wanted to wrap her arms around his waist and lean her head on his chest. She wanted to run fifty miles an hour in the opposite direction.

"Okay," she said. "I'll get my camera."

He smiled, as if he knew she'd agree.

"Should be a fun night for the kids," he said, once they were in the car and on their way out of town.

"I hope so. Jon was so excited. And he looked so handsome in his tuxedo."

"Gates Department Store must have done quite a lot of business this week," Clint drawled. "Between renting tuxes and selling prom gowns, it must have been a busy place."

"I remember my first prom," Marina said. "I wore a blue dress with matching shoes and my date was a boy from my history class."

"I'll bet you were beautiful."

She chuckled. "Oh, I don't know about that. Skinny, yes. Nervous, definitely. We didn't say two words all the way to the gym. Remember when proms were held in the gym?"

"Yeah," he said, glancing toward her with a smile on his face. "The girls would spend two days making paper flowers."

"That's right." She sighed. "It's all so much more complicated now."

"Oh, I don't know. They're still kids. The girls are thrilled with their dresses and the boys have been complaining about wearing tuxedos, so things haven't changed all that much."

"I hope you're right. I want Jon to have a good time, so he has something special to remember."

"I think he's so glad to have a date with Christy Hansen that he wouldn't care where he was going."

She shook her head. "I can't believe he's all grown-up."

"He is," Clint assured her.

But I don't want him to be. Marina looked out the window. It was a beautiful evening for a prom. No wind to disturb the girls' hair, no rain to hurt the dresses.

"Want to get something to eat after this?"

"I don't know." Marina looked down at her jeans and T-shirt. "I'm not exactly dressed for dinner."

"We can get a pizza and eat at my house."

Oops. She should have seen that coming. She'd avoided him all week, hoping that she could forget what had happened in that St. Paul motel room. Hoping that *he* would forget what had happened in that St. Paul motel room.

"Unless you'd rather not," he said.

"No, that sounds good." She wasn't some scared spinster who was afraid to be alone with a man, for heaven's sake. And it was tempting to have an evening alone with him. Being with him didn't mean she was in danger of jumping into bed with him, of course. She had more control than that. Didn't she? "What time do you have to be at the post-prom?"

"Not until midnight. It lasts till four, so don't expect Jon home before that."

"He already warned me not to look for him before dawn."

Clint pulled into the driveway of the farm and found a place to park amidst an assortment of trucks and cars. "Looks like everyone is here," he said.

Marina slung her purse over her shoulder and picked up her camera. Britt met them at the door.

"Come on in," she said, stepping back to let them enter

the large kitchen. "They're being very patient letting us take pictures."

Jake, busy posing the two couples near the living-room fireplace, waved. Christy looked elegant in a short black cocktail dress. Her long hair was loose, a rhinestone barrette holding the gleaming waves from her face. A tall blonde in a navy blue sheath stood beside Matt. Silver earrings hung to her bare shoulders, and she appeared to be at least twenty-five, Marina decided, preferring Christy's outfit. Jon and Matt looked as if they'd worn tuxedos all their lives. Somehow they'd turned into men of the world.

"You all look wonderful," Marina said.

"Thanks, Mrs. Weiss," Christy said. The kids gazed past her to the principal. Tina's eyes grew wide; she was the only one who hadn't known that Jon's mother was friends with Mr. Stanford, Marina guessed.

"Hi," the other three said.

"I promise I won't take long," she said, getting her camera ready.

"Take your time," Jake said, grinning. "They're getting used to it."

"Jake," Christy groaned. "You've used two rolls of film so far."

He didn't look the least bit concerned. He shook hands with Clint, offered him a cold drink, and the men disappeared into the kitchen while Britt watched the two couples pose for another round of pictures. Marina was quick: after photographing the foursome, she had Jon and Christy pose together by the fireplace, then again near the door.

"That's it," Marina said, putting her camera down. "You were great."

Jon grinned. "Can we go now?"

"We should leave," Matt said, speaking for the first time. He was a tall boy with a serious expression on his tanned face. He looked like a kid who was used to working outside and had the shoulders to prove it.

"We don't want to be late," Tina added, smoothing her dress. She turned to Christy. "Is my hair still up?"

The sophisticated twist showed no signs of disintegrating. "It's fine," Christy assured her. She picked up her evening purse and the nosegay of peach roses and baby's breath Jon had brought her and tickled her little brother's nose with the flowers. Marina hid a sigh of relief; Jon had picked a lovely girl to have a crush on.

"Have a good time," Marina said, resisting the urge to straighten Jon's tie and kiss him goodbye. He would never forgive her if she came near him.

"See ya," he said, standing tall in that grown-up tux. He took Christy's hand in a casually protective manner and waved goodbye to the parents.

Britt stood beside Marina and watched the youngsters get into Jake's car. "Matt spent all afternoon polishing that vehicle," she said. "Tina's a senior. I was surprised that he asked her to go to the prom. They've known each other forever, I guess, and he doesn't have a steady girlfriend."

"Christy looked so pretty," Marina replied. They watched as the car disappeared down the driveway, a trail of dust puffing behind.

"She's so excited." Britt smiled. "You'll never know how many stores we went to in order to find the perfect dress." She bent down to pick up Jacob, who held his arms up to his mother. "Can you say hi to Marina?" she asked the little boy. He grinned and, overcome with shyness, buried his face in Britt's neck.

"Hi, Jacob," Marina said, trying not to laugh. She looked back at Britt. "Thanks for having us over."

"Anytime, Marina. You know that."

Clint and Jake were deep in a quiet discussion at the kitchen table, but broke off the conversation when the women approached. "You're ready for that dinner I promised?" Clint asked.

"Yes. Is there a one-hour photo-developing place in town? I don't know if I can wait to see the pictures."

Jake smiled at her. "The drugstore on Elm Street has 'next day' service. And I'll make sure you get copies of my best shots, too."

"Thanks. It's my first prom."

"Mine, too," Jake said, as Britt put his young son in his lap. "I hope we behaved okay. We'll hear about it tomorrow if we did anything embarrassing, I suppose."

Clint stood up and shook hands with Jake, promising to call him next time he needed a fishing partner. Britt walked Marina to the door. "Did Jon tell you the kids are coming back here for breakfast?"

"Yes. That's really nice of you to do that."

She chuckled. "I'm up early anyway, and Christy invited about six couples, so it's not going to be a lot of work."

"Bye," Marina said.

"Don't worry," Clint assured the Marshacks. "I'll be keeping an eye on them for most of the night."

"You're a brave man," Jake said.

Clint put his hand on Marina's shoulder and guided her outside. He was gentle for such a big man, she thought, liking the warmth of his hand touching her. This was ridiculous, she thought. She had to get a grip.

OLSEN'S SUPERMARKET had frozen pizzas that looked pretty good, for frozen pizzas. Clint was obviously experienced at buying frozen food that didn't take long to cook.

As they pulled up to his house, Marina remembered the one other occasion she'd been there, that time Jon had set up the computer and Clint had made his special Texas chili. The house looked similar to hers and was only a few blocks south. She could walk home, if she wanted to.

She didn't want to.

"Pepperoni and mushroom," Clint announced, sliding one pizza into the oven. "And pepperoni and sausage." He shut the door and set the timer. "That should do it."

"Tyler needs a pizza parlor."

"It would get my business," Clint said, turning to face her. Their gazes caught and locked. He held his arms out and moved toward her, and Marina went into his embrace as if she was coming home.

The thick pot holders touched her back. Clint muttered an oath near her lips and swept the mitts from his hands before he kissed her. He held her against him, his arms wrapped around her waist.

"I've thought about this all week," he said, then touched her lips with his in a gentle, teasing kiss.

"I tried not to," she replied, when he lifted his mouth and looked down into her eyes.

His back to the counter, Clint hooked his hands behind her hips and let her lean against him, between his thighs. "Why, darlin'?"

He was hard against her, making it difficult to think clearly. He felt good, all warm and male and solid, and Marina didn't want to lean on him. But she did.

"No answer?"

"No," she admitted. "I'm not used to this."

His lips touched her forehead. "Neither am I," he said, in a voice so soft she barely heard the words. Then a little louder, "Are we going too fast?"

"Yes. No." She couldn't resist touching her lips to the skin at the open collar of his short-sleeved shirt. She felt brave and crazy at the same time, staying in his arms.

"I don't want dinner," he said. "At least not right now." He smiled, but he looked uncertain. "I want to start kissing you and I don't want to stop. Not for hours," he added.

"Hours?"

"Hours," he declared, daring her to protest.

She didn't want to. She wanted to be kissed for hours, even if it was a crazy thing to do. Leaving his motel room had been difficult; walking out of his house would be impossible. Her traitorous body had other ideas, and eating pizza wasn't one of them, especially when his hands caressed her spine.

"This time," he said, stretching one arm to the stove to turn the dial to Off, "I don't intend to let you go so easily."

"Are all Texans bossy?"

"Yeah." His large hands held her face while he bent to take her mouth. It was a kiss full of promise and passion, a kiss to claim her as his, Marina realized. And she kissed him back with promises and passion of her own, daring him to understand that she wanted him, too.

It didn't take long to climb the stairs to Clint's bedroom. It was like the rest of the house, simply decorated and neat to the point of being sparse. There was no clutter, no dust, just a simple, silver-framed picture on the dresser next to a ceramic dish full of pennies.

Clint followed the direction of her gaze. "That's Judy," he said. "Does the picture bother you?"

"No," Marina said, turning around to look at the rest of the large room. A king-size bed took up most of the space, while pine shutters covered three small-paned windows above the headboard. Closet doors covered the opposite wall, with the dresser on one side and nothing on the other but a nightstand tucked at an angle into the corner.

"I've pictured you here," he said, stepping up behind her and putting his arms around her waist. His breath tickled her neck. "I didn't think it would come true."

"It feels strange," she confessed, wishing her knees wouldn't tremble. She rested her hands on his clasped ones; she rubbed his knuckles with her palms in a nervous motion.

"I haven't made love in a hundred years and I'm scared to death."

"It'll come back to you," he whispered. "Even after a century."

His assurance did little to assuage her nerves. "Promise?"

"Promise." He turned her around to face him. "Would it terrify you to take your T-shirt off?"

Marina took a deep breath. "I will if you will."

"That's a deal."

She backed up a step, gripped the hem of her shirt and pulled it over her head. Thank goodness the light was dim. Some sunlight filtered through the louvered shutters, but not enough to make her want to run screaming from the room. Clint tossed his shirt on the floor, so Marina let hers drop on top of it in what she hoped was a casual gesture. Her heart felt as if it were going to pound through her skin.

He planted a kiss above her right breast. "Okay so far?"

She nodded. His chest was brown and wide and solid, covered with a mat of dark hair that made her long to run her fingers across the muscled skin.

"Shoes, then," he said. She kicked off her sandals, and Clint sat down on the bed and pulled off his boots, then his socks, and tossed them aside. "Come here," he said, pulling her to him. She stood in the vee of his legs, between his knees. He reached for the waistband of her jeans and unsnapped the metal fastener, then slowly unzipped the fly. His fingers slid between the denim and her skin, then along the silky underpants and down, to slip the jeans from her hips. Marina, legs shaking, bent to remove them and kick them aside. Then she stood facing him, clad only in her bra and panties, while his fingers teased the lace waistband that crossed her abdomen.

"Your turn," she whispered. "Stand up."

He did, giving her a questioning look, and she bravely

reached for his jeans and imitated the way he had undressed her. Her fingers found cotton briefs and briefly swept over the hard bulge beneath as she tried to push the denim past his hips. He took over for her, tugging his jeans off in a rough motion, his briefs following quickly. Then he took her in his arms for a searing kiss; he was hard and hot against her thigh and Marina closed her eyes and wondered how she could have lived without this for so long. She wasn't sure how they ended up in the bed. Somehow Clint managed to pull back the covers. Somehow she was sprawled on top of him and he was unhooking her bra and moving the straps down her shoulders. Then she was on her side, the scrap of lace tossed across the bed, and Clint was caressing her breasts with his hands and then his lips.

He didn't stop there. He kissed a trail lower along her skin, slipped his hand beneath her panties and eased them away from the part of her that was aching with need. He touched her with gentle fingers, then moved over her.

"Still scared?" he asked, looking down into her eyes.

"Just a little. I think it's all coming back to me now," she managed to say, and he smiled.

"This time I'm prepared," he said, reaching toward the nightstand. Seconds later he hovered above her, looking into her face as he paused before entering her.

"So beautiful," he whispered, then he eased inside of her. He moved slowly, as if he was afraid to hurt her. Then, as she shifted slightly to pull him farther inside, he moved into her completely, claiming her as his. It was heaven, Marina decided, while she could still think a coherent thought. Heaven, she thought once more, and then nothing but sensation swept over her.

CHAPTER ELEVEN

"ARE YOU STILL BREATHING?" Clint nuzzled Marina's shoulder and inhaled the faint smell of roses. He wondered if it was from her soap or from perfume. He would never forget the fragrance, that much he knew.

"Mmm," was her sleepy response as she rolled toward him and snuggled against him. Her soft, sweet body fit into his arms the way he'd imagined it would. Her eyes were closed and her hair was a tumble of dark waves along her shoulders. All in all, a very enticing picture.

He wondered if making love to her a third time would be pushing the limits of good taste and common sense. He looked at her breasts and felt her sleek thighs against his legs and seriously considered the possibility.

Then he closed his eyes and sighed with contentment. As sure as God made Texas, Marina Weiss had been worth waiting for.

She woke him up after what seemed like only minutes. He pulled her closer, relishing the feel of a naked woman in his bed.

"It's almost eleven-thirty," she whispered. "Don't you have to chaperon the party at midnight?"

He groaned. "I'm never leaving this bed."

"But—"

"And neither are you." He opened his eyes and gently bit her neck. "You taste good."

She laughed softly, another female sound he liked in his bed. All in all, this was working out real well. He shifted his weight and rolled her onto her back, then prepared to move over her.

"We have to go," she said, and she sounded like she meant it.

Damn. He nudged her legs apart with his knee. "Five minutes," he said, looking down into those sleepy hazel eyes.

She smiled. "Fifteen," she countered.

"You're on," he agreed, and proceeded to make love to her again.

THE PHONE RANG when Marina was still in the shower. Clint wrapped a towel around his waist and reached for it. *The prom,* he thought. There was something wrong. "Hello?"

"Clint," Brick Bauer said. "I'm glad I caught you. I've got a carful of your kids who are going to be a little late for the postprom."

"What's going on?"

"No one's hurt. They ended up in a ditch out on the highway, about a mile west of the Dairy King."

"Have they been drinking?"

"No sign of it. I'm not sure what was going on, but you might want to come down here and see for yourself. I called a tow truck, and Jake Marshack is on his way, too."

"Who are the kids?"

"The Hansen kid was driving, and our friend Mr. Weiss was in the back seat with Christy. How does that kid get into so much trouble?"

"Beats me. I'll be right there," Clint promised, and hung up the phone as Marina entered the room, a towel wrapped around her body, and smiled at him.

She gave him a questioning look as she bent to pick up her jeans. "What's going on?"

"Some of the kids drove into a ditch on their way to the postprom. I have to go check it out."

Marina stopped. "Jon?"

He nodded, and watched the color drain out of her face. "No one is hurt. Brick said they're just shook up."

"Are you sure?"

"Positive. I'm going out there to see for myself."

"I'll go with you."

It was useless to argue, and besides, he didn't blame her for wanting to see for herself that her son wasn't hurt. Damn kids. He put his clothes back on faster than he'd taken them off.

THEY WERE MAKING a federal case out of it. All of them, even Christy's stepfather. Mr. Marshack had taken Matt aside for some heavy interrogation, but it didn't look as if he was getting anywhere. The policemen relaxed a little when the tow truck showed up. Jon stood close to Christy and watched the mechanic hook up the bumper of Mr. Marshack's Ford Taurus.

Headlights came from town and pulled over to the other side of the road. Blast it, Jon thought, someone else to gawk at them and ask a lot of questions. He groaned out loud when Stanford got out of the white Jeep. And then Jon wanted to sink into the ground when his own mother followed close behind, crossing the road as fast as she could, heading toward them with a worried look on her face.

Why in hell did Stanford think he had to call her?

Jon braced himself. "I'm all right," he said, hoping to wipe the worried look from her face.

She did relax a little after he spoke, after she touched his shoulder as if she had to make certain he was alive. "Are you sure?" She looked at Christy. "Are you okay, too?"

"We're fine, Mrs. Weiss," Christy assured her. "We were on our way back to my house to change for the post-prom. I guess we're going to be really late now."

"What on earth happened?"

Christy bit her lip, and Jon answered for her. "I'm not really sure. I think we hit some gravel and Matt lost control for a second."

"Were you speeding?"

"Oh, no," Jon said, not wanting her to get off on that track. "If we'd been going too fast we'd have hit the ditch real hard. This was nothing. I don't know why everyone's making such a big deal out of it."

Marina put her hands on her hips and surveyed the scene. Two police cars, one tow truck, a principal, stepfather, mother and three teenagers. "It looks like a big deal to me. Where's Matt's date?"

Christy pointed to one of the police cars, where Clint and a policeman stood talking. "Tina's in there, crying. I think she's waiting for her mother to come pick her up."

Marina turned back to the kids. "What about you? Are you still going on with this night?"

"Yeah, sure," Jon said, suddenly afraid she'd pull the plug and take him home.

His mother paused. "Okay. If you're bent on going to the postprom, Mr. Stanford can give you a ride."

"We have to go back to Christy's for our clothes," Jon said. "Mr. Marshack said he'd take us in a few minutes, as soon as he made sure everything was okay here."

"There," Christy said, pointing across the road. The tow truck pulled the car out of the ditch and settled it on the road. Jake and Matt went over to it and checked out the tires. "It looks okay, doesn't it?"

"I suppose so," Marina said. "Stay right here. I'm going to talk to Clint and I'll be back."

Jon and Christy watched her cross the road and head toward Mr. Stanford.

"Does she go out with him?"

"What do you mean?"

"Your mother is so pretty. Does she goes out with Mr. Stanford? You know, date him?"

"Sort of. They go out to dinner sometimes."

"That's so neat."

"Why? It's kind of a pain having him hanging around the house."

Christy shrugged. "He's nice. I like him." She poked him in the ribs. "Maybe he'll be your stepfather someday."

"Ouch," he said, secretly enjoying her teasing. She went to poke him again, but he caught her hand in his and hung on to it. "My mother doesn't want to get married again, that's for sure."

"Why not?"

"She says she'll never give up her freedom for a man again. She says she likes being on her own."

"And she likes Mr. Stanford." Christy pointed to the police car. Mr. Stanford stood close to Marina and had draped a comforting arm around her shoulders. "It looks like he likes her, too. Do you mind?"

"It doesn't matter." Jon shook his head. "He'll never get anywhere. No one ever has."

Still, he watched his mother when Christy left his side to check on Tina. His mom and Stanford did seem awfully friendly, all right. They'd *really* freak if they knew what had happened tonight. Maybe now Matt would believe him.

Maybe now Matt would understand.

"IF I SEE SCHMIDT, I'm beating the living crap out of him." Matt's hands were balled into fists and he looked as if he were going to start tearing down the gym walls. Loud music blasted through the room, but Jon looked around, hoping no one would overhear their conversation.

"You can try, I guess," he said, wishing Matt would keep his voice down. They didn't want this story to get around school. "You're almost as big as him."

"I'm a hell of a lot madder, too." Matt watched the double doors. "Where do you think he is?"

"He can't come here. He's a senior and he doesn't have a date with a junior." Jon shoved his hands in his pockets and wished Christy would come back from having her fortune told. Miss Henson, one of the English teachers, was reading palms in a gold tent under the basketball hoop. "You'll see him soon enough. He'll be gloating, too."

"Not for long," Matt said, flexing his fingers. "Not for long."

"Are you sure it was him?"

"Yeah. Pretty sure."

"Did Tina see?"

"She wouldn't say. She just started crying and that was that. Her mom took her home, so I didn't get to talk to her. She said she'd try to come here in a little while." He ran a hand through his rumpled hair and looked toward the double doors. "He could have killed us all."

"Yeah." Jon swallowed. Hard. Brad Schmidt had deliberately run them off the road tonight. Maybe he hadn't tried to kill them, but he'd certainly planned to ruin their evening. And he had, at least where Matt was concerned. Now the guy didn't even have a date.

The boys stood silently for a long minute, until Matt finally spoke. "Why'd you have to drag us into this, Weiss?"

Jon looked up, surprised. "You think this is all because of me?"

"Brad's been a friend of mine since we were little kids. He wouldn't have turned on me, unless you were in the car."

"It's not about me," Jon insisted. "Not really."

Matt shook his head and moved away. "He's trying to get to you and you're still lying. This feud could've gotten us all in a lot of trouble."

"I told you—"

"You told me nothing." He lowered his voice as Christy approached them. "If she gets hurt, it'll be your fault. And I'll see that you pay for it."

"You'll never believe what she said," Christy said, giggling. "My palm shows a strong life line and four children!"

"So you'll be an old lady with a lot of kids," Jon teased, grateful to end the conversation with Matt. "And you're *excited* about that?"

"I'm not going to tell you what else she said," Christy said. "Just that there was a green-eyed boy in my life."

Matt frowned as Christy took Jon's hand. "When you two are ready to leave, let me know. I'm gonna call Tina and see if she's okay."

Christy gave her brother a worried look. "It wasn't your fault," she said. "Some idiot ran us off the road. It was an accident."

"Yeah," Matt replied. "An accident." He looked over at Jon. "Remember what I said," he told him before disappearing in the crowd of dancers.

Christy turned to Jon. "What did he say that you're supposed to remember?"

He was too tired to do anything but be honest. "To see that you don't get hurt."

"Why would I get hurt?"

He tugged her away from the crowd, to a corner of the bleachers. "You didn't see the driver of the car, did you?"

"No." Her eyes were wide. "You mean, you and Matt know who did it?"

"Yeah."

"Well, *who?*"

"Brad Schmidt."

Christy stared up at him. "Why didn't you tell Mr. Bauer? Or Mr. Stanford? He can't get away with—"

"He won't get away with anything," Jon said, wishing

he knew that for sure. "Matt thinks he's gonna take care of it."

"It's because Tina went out with Matt tonight, isn't it?"

Smart girl. Smarter than her brother, who didn't want to face the truth. "Yeah, that's part of it."

"What's the other part?"

"Doesn't matter." Jon tried to smile, tried to look like Keanu Reeves. "Tell me about your fortune? I have green eyes, you know."

"I noticed. They're very nice," she informed him. "And you should smile more often."

"There's not a lot to smile about."

"Sure there is," she said, pulling him into the crowd of dancing teenagers. "For one thing, we don't have to go home till dawn."

The music shifted into a slow song, Rod Stewart singing "In Your Eyes" for the fifty-millionth time. Christy went into Jon's arms and suddenly there was a lot to smile about.

THERE WAS A LOT to be said for great sex, Marina decided, climbing into her bed and pulling the covers over her shoulders. More than she remembered, actually. And it had never been as good as it had been tonight, with Clint.

She grew warm remembering.

It wasn't love. Of course not. That tingly feeling when she looked at him was lust, pure and simple. They'd proved that tonight.

It had been good to touch a man's body, to be touched by a man. And not just any man, but one like Clint Stanford.

She wondered if all Texans made love with such... abandon. She wondered if she should ask him. He would laugh, of course. Next time she would ask him.

Next time. Marina rolled onto her back and looked up at the ceiling. Would there be a next time? *Should* there be?

Good question. Marina sighed. She could easily imagine

making love to him again. And that's what it was: love-making. Was she falling in love with the man? That soft look he sometimes gave her tended to weaken her knees. Clint Stanford was an incredibly *nice* man, a man with gentle hands and an easy smile. He treated her with a tenderness that made her long to rest her head on his very broad shoulder and tell him all her troubles, big or small. He was the kind of man who would stand by his woman, of that much she was certain.

MARINA WAS AWAKE, drinking her second cup of coffee, when Jon walked into the kitchen. He carried his tuxedo, on its hanger, over his arm and dropped it on a kitchen chair. "Hi, Mom!"

"Hi, yourself. Did you have a good time?"

"Yeah. It was pretty cool. There was a hypnotist who made kids do all sorts of funny things—"

"A hypnotist? Really?"

"They got him from Milwaukee, I think. And a deejay who had a Golden Oldies contest and an auction, too. Christy and I put our money together and bid on a portable CD player." He grinned. "Don't worry, Mom. It was fake money they gave us for different things. I guess stores donated the stuff for the auction. It was pretty cool." He sat down, straddling the chair backward.

"And you went back to Christy's for breakfast?"

"With a bunch of other people. Mrs. Marshack made pancakes for everyone." He yawned. "Man, am I tired."

"You look it." He also looked happy. Obviously, dating Christy Hansen was good for his temperament. "I'm glad you had fun. Everyone should have fun at their prom."

"Tell Matt that. Tina didn't show up at the postprom."

"She looked pretty upset. She must be a very, um, sensitive girl."

Jon shrugged. "She's okay. Christy called her this morning."

"How'd you get home?"

"Mr. Marshack dropped me off. Matt went to bed early."

It didn't sound like Matt had had such a good time. "That's too bad."

Jon yawned again. "I'm going to bed."

"Good idea." Marina took another sip of her coffee and wondered if Clint was as tired as her son. He hadn't had much rest before chaperoning the late-night party, after all.

"Mom. Hey, Mom."

She looked over to him. "Hmm?"

"You okay?"

Marina tried not to look like a grinning fool. She covered her smile by taking another sip of her coffee. "Never better. Why?"

"I don't know. You look different or something."

It showed? She swept her hair back from her face. "I think I need a haircut, that's all."

"No," he said, standing up. "That's not it. Never mind, I'm going to bed for a while. I'm really tired."

"Sleep well," Marina told him, watching Tex follow the boy out of the room. Then, alone in the quiet kitchen, she finished her coffee and wondered what Clint was doing. Sleeping, of course. Did he regret last night or would he expect to see her again? Dating in the nineties was certainly a difficult thing to figure out. She turned and eyed her yellow walls. Maybe it was time to get her mind off sex.

SURELY HE COULD COME up with something. Clint poured himself another cup of coffee and looked at his watch. Noon. He'd slept late enough. Marina would have been up for hours. Or, he thought, remembering last night, maybe she'd overslept, too.

He had to think. He took his coffee into the dining room

and looked at his computer. That was the last thing he wanted to play with today. He wanted to call Marina and go out to the lake and hold hands and take her to bed. But that was probably rushing things. But there had to be a way he could see her today, just to make sure everything was okay between them. She could be having second thoughts.

Worse, she could be thinking it was a one-night stand. If people still called them that.

He would phone her, he decided, checking his watch again. He would ask her out to the lake. He would tell her he had to check on the cabin and ask her if she wanted to ride out there with him. Jon would be sleeping; every kid who was at the prom would be sleeping late.

Maybe he should keep it casual. He would go over there to take Tex for a run. He could say he knew Jon wouldn't be walking the dog today. It would be very casual, not as if he'd planned it over two cups of coffee.

"HELLO?"

Marina balanced herself on the ladder and leaned over to see if that was really Clint's voice she'd heard at the back door. "Clint?"

"Yeah." The door opened and shut, then he appeared next to the open cupboard door. "What are you doing?"

That seemed like an unnecessary question, considering she held a paintbrush in her hand and a can of paint sat on the newspaper-covered counter, but Marina simply smiled at him. "Painting my kitchen. I've been waiting for spring."

He surveyed the two cupboards she'd finished. "It looks nice," he said. "Better than the yellow."

"I think so."

"Shouldn't you take the cupboard doors off first?"

She dipped her brush into the paint and continued to paint door number three. If he could act casual, she could, too.

"No. I didn't think I could get the hinges off. And even if I could, I was afraid I'd never get them on again."

She saw him wince as he looked at the paint-covered hinges.

"I'm not sure you really want to do this," he said.

"The hinges have been painted over before." She pointed to the door she was working on. "See?"

"I see."

"I'll be done with this in a minute. Do you want a cold drink or anything?"

"I came to take Tex for her walk."

"Oh. She's upstairs, in Jon's room." He'd come to see the dog. Not her. She pretended to be vitally interested in the back of the door. This was becoming embarrassing. They'd made love three times last night and he came to see Tex.

She heard him clear his throat. "That's not true."

Marina turned to look down at him. He'd approached the bottom of the ladder and reached for her waist, lifting her off. "It's not?"

"Hell, no." He set her feet on the floor and kissed her, long and hard, before he raised his head and looked into her face. "I came because I had to see you."

The paint fumes had made her dizzy. "You did?"

"The damn dog was just an excuse."

She hooked her hands around his neck, careful to keep her brush away from his hair. "I wondered if you'd call."

"I had to find out for myself that last night really happened."

"It really happened," she assured him. "And it was very nice, too."

"Very nice? That's all you can say?"

"Very, very nice," she said, planting a kiss on his chin. "How about that?"

He tightened his grip around her. "Want to go out to the lake for a while?"

"I can't," Marina said, wishing she hadn't started such a big project, after all. Still, the kitchen cupboards would surround her long after Clint had moved on. Kitchens were permanent; men were not. "I'm in the middle of this and I need to get it done."

"Do you have an extra brush?"

"Yes, but—"

"I'll help then."

"You don't—"

He kissed her briefly, then released her. "I wouldn't mind the work. I could use the exercise."

No, he couldn't. Every inch of his body was perfect. She'd discovered that for herself last night. "You really don't have to get involved with this."

"I'd like to." He was already picking up a brush from the pile of supplies she'd assembled on the table. "Where do you want me to start?"

She pointed to other end of the kitchen, to the cabinets above the stove. "How about over there? Then we'll be out of each other's way." She eyed his white T-shirt and clean jeans. "You're going to be covered in paint."

"That doesn't matter. Should I open another can?"

"Okay."

They painted for hours, stopping only for sandwiches when they were hungry. He told her Air Force stories. She told him about growing up in the suburbs of Chicago. They didn't talk about teenagers or school or the future.

Marina realized she enjoyed the help. She wasn't used to having anyone but Jon help her.

Her son woke up before they were done. "Hey, neat," he said, looking at the paint job. "Hi, Mr. Stanford." Tex wagged her tail when she spotted Clint and stepped around newspapers to greet him personally.

"Hi, Jon," Clint replied.

"That dog knows who she belongs to," Marina said, watching the way the animal hurried over to Clint.

"Doesn't look like long now, does it, girl?" He stroked her head and eyed her sagging belly.

Jon sprawled into a chair. "I wonder how many she'll have."

"No telling," Clint said. "Five or six?"

Marina gulped. "Where are we going to put five or six puppies?"

"I'll build a shelter outside," Clint offered. "Something temporary. I know you can't have all those dogs in the house."

"Okay. But then what? What do we do with the puppies?"

"We'll find homes for them," he said, turning to Jon. "Right?"

"Right. It'll be real easy."

The whole scene was just too cozy. Anyone would have thought they were a family, the way they were acting. It made Marina very, very nervous. "I'd better get this mess cleaned up," she said, not looking at either one of them. It wasn't going to last, she reminded herself. But, oh, she wanted it to.

"SO, HOW'S IT GOING?" Ethan reached for the pitcher of cream that the waitress at Marge's had set near the edge of the table. "I understand you went to the prom."

"Postprom," Clint said. He pushed his half-eaten breakfast to one side of the table and picked up the thick mug of coffee. "I took the midnight-to-four shift."

"Ouch."

"It wasn't that bad." *Except all I wanted to do was crawl back in bed with Marina,* he added silently.

"Jake said the kids had a problem out on the highway."

"No one was hurt. The Mallory girl was pretty shook up, but the others seemed to take it in stride."

"That's a relief." Ethan stirred his coffee. "These Monday mornings are rough. Did you get out to the cabin this weekend? I meant to ask you if the fishing was any good."

"I didn't make it. I spent yesterday helping Marina paint her kitchen."

Ethan's eyebrows rose. "Really? Sounds like you're making progress with the lady."

Clint didn't say anything right away. He certainly wouldn't discuss what had happened Saturday night. No true gentleman would. "Maybe. I don't know where it's going. I can't get her to myself very often."

"You look miserable. Like a man in love."

Clint glanced up. His friend's expression was serious. "I'm beyond all that," he said.

"I see." Ethan picked up his mug and took another swallow.

"I'm nearly fifty. That's too old for mooning around like a lovesick calf." Ethan looked at him as if he waited for Clint to continue. "She has a son," he added. "A son who's spent the past month in detention. I'm too old to be a father."

"Not really, but go on."

"I'm used to living alone. I'm set in my ways."

"True," Ethan stated, sounding very much like a judge. He turned his direct gaze on his friend. "And you've spent the past month trying to figure out how to get that woman to go out with you. There must be a reason why you went to so much trouble."

"I'm attracted to her, I admit it."

"Then what's the problem?" Ethan pulled his wallet from his inside jacket pocket and tossed some bills on the table. "I think it's my turn today."

"Thanks." Clint considered the question. "I don't have a problem."

His friend grinned. "Sure you do. You're in love with her. The way I see it, you've got one *hell* of a problem." He slid out of the booth and clapped Clint on the shoulder. "Good luck."

"Thanks." Clint looked at the wall clock above the cash register. Seven o'clock. Time to go to work and forget all about women.

"CLINT CALLED," Amanda said, when Marina returned to the office. She'd walked across the town square to Carl's Garage to retrieve her car. "Right as rain," Carl had pronounced, handing her the keys and the bill. She'd written the check, swallowed hard and drove her car to the lot behind the office.

Amanda smiled. "He sounded disappointed that you weren't here."

Marina tried not to grin like an idiot. "I'll call him back in a few minutes. Did you want to go over the Carter notes?"

"Not really. I think you should call Clint first." She winked at her and headed toward her office. "When you're done, just come on in. I'll be working on that file."

"All right." Marina dialed the school's number and the secretary connected her with Clint right away.

"Stanford," he said, sounding very official.

"Weiss," she answered. "Returning your call."

"Marina." He sounded pleased, which made her smile into the telephone. "I'm glad you called back. I wanted to…just a minute." She heard him talking to another person, then he got back on the phone. "Sorry about that. Mrs. Donelly came in with some papers for me to sign."

"That's all right. What's up? Nothing with Jon, I hope."

"No. It's personal. I wondered if you wanted to go out

to the cabin tomorrow night. We could have a cold supper and I could teach you to fish.''

"I'm not sure.''

"Think about it," he urged. "I'll supply supper, of course.''

Marina smiled into the telephone receiver. This was all about being alone together. This was all about sex. And boy, was she tempted to say yes. "Do we have to fish?''

He chuckled. "No. In fact, I'd prefer not to.''

"Me, too. What time?''

"I have a baseball game after school, so I'll pick you up at six-thirty. How's that?''

"That's fine." She would have time to shower and change clothes and fix something for Jon to eat before she went off to make love to the principal.

"Did you get your car fixed?''

"I picked it up this morning. Thanks again for helping me with that.''

"No problem," he drawled. "I'm at your service, ma'am.''

"Ma'am?"

There was a brief silence. "Just habit," he said.

"No problem, Tex," she said, trying not to laugh. "I'll see you tomorrow.''

"Yes, ma'am," he said. "I'll be lookin' forward to it.''

She hung up the phone and rested her chin on her hand. The front windows needed cleaning and the plant in the corner looked as if it was dying of thirst. She really should get up and water the poor thing, and then there were those briefs that Amanda needed to go over. Marina didn't move. She had another date with him, a date that would end up where they both wanted it to: in bed.

Oh, Lord. She couldn't possibly be in love with him. And

he wasn't in love with her. The man kept his feelings carefully hidden.

So what on earth was she doing? Whatever it was, she was enjoying herself.

"MOM, WHAT ARE YOU doing?"

Marina looked up as her son entered her bedroom and caught her brushing her hair for the fiftieth time this afternoon. She put an innocent look on her face. "What do you mean, honey?"

"Are you going out?"

"Um, yes. Clint's taking me fishing out at the cabin tonight. I thought I told you."

"You said you left my dinner in the fridge but you didn't say why." He came into the room and sat on the bed. "Can I come?"

"No."

He gave her a funny look. "You're really dating the guy, huh?"

"I guess so." She turned from the mirror over the dresser and faced her son. "Do you have a problem with that?"

"I'm not crazy about it," he said. "I don't like him knowing my business."

"You didn't mind when he drove us to St. Paul."

"That was different."

"Why?"

"It wasn't as if you were going out with him. It was...more like friends."

"It still is," Marina assured him. "He's a friend, and I'm going out with him."

Jon gave her a worried look. "It's not serious, is it?"

Marina answered as honestly as she could. "I don't know what it is, Jon. Clint and I...enjoy being together. That's all it is right now."

"Really?"

"Really."

He looked relieved. "I'm not used to you going out," he said.

"And I'm not used to *your* going out, either," Marina teased. "You looked so handsome in your tuxedo."

"Mom," he groaned, and hopped off the bed. "I'm gonna go get something to eat."

Marina turned back to the mirror and made a face. She was queasy and nervous and couldn't stop looking at her watch. She wished she could remember what being in love felt like. She didn't think this was it, though. This was lust, pure and simple.

"DO THAT AGAIN," Clint murmured, pulling her toward him for another kiss.

"Mmm," she said, lifting her lips to his. "I thought we were going to eat dinner."

"Later."

"How much later?"

"At this rate, you'll be eating dinner in about fifteen minutes." He grinned and set her away from him.

"We're crazy."

"Yeah," he said, tucking her hand in his and leading her toward the bedroom. "I've thought that, too."

Much later, they took their sandwiches out to the porch. The sky was showing off its sunset colors in the last minutes before dark, and Clint sat beside Marina in a comfortable silence. There didn't seem to be anything to say, yet at the same time there were a million words he wanted to share.

The problem, he thought, choking down the roast beef sandwich, was that he couldn't remember how it felt to be in love. He could only guess that wanting this woman day and night might be his first clue.

CHAPTER TWELVE

"WHERE DO YOU WANT IT?"

Marina stood beside Clint's Jeep and looked at the partially assembled doghouse in the back. "I don't know. It looks pretty big."

He reached in and slid it onto the tailgate. "I wanted it to be comfortable. It has to hold them for at least six weeks."

"I think you're just in time. That dog has been acting pretty quiet today. She didn't even whine when Jon left after dinner."

"Where'd he go?"

"Christy's. There's a big chemistry test coming up on Friday. They're getting a head start on studying." She watched as he lifted one end of the wooden structure. "Can I help?"

"Sure. Grab the other end and follow me. It shouldn't be too heavy."

"I'm stronger than I look," she said, getting a grip on the bottom corners of the doghouse.

"I won't argue with that. Am I going too fast?"

"A little." It wasn't easy keeping up with those long legs of his as they crossed the lawn.

When they rounded the house, Clint hesitated. "How about in that corner?" He nodded toward the one part of the yard that hadn't been converted to a flower garden. "I can add a temporary fence, too, if the puppies get out of hand."

"What have I gotten myself into?" Marina meant the question in more ways than one. She helped him carry the structure to the corner, then they set it down and positioned it with the door facing the house.

"So you can see the puppies go in and out," Clint explained.

Why? she wanted to ask. But she didn't. She watched as he adjusted the house.

"I brought an old blanket, and we should spread newspapers around, too, for the birth."

"All right." Marina retrieved a stack of newspapers from the basement while Clint got the roof and the blanket from his car. She opened the kitchen door and called Tex to come out and see her new home.

The dog was not impressed. She sniffed it a couple of times, then lay on the grass and watched Clint line the wooden floor with a blanket. He called her over to try it out, but she wasn't interested. Marina eyed the doghouse. It looked better now that it had a roof, and the fresh coat of yellow paint matched the house.

"Did you paint it yellow on purpose?"

"Yeah. I thought you might like it better that way."

"I do, thanks."

He sat beside Marina on the grass and leaned back on his elbows. "Have you had dinner?"

"An hour ago. What about you?"

"I ate, too. I have a meeting at school in an hour with the parents of seniors."

She tried not to feel disappointed that he couldn't stay. This was ridiculous. She was growing used to seeing him and, even worse, she was beginning to count on it.

"I could come over later," he offered.

She shook her head. "Jon will be home."

They sat in silence on the lawn, as Tex ignored her new home.

"Can you get away for the weekend? We could go to an inn up near Lake Winnebago."

"I can't." She hoped he'd understand. "It's just too awkward. How would I explain that to Jon?"

"He's seventeen."

"Exactly." She smiled, and pushed his foot with her own. "Wouldn't you have been shocked when you were seventeen and your mother went away for the weekend with a man?"

"I would have been shocked if my mother ever left the kitchen," he admitted. "I wish you could have met her. She died almost four years ago, right before Judy got sick." He leaned back in the grass. "That woman loved to bake."

"My mother did, too," Marina said. "But she died when she was quite young, in her fifties."

"And your father?"

"He was killed in an accident when I was ten. It was just my mother and me growing up."

"Like you and Jon."

"Yes."

He sighed and closed his eyes. "No wonder."

"No wonder what?"

"No wonder you're so damn used to being alone."

Marina stared at him for a second, but he didn't open his eyes. His breathing grew quiet and steady, and she wondered if he was asleep. Sure, she was used to being alone. There was nothing wrong with that. It made her strong. It made her independent.

And it made her glad when someone drove her to the garage and built her a doghouse and helped her paint her kitchen. And held her in his arms.

"YOU COULD TELL ME what's going on, you know," Christy said, closing her chemistry book. "I'm a good listener."

Jon didn't look up from the equation he was trying to finish. "There's nothing to tell," he lied.

"Oh, really?"

"Brad hasn't been in school, Matt's cooled down and things are pretty quiet, don't you think?" He looked up at her then. She frowned at him.

"I heard Brad and Tina are back together again."

"See?" He tossed his pencil on the table. "The guy always gets what he wants. Maybe now he'll leave me alone."

"Why was he after you in the first place, Jon? He and Matt had a long talk the other day. Brad apologized for what happened after the prom. He said it was an accident, that he was upset over Tina and that he was really sorry for being such a jerk. Matt says it has to do with the fire. Is that the truth?"

Jon didn't want to talk about this. The serious expression in Christy's blue eyes made his stomach sink. He dared a question. "What if I told you it had *everything* to do with the fire?"

She blinked and leaned back in her chair. "I can't believe you had anything to do with burning down the F and M."

His heart started beating again. "Well, you're the only one," he said. Not counting his mother.

"I couldn't believe a lie like that, Jon. You should know that." She leaned her chin on her hand and studied him. "Why do you think Brad hasn't been in school?"

"I don't know. Maybe he's sick."

She shook her head. "Tina said he went to M.I.T. They asked him to interview. He's the winner of the science scholarship this year, you know."

"I heard." Brad was the kind of guy who won everything. The kind of guy who knew how to get his own way.

"You'll probably get it next year, even without the F and M project. You get higher marks in chemistry than anyone else I know."

"There's more to it than just grades," he said, trying not to sound bitter. "You figured out this equation yet?"

"No." She smiled, and suddenly life didn't seem so bad. "But I'll bet you have, right?"

"Right. But you have to do it yourself so you can do it on the test Friday."

She picked up her pencil and turned to the figures on the legal pad in front of her. "Okay, but after this we'll have some cheesecake."

"Great." He was getting addicted to the stuff. The Hansen refrigerator was always stuffed full of great food.

"Whether or not I get this right," Christy muttered, making him smile.

"You'll get it right."

And she did. And later, when they'd raided the refrigerator and finished studying, Christy walked him to his car. Jon looked around for Matt, hoping the guy wasn't going to show up and give him a hard time.

"He's at baseball practice," Christy said, guessing who he was looking for. "It's safe."

"You never know," Jon said. "He could be waiting behind the barn or something."

"Nope." She put her arms around his neck and kissed him. It was a brief kiss, just a sweet brushing of the lips, but it stunned him.

"Bye," she said, smiling at him. "Thanks for the help."

"Bye." He tossed his books on the passenger seat and got into the car. He pretended a casualness he didn't feel as he drove out of the farm's driveway. He hadn't kissed her the night of the prom—the morning, actually—because it was daylight and everyone could see. He'd planned to; it just hadn't worked out. But she'd kissed him. Softly. Quickly.

He couldn't believe his luck.

Finally something good had happened to him in Tyler.

TEX IGNORED her new home, preferring instead to lie on the porch and guard the backyard from a distance.

"She's stopped eating," Jon noted as he finished a bowl of cereal. "Do you think she's sick?"

"No. I think dogs lose their appetite before giving birth. She must be very close to having those puppies," Marina said.

"How close?"

"I don't know, Jon." The dog was restless, though. She moved from one end of the porch and back again. "Just make sure she has plenty of drinking water. It looks like it's going to be really warm today." Morning sun poured through the kitchen window, and the air was fragrant with the neighbor's lilacs.

"Okay." He stood up, put his bowl and spoon in the dishwasher and grabbed his backpack. "See ya."

"Have a good day."

"Yeah, Mom. Sure." But he smiled to show he wasn't serious. "What about Tex? What if she has the puppies when we're not here?"

That wouldn't exactly be the end of the world, Marina thought, but she didn't voice the words. She was a little squeamish just thinking about it. "I'll check on her at lunchtime."

"I'll be home right after school."

"Good. I won't be late tonight, either."

He was out the door, talking to the dog, as Marina poured the rest of her coffee down the sink. Jon had become attached to the animal in the past few weeks. Boys and dogs— what a combination. And it didn't seem to matter how old the boy was, either.

Jon had missed so much growing up. And yet, Marina knew, if she had it to do over again, she couldn't have done it any other way. She'd had to leave James. She couldn't have let Jon grow up with that kind of abuse; she couldn't have lived with it, either.

It frightened her to think of loving again, giving someone else power over her life and that of her son's. Maybe it was time to slow down, take some time to think about what she was doing, what she wanted from this relationship with Clint. Maybe it was time to talk to someone who knew about love.

AMANDA POPPED out of her office and poured herself another cup of coffee. "Want to go out to lunch today? We could be really decadent and have hamburgers and fries at Marge's."

Marina turned from the computer screen. "That sounds good, but I have to go home and check on my—Clint's dog first. I think she's close to having her puppies."

"Really? That's exciting." Amanda leaned in the doorway. "You can run home, and if she's okay, you can meet me at the diner."

"All right." She looked at her watch. "How about in an hour?"

"Good. We'll put the Closed sign on the door and turn the answering machine on and figure we deserve an hour off." Amanda hesitated before returning to her office. "Are you okay, Marina? You've been so quiet all week. Is everything all right?"

"I think so." She smiled apologetically. "I'm sorry you noticed."

"Why?" Amanda came over and sat down by Marina's desk. "We're friends, aren't we?"

"Yes," Marina said, and realized it was true. "I'm, um, dating Clint Stanford."

Amanda grinned. "I know, Marina. The whole *town* knows. Even my mother asked me about it on Sunday."

"Your mother? She doesn't even know me."

"Don't let that quiet exterior fool you. She knows everything that goes on in town. Is it serious?"

"I don't know. That's what I'm trying to figure out. I have no idea how he feels and no idea how I feel and sometimes I think it's just not worth it."

"What isn't worth it?"

"I think I'm scared," Marina admitted. "He's too good to be true."

Amanda laughed. "Sorry," she said, "but you look so *sad* about it. He's a nice guy. I don't know any more than that. Maybe he has deep dark secrets in his closet, but I doubt it."

"It was cancer his wife died of—four years ago, like you told me. That's why he came to Tyler. It was a chance to start over."

Amanda nodded. "Ethan mentioned that. So, how do you feel about him?"

"I don't know. That's the trouble. I really didn't plan on…" She stopped before saying the words.

"Falling in love?" Amanda finished for her. "No one does, do they? I mean, doesn't it usually take you by surprise?"

"I don't know," Marina said, shrugging her shoulders. "I'm too old to remember."

Amanda laughed and stood up. "I think you're just nervous. Don't worry about it so much. Just enjoy the man and see what happens."

She'd been enjoying the man a little too much, Marina thought, as Amanda returned to her office. So much that it clouded her normally rational way of thinking. It was time to back off for a while.

TEX WASN'T on the back porch or the front porch at noon. Marina checked the doghouse, then started to call the dog's name. Surely in her condition the animal wouldn't have run away. This morning she hadn't looked as if she had the energy to run across the yard, never mind cruise around town. A low whimper answered her call, and Marina found Tex stretched out under the blooming forsythia bush. She lay panting, her body in the throes of giving birth.

Marina wanted to faint.

"Nice girl," she crooned, hoping to soothe the panicky look in the dog's eyes. "Good girl."

Now what was she supposed to do? Call the vet. That was a good idea.

The receptionist for Dr. Phelps didn't seem concerned. "He's north of town with a cow right now, Mrs. Weiss. Is the dog in distress?"

"Well, she seems a little scared."

"Any unusual bleeding?"

"Not that I can see."

"Just let nature take its course," the woman told her. "Everything should be fine, but if you have any problems you can call back and I can page the doctor. But usually these things go fine, especially with a dog that size."

Marina hung up the phone feeling a little better, but not much. She couldn't leave the dog alone, so she looked up Marge's Diner in the telephone book and dialed the restaurant. It didn't take long to get Amanda on the line, though it wasn't easy to hear her over the background noise.

"She's going to have the puppies any minute now, I think. I'd better spend my lunch hour here."

"Take as long as you want," Amanda said. "I have to drive into Sugar Creek, so I'll just leave the answering machine on. You have your key?"

"Yes. I'll be in as soon as I can."

"Good luck! I'll stop by in a little while to see how you're doing."

"You know about having puppies?" Marina asked.

"Not a thing," Amanda replied cheerfully. "But I'll offer moral support."

"Thanks."

She returned to Tex, who didn't look any better or worse than she had ten minutes earlier. Taking the blanket from the doghouse, Marina spread it around the dog. The puppies couldn't be born in the dirt, she decided. She didn't dare lift Tex's haunches to slide the blanket under her, so she settled for putting the soft material as close to her as possible. Satisfied, Marina moved a lawn chair over to the forsythia bush and sat down to wait. Even though she wasn't sure what she was supposed to do as the puppies were born.

They weren't even her puppies.

Marina hurried back to the house and dialed the number of the high school. "Clint Stanford, please," she said in her most official voice when a woman answered.

"He's in a meeting. May I take a message?"

"This is Mrs. Weiss calling. Would you have him phone me at home, please?" She debated whether or not to mention the dog, then decided it would sound a little too dramatic. "Would you tell him it's important?"

"Certainly, Mrs. Weiss. May I have your number?"

Marina gave it to her, then thanked her for helping and hung up. If Clint could come over, then she could go back to work. And Tex was his responsibility, darn it. She hurried back to the dog and talked to her in what she hoped was a soothing voice. She didn't want Tex to know that her temporary owner was just as frightened as she was.

"YOU'D BETTER TELL ME what you know, Matt," Clint advised.

The boy sat on the other side of the desk, his hands clasped on his knees. "I don't know anything."

"I think you do. You were on the science team with Jon Weiss, Tina Mallory and Brad Schmidt. Then the building burns down, and I've been led to believe that someone on the science team had something to do with it.'' Clint pushed the note across the table. It was the third one he'd received now, computer-generated on an ink-jet printer and left in the outside office for someone to find and give to him. "Read it."

Matt took the paper, read the sentence and put it back on Clint's desk. "I don't know what that's all about."

"Are you the one who wrote it?"

The boy looked genuinely surprised. "No! Why would I do that?"

"Because you know what happened that weekend of the fire."

"I was sick with the stomach flu. You can ask my mother. I didn't go to the meeting on Saturday. You can ask anyone."

Clint leaned back in his chair and kept his mouth shut. If the boy remained nervous, he might say something helpful. "What about Jon?"

"He was there. With Brad and Tina. We'd been working on our projects and they were starting to look pretty good." Matt sighed. "I wish we could've finished."

Clint waited, but the boy didn't add anything else. "Tell me about the accident Saturday night."

Matt gulped. "I lost control of the car."

"That's it?"

"Yes, sir."

Lying through his teeth. "Brad Schmidt didn't run you off the road?"

Matt paled. "No, sir. I'm not sure what happened."

"Do you think Jon Weiss set the fire at the F and M?"

Matt stared at him. His mouth thinned into an angry line. "That's what I hear, Mr. Stanford."

"That's what you *hear* or that's what you *know?*"

"Hear."

"So you're not aware if it was an accident or not?"

"If it wasn't an accident, the insurance company won't pay to rebuild. That's what Jake said."

Clint gave him a piercing look and watched the boy squirm. "If one of my students set the fire—deliberately or by accident—I need to know about it. Immediately."

"Yes, sir."

He excused the boy, then leaned back in his chair once the door had shut behind Matt. This wasn't getting him anywhere. All signs pointed to Brad Schmidt or Jon Weiss, either setting the fire or knowing who did it. If he brought them in, they would blame each other.

Lee wanted a meeting. Brick wanted the letters.

Marina wanted her son to be innocent.

Brad's father was a longtime F and M foreman. The boy wouldn't burn down his family's source of income. There was nothing in his record to show that he had family problems or behavior disorders or anything else that would lead to arson.

Clint pushed the files aside. None of this made sense.

There was a knock on the door, and Mrs. Donelly peered in. "Mr. Stanford?"

"Yes?"

"A Mrs. Weiss called. She said to call her back as soon as possible. She's at home."

"Thanks." He reached for the phone, then stopped. He could take a few minutes off and find out for himself what she wanted. Besides, he needed to see her. Jon was going to have to be questioned. Officially, this time.

HE KNOCKED on the front door, then rang the bell, but there was no answer. Marina's car was in the driveway, so he hurried down the porch steps and went around to the backyard. He could always pound on the kitchen door and get her attention. He saw her right away, sitting in a chair by one of her yellow bushes.

"Marina?" His heart leaped to his throat. "What in Sam Hill is going on? I got your message—"

Marina turned and waved him over, but there was a tense expression on her lovely face. Then he noticed the dog under the bush in what looked like a pile of blankets.

"Don't upset her," she said. "She's having her puppies. Or at least, she's trying."

He came closer and knelt down at the dog's head. "Hey, girl," he crooned, patting her forehead. "How's it goin'?"

Marina answered for her. "It's not. Nothing's happening. Nothing's been happening for an hour."

"These things take time."

"I had to call you, because I couldn't leave her alone."

He stood up and touched her shoulder. "Of course not. When do you have to be back at work?"

She looked at her watch. "I should be there now, but Amanda told me not to hurry. She's out of the office this afternoon, so I'll just get there when I can."

"Good. You don't want to miss this."

"I don't? I was sort of hoping that's exactly what I could do."

He wanted to laugh at her expression. "You're sure not a country girl, are you?"

She eyed the dog nervously. "Nope."

"Let me call the school and tell them I won't be in for the rest of the afternoon, okay? I'll be right back."

"Okay."

Clint called his office, left a message with the secretary and figured this was a stroke of luck. It was a beautiful afternoon and he was spending it outside, with the woman he wanted to spend time with. Her son was in school, where hopefully he wouldn't get into any more trouble. The question of who started the fire could wait, at least until tomorrow. Clint would call Lee, he would notify Brick, and he would somehow figure out how to tell the woman he loved that her son was mixed up in this, no matter what she wanted to believe.

He turned back to Tex. The dog appeared to be taking the birth process in stride, though Clint would never convince Marina of that. He'd seen enough animals give birth to know when something was going wrong and when it wasn't. Still, he thought, rolling up his sleeves, it would be a good idea to keep an eye on the animal. The vet had guessed this was her first pregnancy, so Tex wouldn't be familiar with the process.

Clint grabbed a plastic chair from against the back of the house and plopped it next to Marina.

"There," he said, stretching his long legs in front of him. "All set."

"I'm so glad."

He took her hand. "This is fun."

"Fun?"

"Sure." He brought her fingers to his lips and kissed them. "Holding hands in the middle of the afternoon is fun."

Tex whimpered, and Clint dropped Marina's hand and knelt beside her. "It's okay, girl. In a few hours you'll be a mother."

Marina chuckled. "That's supposed to make her feel better?"

"Here we go," he said. "Come here and see." Contractions shook the dog's belly, and soon a small puppy was born. Tex cleaned it, a dark slippery bundle with closed eyes.

"Is it alive?"

"Yes," he assured her. She was right next to him, tensely watching the dog clean up her firstborn. "Are you glad you stayed?"

Marina smiled at him. "Yes. I've never seen this before."

"It's damn incredible," he replied. "Damn incredible."

They watched for another hour, as two more puppies were born. Jon came home in time to see the last two arrive in the world. He looked just as awed as his mother.

"We get to keep one, don't we?"

Marina shook her head. "You're going off to school in a little more than a year, remember?"

Jon didn't give up. "You'll need a dog to keep you company."

"I don't think so," Marina assured him. "I think I'll be fine by myself."

Clint didn't agree, but he couldn't argue. Not with her son standing there. But he had no intention of Marina being alone. And he didn't want to wait until a year from next fall, either.

It was almost five by the time they moved Tex and her puppies into the doghouse. The dog didn't seem to mind the protection of the house once she'd settled her puppies into it. Clint didn't look as if he was in a hurry to leave, so Marina decided to heat up sauce and cook spaghetti for the three of them. Then Amanda knocked on the door.

"Well," she asked, stepping into the foyer. "Do you have puppies?"

"Five of them," Marina said. "Come out back and you can peek."

"Will she let me?"

"She's pretty calm about the whole thing. Better than I am." She led Amanda through the dining area and into the kitchen, where Jon was on the phone and Clint stood near the stove stirring the spaghetti sauce.

"Hello, Amanda," Clint said. "Come to pick out your puppy?"

She laughed. "You'd have to talk Ethan into it first."

"Boy or girl? We have three girls and two boys."

"I came over to see for myself." She turned to Marina. "This is a great house," Amanda said.

"You've never been here before?" Marina hid her embarrassment. She should have had her boss over for dinner, she supposed.

"Not inside."

"Come on. I'll show you the puppies. They're pretty small, and their eyes are closed."

Amanda followed her outside and across the lawn. "This is a great doghouse."

"Clint built it. He took the roof off so we could watch the puppies for a while, but he'll put it back on before he goes home."

Amanda peered at the tiny, wriggling babies, snuggled against their mother's warmth. "Maybe Ethan would like a dog."

"You have six weeks to talk him into it."

"I'll have to bring him over to see." She checked her watch. "He should be home soon. Maybe he could stop by."

It seemed natural to say, "Call him up and come over for dinner." Marina didn't think twice, though normally she would have had to think about it for three or four months. "I'm sure Clint's staying for a while. It's nothing fancy, but I have a bottle of wine and some French bread in the freezer."

"That sounds really nice," Amanda said. "Are you sure?"

"Sure I am. We'll get Jon off the phone and you can call your husband and ask him if he wants to pick out a dog."

Amanda laughed and followed Marina back to the house. "We'd better give him a glass of wine first."

"COME HOME with me," Clint whispered. He dried the last pan and set it down on the kitchen counter.

"I can't," Marina said, keeping her voice low. Jon had gone outside to check on the dogs, but he would be returning to the kitchen anytime now.

"Why not?"

She unplugged the sink and let the soapy water run down the drain. "It would just…look odd."

"We'll say we're going out for ice cream." He looped the dish towel around her neck and, holding on to the ends, tugged her toward him. "In fact, we really could go out for ice cream. *Then* we could go back to my house."

She thought about backing away, but it was too much fun to be close to him. "And then what?"

His dark eyes twinkled. "Give me an hour or two and I'll show you."

"We're acting like kids."

"Uh-uh." He shook his head. "We're acting like two mature adults who know exactly what they're doing."

"Speak for yourself, Stanford. I haven't a clue."

"No?" His lips hovered near hers. "I thought you knew."

"Nope." She smiled and ducked out of the embrace. "I think we're crazy."

"Being in love with you isn't crazy."

Marina stopped, uncertain if she'd heard him correctly, but when she looked at him, Clint wasn't smiling, wasn't teasing. "No—no one's mentioned love," she stammered, squeezing water from the sponge and setting it on the side of the sink.

"I just did." He didn't seem the least perturbed.

"Well, don't."

"Why not?"

"Because it's not."

He seemed to think about that for a moment. "All right. For you, maybe it's not. Yet. I told you, Texans are persistent."

"And I told you, I'm not interested in a relationship."

"You've got one whether you're interested or not," he stated. "We've been…" He stopped and looked toward the kitchen door, then lowered his voice to a whisper. "We've been making love for a week. We're going to do it again. *Something*'s going on."

"Lust."

"Lust," he repeated flatly. "You think this is just about sex?"

No, she didn't think that at all. That was the scary part. But she couldn't tell the man that. He was too strong to ever understand why she was so afraid to love him. He would take over her life and her heart and everything else if she wasn't very, very careful. She turned away, afraid he'd see the truth in her eyes.

"Marina?" He took her by the shoulders and turned her around. When he looked down at her his expression was serious. Tender, even. "It's all right," he said. "I'm going too fast. It's just…" He stopped, and a look of pain crossed his handsome face.

"What?"

He smiled. Or tried to. "I didn't expect to be happy again. I didn't expect to find someone like you. I guess I should pull back on the reins a little."

"You mean, slow down?"

"Yeah."

"That would help." She ducked out of his grasp when she heard Jon's footsteps on the porch. She raised her voice. "I'm glad Ethan and Amanda came for dinner. That was really fun."

"They're nice people," Clint agreed, a twinkle in his eyes as he went along with her attempt to chat.

"The puppies are doing great," her son announced, a grin on his face. "Tex looks real happy, too."

Marina put away the last clean pot and turned on the dishwasher. "I'll bet she's glad that's over. I know I am."

"I hafta go study." Jon started out of the room, then turned. "Good night, Mr. Stanford. Night, Mom."

"Good night, Jon," Clint murmured.

"Night, honey." She hesitated, then called after him. "Clint and I are going out for ice cream. Leave the light on, okay?"

"Yeah, sure," he said, and soon they heard him taking the stairs two at a time.

"We're going out for ice cream?"

Marina turned to Clint and took his hand. "In a manner of speaking, yes."

He tugged her toward the foyer. "I like a woman who can change her mind."

"I don't do it often," she warned.

He opened the front door and ushered her outside. "This is a good start, darlin'."

MUCH LATER, in the privacy of her dark bedroom, Marina repeated the conversation in her mind. He had told her he loved her. No, he had said "in love." There was a difference. And she'd told him it was lust.

She'd lied. It wasn't just lust. Making love to that man transcended something that was merely a sexual act. It was special, and she certainly knew it. Her body still hummed from their lovemaking.

But being in love required more than she could give. Or did it? Was there a way to love the Texan without her entire world changing?

CHAPTER THIRTEEN

"PROM NIGHT WAS JUST a warning, Weiss."

Oh, cripes. He was back. Jon didn't have to turn around to know that Brad stood behind him. Now he was trapped between a football player and a row of metal lockers. Friday was sure starting out with a bang. He reached for his history book, then slammed the locker shut. "What do you want now?"

"Tina."

Jon turned around very carefully. "I can't help you with that."

"No?" Brad's red face grew redder. "She's acting weird."

"She's a *woman*." Sometimes it was necessary to point out the obvious.

"So?"

So far so good. He was still alive. "So, women act weird. It's just the way they are."

"You're a real smart-ass, Weiss." Brad's eyes narrowed. "You've done something else, haven't you?" He took one meaty hand and pushed it into Jon's chest, pinning him against the row of lockers. The history book fell to the floor, along with a spiral notebook. "Nielsen's here, in Stanford's office. They know, don't they?"

Yikes. The fire investigator and the principal together. This wasn't good news. And Brad's fist in his chest was threatening to cut off Jon's breathing. "I haven't—said anything."

"Confess," Brad hissed. "Say it was an accident."

"No."

The hand pushed harder, spreading a layer of pain across Jon's chest. But he looked Brad in the eye and said the one phrase that was guaranteed to get him killed, right here in the halls of Tyler High. "Shove it up your ass, Schmidt. I'm not saying it. I won't tell on you—"

"*Shut up!* There's nothing to tell."

The late bell rang. The corridor had emptied and first period was going to begin in one minute. Brad released his hold and backed away. "Tell Christy Hansen to mind her own business or next time I won't just run you into a ditch." He turned around and hurried around the corner.

Jon took a deep breath and bent down to pick up his stuff. He was going to be late for class now. And he'd have detention for it, too. He'd bet ten bucks that Brad wouldn't be there. He'd have charmed the teacher with some excuse and be let off the hook.

"Here," a voice said. Jon looked up to see Matt handing him a spiral notebook.

"Thanks." He reached for it with trembling hands. He shook with anger, not fear this time, but he didn't bother to hide it. Let Matt think what he wanted to think. Jon stood up and started to move away.

"Wait," Matt said, his voice low. Jon turned to look at him. "Schmidt threatened my sister."

"You heard?" Matt nodded, and Jon added, "Yeah, well, he tends to do that. It's becoming a habit."

Matt paled. Both boys ignored the late bell's shrill call as they faced each other in the empty corridor.

"He's gone too far," Matt said. "I didn't think he would hurt anyone."

Jon snorted. "Yeah, he ran us off the road after the prom just for fun, not because you were with Tina. And he set fire to…'' He stopped. "Never mind." Jon turned away. "You'll believe what you want to believe."

"Weiss?"

Jon stopped and looked over his shoulder. The other boy stood there, his fists clenched by his side. "What?"

"Is Christy in danger?"

"Not as long as I keep my mouth shut."

Matt didn't say anything, so Jon turned and headed toward class. Matt Hansen would have to figure it out for himself. If he was smart enough.

"BRING HIM IN," Lee insisted. "Now."

"No." Clint turned away from the window and faced the investigator. "Not here."

The other man gave a snort of frustration. "Then where, Stanford? I'm at the end of my rope. Practically everyone in town is on my case since I sent my report to the insurance company. They think I should have found the culprit *and* gotten the company to pay off."

"I'm aware of that, Lee. I'm trying to be fair." He couldn't have Jon confronted officially here at the school. He had to talk to him first and see what could be done.

"Let me see the letters again."

Clint stepped over to his desk and opened the side drawer. He pulled out the three letters and handed them over.

"*Three?*"

"One arrived this morning."

Lee scanned them, then tossed them back on the desk. "They don't say anything, not really."

"They point the finger at one of the boys."

"We eliminate Hansen, since he was sick. I asked his mother, and it's true. The boy couldn't have lit a match on Saturday. Supposedly he couldn't have gotten out of bed, except to vomit."

"That's what I understand." Clint sat down and felt a

little sick himself. All this time he'd suspected that something was wrong between Jon and Brad, but he hated the fact that he was right.

"So, we have the new guy in town. A quiet kid, keeps to himself. And then we have one of the most popular guys in school—"

"Sports makes strange heroes," Clint interjected.

"Granted. But still…"

"Still, you're saying he's a known quantity and Jon isn't."

Lee gave him a sympathetic look. "I don't like this any more than you do. Are you still dating the boy's mother?"

"Yes."

"Is it serious?"

"Definitely."

"Sorry."

"Yeah. It complicates things."

"I'll give you the day, but you'll have to set up a meeting with the boy and the mother tonight."

"All right." Sometimes he hated his job. "Do me a favor. Talk to Brad first and see if he'll crack."

Lee nodded. "Sure. Call him in."

Clint switched on the intercom and talked to Mrs. Donelly, who promised to find out which class Brad Schmidt was attending at the moment. Then he turned back to Lee. "What about Tina Mallory? Do you want to talk to her again?"

"Girls don't set fires," Lee said.

Clint didn't bother to argue, but in his experience girls were capable of just about anything.

CLINT HAD a difficult time reaching Marina. According to the answering machine, she and Amanda had gone to the courthouse at Sugar Creek and would be back at three. He left a message saying he'd called. He couldn't discuss this over the phone, anyway.

It had been an interesting conversation, with Brad facing Lee's questions with wide-eyed innocence and charm. Clint had been called out in the middle of the interview to attend to a fistfight in the second-floor boys' bathroom. Two freshmen would be in detention for a while.

Lee was gone when Clint returned. He'd left a message, a message Clint didn't want to read. *Set it up for seven. I'll meet you there unless there's a problem.*

Clint crumpled the note and tossed it into the garbage can. There was a problem, all right. The woman he loved was going to be terribly hurt tonight, and there wasn't a damn thing Clint could do to stop it.

Unless Jon himself could come up with an explanation. Would the boy talk? Clint had to give him one more chance.

"I DON'T KNOW what you're talking about," Jon said. "I didn't have anything to do with the fire."

"Are you sure?"

"Yep." He pretended a nonchalance he didn't feel. Stanford looked serious. Too serious. Something was going on. "I've said that about a hundred times before, remember?"

"Yes. I remember."

Jon leaned against the wall and waited for Stanford to explain why he'd hauled him out of detention.

"Lee Nielsen, the investigator of the fire, was here this afternoon to talk to the students assigned to the science team. He's reopened the investigation."

"He didn't talk to me."

Clint gave him a level look. "Maybe he's saving the best for last."

Damn. Here it goes. "Is he going to say I did it?"

"I don't know what happened with the others, Jon. I'm

just trying to do you a favor and give you a chance to talk to me first.''

''I am talking to you, Mr. Stanford.'' Jon met his gaze. ''I didn't do anything wrong. I swear it.'' *I'm just trying to get through this year in one piece.*

''Then who did?''

Jon stayed silent. It would be so easy to tell Stanford that Brad Schmidt burned the place down. But what would happen then? Would anyone believe him? Jon doubted it. He had tried telling Matt and got nowhere. If Matt wouldn't believe him, then who in this godforsaken town would? Besides his mother and Christy, of course.

''What are you afraid of, Jon?''

''You want a list?''

''It's a start.''

Jon sighed. The man didn't understand sarcasm. ''Look, I've told you the truth. I can't help it if no one believes me.''

''Okay.'' Clint didn't move. ''How are the puppies?''

Jon blinked at the rapid change of subject. ''They're fine. Tex is a real good mother.''

''Is she staying in her house?''

''Yeah. We put her food and water outside so the pups wouldn't fall into it.''

''Good idea.'' He shoved his hands in his pockets. ''Go home. I'll tell Mr. Wagner that you're done here today.''

''Hey, thanks.''

''No problem.''

''I'll go get my stuff.''

''Yeah, you do that.''

Jon gathered up his books, shoved them into his backpack and was out the door before Mr. Stanford could change his mind. Before Mr. Stanford could ask him any more questions. He left the school as quickly as he could and headed toward home. Could he tell the truth and still keep Christy safe? Brad had proved he was capable of anything.

CHRISTY CALLED HIM back after supper. Jon took the phone into his room and shut the door. "Did you talk Jake into taking a puppy?"

"No. Listen. You're in big trouble. The police are coming to your house tonight to ask you about the fire."

"How do you know that?"

"Tina. She heard Mr. Nielsen talking on the phone in Mr. Stanford's office. She thinks he was talking to the police."

He swallowed the lump of fear that threatened to choke him. "I'm not taking the blame for this."

"Then tell them what you know."

"That's the trouble. I don't *know* what happened that weekend. Brad and Tina had a fight and then we left. I took Tina home and Brad stormed off in his own car."

"If you didn't start the fire, then no one can prove you did."

"I wish that was true. But Brad can say anything and they'll believe him."

Christy was silent for a minute. "You have to get out of your house until we can figure out what to do."

Jon thought for a moment. He was so tired of being afraid. "Okay," he said, knowing Christy would help him. "Maybe I can hitch a ride to your house."

"I'll get Matt to pick you up. We could meet you at the library."

"Matt's gonna help?"

"Yep. All we have to do is come up with a plan."

"A plan," Jon repeated. "I could use a plan."

"No kidding," Christy said. "You need all the help you can get."

Relief flooded his voice. He wasn't alone. "Damn right,"

he said. "What time should I be there?" The three of them should be able to come up with a way to get out of this.

"CLINT!" MARINA OPENED the door wider to let him in. She felt ridiculously happy to see him. "I got your message, but it was too late to call you at school. I was going to try tonight—"

He kissed her, and she wrapped her arms around him and held on as tightly as she could, despite the fact that Jon could come down the stairs at any second.

"There," he said. "I feel better now."

Why did he look so serious? "Want some coffee? I just made a fresh pot. I've been in the kitchen paying bills."

He started to follow her into the kitchen, but halfway through the dining room he took her in his arms again. "Marry me," he said.

Marina stared at him. "What are you talking about?"

"Marry me," he repeated, a determined expression on his face. She reached up and touched his cheek.

"This is pretty fast."

"You need…" He stopped, as if he'd been about to say something he shouldn't.

"I need what?"

"Me."

The doorbell rang, making them both jump. Clint took her arm. "Say yes, Marina. I promise I'll help you through this."

"Through what?" she asked, suddenly feeling very frightened. But Clint didn't answer her question. He followed her as she went to the door and opened it. Lee Nielsen and Brick Bauer stood on her front step.

"Good evening," Brick said. "May we come in?"

"Of course." She stepped back to let them enter. Clint stood next to her.

"I'm sure Clint has told you why we're here," Lee began.

"No, he hasn't."

Clint cleared his throat. "I was just about to. You're a little early."

Marina didn't look at him. "Lee. Brick. What do you want?" She didn't care if she sounded harsh. She just wanted to know why these men were here before she passed out from fear.

"We came to ask Jon a few questions," Brick said. "Is he home?"

"He's upstairs doing his homework. What is all this about?"

"We have to talk to Jon," Clint said. "Maybe we can get this whole thing cleared up quickly."

"Talk to Jon about what?"

Clint took her elbow and tried to lead her into the living room. "Marina, it would be best if you would—"

She pulled her arm away, unwilling to let him help her. Whatever was going on, he was part of it. Whatever was going on wasn't going to make her happy. She stayed where she was. "I think you'd better talk to me first."

Lee nodded. "May we sit down?"

Marina hesitated, then led them into the living room. Clint sat beside her on one love seat, while the other men sat across from them on the matching sofa. She looked at Lee and waited for an explanation.

"It's about the fire at the F and M last December," he began. "We now have reason to believe that Jon set the fire."

"That's ridiculous." She turned to Clint. "Tell him. Tell him Jon couldn't be capable of something like that."

Clint shook his head. "It won't do any good, sweetheart. I think it's time Jon talked to us."

He wasn't going to be any help. He could call her

"sweetheart" from now till Christmas and it wasn't going to help her. Marina took a deep breath and turned back to the other men. "Just exactly why do you think my son set the fire?"

"According to one of the other boys on the science team, there was an argument the day before, at the plant. Something about an experiment that had been tampered with. Jon was very angry about that. He made threats about getting revenge."

"Jon isn't that kind of boy."

"We've spent the past couple of days talking to the other members of the science team. Clint can vouch for that. We think Jon has the answers, Mrs. Weiss."

"He couldn't have done anything wrong."

"Could we talk to him, Marina?"

She shook her head. "Not without a lawyer."

Brick leaned forward, his hands clasped between his knees. "We're not arresting him. We just want to ask him a few questions."

"And you can," she said, standing up. "As soon as Amanda gets here. I'm not going through this alone."

Clint stood, too, and followed her out of the room. She glanced up at the stairs and prayed Jon wouldn't come down to see who was here. Maybe he was in his room with the door shut, with those headphones on. She walked quickly through the dining room and into the kitchen to the phone.

"You're not alone, Marina," Clint said.

She ignored him. She was so nervous she couldn't remember Amanda's phone number and had to look it up in the telephone directory. Her hand shook as she punched the buttons, but she didn't look at Clint. "You knew they were coming."

"Yes."

"You couldn't have warned me?" Clint didn't answer as she waited for Amanda's phone to ring. Clint had asked her to marry him instead, as if that was supposed to solve everything. She heard Amanda's voice and felt a rush of relief. "Amanda? This is Marina. I need your help."

"What's the matter?"

"It's Jon." She quickly explained the situation, while Clint leaned against the counter and listened.

"I'll be right over," her friend said, and hung up the phone. Marina replaced the receiver and took a deep breath.

Clint didn't move. He didn't put his arms around her or tell her it was going to be all right. She didn't know what to expect anymore.

"Is she coming?" he asked.

"Yes." He had asked her to marry him. He had held her in his arms and asked twice, when he should have been telling her that the police were coming for her son. How could he have done that?

She started to leave the kitchen, but he touched her arm to stop her. "Marina," he began, his eyes dark and worried. "You knew this was going to happen."

"Yes."

"When?"

"This morning."

"You didn't think of telling me?"

"I called the office. You weren't there. I talked—"

"Don't," she said, cutting off his words. "I thought you were our friend."

"I am."

"I trusted you," she whispered. "I trusted you not to hurt my son."

"I tried to help him," he insisted. "He wouldn't let me."

"He wouldn't confess, you mean. You turned him in, didn't you?"

Clint looked as if he wanted to punch a hole through the ivory wall. "I told you, I tried to help him."

"How?" She waited for him to explain. Waited for him

to say something to make it all better, to prove this was all a mistake.

"I gave him one last chance this afternoon, Marina. I tried to get him to tell what he knows."

"He doesn't *know* anything."

Clint shook his head. "That's where you're wrong, sweetheart. He knows a lot more than he's telling, and it's time he talked."

"I trusted you," she whispered. *I loved you.*

His lips thinned into an angry line. "And you think I let you down?"

She nodded, and his eyes darkened.

"I wouldn't—couldn't—do that." He hesitated, then moved toward the living room. "Let's get this over with," he said, shoving his hands in his pockets.

"All right." Marina turned away from him and left the room. She couldn't bear to hear another word. She waited by the foot of the stairs, as if daring any of the men to cross her path to get to Jon.

Marina had avoided calling Jon downstairs. Let him study and listen to his music. He didn't have to know that there was all hell breaking loose in the living room.

Amanda arrived after long, agonizing minutes of waiting. "I think it would be a good idea if I talked to Jon first," she said, in a voice that dared any of the men to argue with her.

"Fine." Lee sighed. "Just get him down here as soon as you can. This thing doesn't need to drag out any longer."

Amanda nodded. "I couldn't agree with you more, Lee."

Marina took her friend upstairs and knocked on the door of Jon's room. "Jon," she called. "I need to talk to you."

There was no answer, so Marina called again, this time louder. Finally she opened the door, expecting to see her son with his headphones on, seated at his desk. The lights were on, but the room was empty.

"Maybe he's in the bathroom." A quick check of the rest of the upstairs proved that Jon wasn't there, either.

"He's gone," Marina whispered, turning to her friend. "What on earth is going on around here?"

Amanda put her arm around her shoulder. "I don't know, Marina. But we've got to tell them that Jon is gone. It's not going to look good."

The women went down the stairs and Marina told the three men that her son was gone. Brick lost no time notifying his office, instructing the policemen on duty to look for Jon Weiss.

"What will you do when you find him?"

Brick gave Marina a sympathetic look. "Exactly what we'd planned to do, which is ask him some questions about the fire." He nodded toward Amanda. "With his attorney present, of course."

"You won't hurt him?"

Brick's tone was patient. "He's not a fugitive, Marina. He's just a missing teenager. He could be sitting in a car in front of the Dairy King right now. We'll find him and we'll bring him home and we'll get to the bottom of this whole thing, all right?"

Marina took a deep breath. "All right."

Clint watched the whole thing from his position in the foyer. He was too nervous to sit down. He wanted to pace. He wanted to get in his Jeep and find that damn kid before Marina crumbled into a thousand pieces right before his eyes. And when he found him he wanted to tan his hide with a willow switch until Jon promised he would never worry his mother again.

"We'll start with the usual teen hangouts," Brick told Marina. "Did Jon talk about going out tonight?"

"He doesn't have his own car."

"Does he take walks?"

"Not without the dog."

Clint had already checked to see if Tex was in her house. "The dog is here," he said, raising his voice across the other conversations in the foyer. Lee was talking to another policeman. Amanda was speaking into a cell phone in the dining room and keeping an eye on Marina at the same time.

"And so is my car," Marina said.

"And you didn't see him leave?"

"No."

"When was the last time you saw him?"

"After dinner. Around six. We ate early."

Brick made a few more notations on his pad. "I'll check around town. Why don't you call the Hansen girl and see if she knows anything? Maybe they had a date."

Clint would have bet a hundred dollars that Amanda had already done that and knew exactly where the Hansen teenagers were right now. Damn. He hoped the kid hadn't done anything stupid. Running away made him look guilty as hell, which wasn't going to help at all.

At this point, Clint didn't know what would, but there was one teenager he would like to talk to again. And as soon as possible. Clint slipped out the back door. No one but Marina noticed he'd left.

"This had better work, Weiss," Matt hissed. They watched headlights enter the farm driveway and bounce along the road to the barn. Then the lights went off, and a car door slammed.

"He's here," Christy said, clearly enjoying the thought of the drama that was about to take place. "Tina was right."

Matt shook his head. "I can't believe he fell for it."

Jon could. Brad was clever, and a good liar. But he had one blind spot: Tina Mallory. "He's not as smart as he looks."

"I guess," the boy said, watching his friend come

through the open barn door. "Turn that thing on and let's get this over with."

Christy pressed the record button and the machine started. "We're all set," Christy whispered. "Good luck."

Matt held his electric lantern high and stepped out into the middle of the barn. It was a large space, with stalls against one wall and machinery against another. One of the stalls held a curious horse; another concealed the onlookers. They'd considered hiding in the loft above, but Jon had been afraid they wouldn't be able to record the conversation from that high up.

"Hey," Brad called, stepping forward. The barn had electric lights, but Christy thought they might be seen if the place was brighter. "What's goin' on?"

Matt sat on a bale of hay, the lantern at his feet. "Haven't you heard?"

"What?"

"The police figure they know who set the fire."

Brad's fists clenched. "Yeah? Did Weiss talk?"

"No. Not Weiss. You'll never believe it."

"Cut the crap, Hansen. Where's Tina?" He looked around the dark barn. "She said she had to meet me here. We're back together again, y'know."

Jon watched Matt give Brad a dumbfounded look. He was wasting his time playing baseball, when the drama club could use him. "*Tina's* the one being accused, butthead."

"No way."

"Yeah. She's in the house with Christy. She hasn't stopped crying since she got here."

Brad sank down onto a dust-covered bench. "Oh, shit."

"Yeah." Matt looked sympathetic. "Why in hell did she do it?"

"She didn't do it," Brad insisted. "Weiss did. He must have blamed her and they were stupid enough to believe him."

"I don't think so. Tina said they were on their way to Jon's house after they saw her. She figures you told on her. Set her up."

"Me?"

Christy leaned closer. "Brad looks like he's going to cry," she whispered.

"It's working," Jon said incredulously. "Matt's doing great. *And the Academy Award goes to...*"

"Yeah," Matt was saying. "That's what she told Christy."

"I wouldn't do that," Brad said. "She knows how I feel about her." He stood up. "I've gotta go talk to her. Come on." Matt didn't move. "Come *on*."

Matt stood. "She already told the truth, Brad. Pretty soon everyone's going to know who really set the fire."

"An accident," Brad said, looking panicked. "It was an accident."

"Yeah?" Jon stood and stepped out of the stall. "Who's gonna believe you?"

"What the hell are you doing here? Did Tina call you, too?" His eyes narrowed. "I told you to stay away from her."

"Yeah?" Jon suddenly didn't care that Brad was bigger, taller, wider and tougher than he was. "Well, I'm sick of you telling me what to do. I'm sick of your ugly *face*."

Brad laughed. "Yeah? Well, come a little closer and we'll see how *your* face looks after I get through beating the crap out of you."

Matt stood up. "Hey—"

"It's okay," Jon assured his friend. And Matt was his friend. He'd come through for him, when it mattered. "This has been coming for a long time."

He put his fists up and approached Brad, who grinned with anticipation. Jon avoided the first two punches, ducking and moving. Still, Brad landed the first blow, a punch in the nose that left Jon tasting his own blood. He retaliated fast, hitting Brad with a punch to the jaw that sent him sprawling into the hay.

Jon flexed his fingers. That had hurt like hell. But, damn, it had felt good! He waited while Brad got to his feet. "Who set the fire, Schmidt?"

"Screw you," the older boy answered, only he was holding his jaw and it sounded more like "ooh-yoo." Then he put up his fists and came closer.

Jon stood his ground and waited for the next blow. It came fast, but Jon took it on the chin without falling down. He even landed another punch of his own. It connected with flesh, but he didn't know where. And didn't care. He was sick and tired of being scared. He was sick of hoping the whole damn thing would go away. Brad staggered, and Jon saw his chance. He hit Brad's face with all his strength, ignoring the crunch of pain in his own fingers when the punch connected. "That's for threatening Christy," Jon said, panting.

Brad came at him and with one blow, knocked Jon to the wooden floor. "That's for going after my girl," Brad retorted, wiping a stream of blood from his nose.

Jon couldn't move; his legs wouldn't support him. Brad bent over, his fist ready to land the final blow, but he never got to throw the punch. Matt stepped forward, his fist landing in Brad's face.

"And *that*'s for the prom," he said.

Brad collapsed into the straw. Jon struggled to sit up. "You didn't kill him, did you?"

"Nah." Matt grinned. "I just knocked him out. He'll come around."

Christy stepped out of the shadows. She knelt beside Jon and gave him a worried look. "You're going to need some ice. Where'd you learn to fight?"

"I didn't." He tried to grin, but the right side of his face hurt too much. "It just came naturally." She looked as if she wanted to hug him, so he groaned a little, hoping she'd put her arms around him. She didn't, so he tugged her down beside him and threw a proprietary arm around her shoulders.

Matt flexed his fingers. "Now what? We beat the crap out of him but we didn't get him to confess to setting the fire."

"You don't have to," a familiar voice declared. The three teenagers turned to see Mr. Stanford standing in the door of the barn.

It had taken Clint a while to piece it all together. He'd gone to Tina's house and talked her into telling him what she knew about the fire. She'd also answered another important question, which had led him to the Hansens' barn. The kids had come up with a way to confront Brad, and Tina had been in on it. Her job had been to convince Brad to meet her at the farm, and she was sure he'd fallen for the lie. Supposedly Christy had a tape recorder and would tape the confession, therefore getting Jon off the hook once and for all.

Clint found a light switch, so the dark barn was fully lit. Jon looked as though he'd tangled with a bronco and Brad was out cold on the wooden floor. So much for the plan to record a confession. Brad didn't look as if he'd given up without a fight.

"We don't?" Christy asked. "I've got some stuff on tape—"

"Tina finally talked," Clint said, stepping over to see Brad's eyelids fluttering. "I'm sure we can place the blame where it's deserved."

Matt and Jon gave each other a relieved look and Christy ran to the house for an ice pack, bringing back her mother and stepfather. The others arrived a few minutes later, which Clint had expected. Jake demanded to know what was going on, Britt talked to Amanda and Brick stood in the door and informed the boys he wanted a complete accounting of the evening's activities. Lee, sensing an end to his investigation, stayed close to Clint.

Marina turned white when she saw the blood coming from Jon's nose, but to her credit she didn't say anything to embarrass the boy, especially when she saw that Jon was content to have Christy hold an ice bag to his face. Clint watched Marina head to her son. She spoke softly as she knelt near him, and he smiled and shook his head. Probably asking if he should see a doctor, Clint supposed. He started to move toward them, but Britt was already speaking to Marina.

"We should put something on those cuts," Britt offered. "I've got some iodine in the house."

"Come on," Marina said, urging her son to stand. "We're going to go into the house and get you cleaned up."

Brad groaned, opened his eyes and groaned again when he saw Clint.

Clint bent over him. "You okay?"

"Yeah."

"Here," Clint said, giving Brad his hand. "Sit up and clear your head. You've got some talking to do."

"I didn't do anything," he said, sitting up and hanging his head between his knees.

"How about this?" Clint straightened. "Last fall you thought that Tina was interested in the new kid in school. And when she was tired of your jealousy, she broke up with you. That was the Saturday before the fire. You two had a fight that afternoon."

Clint kept his eye on the boy in front of him. "Here's the part I don't understand. Somehow you sneaked back into the plant, with your father's keys, and, what—tried to destroy Tina's experiment?"

"Not hers," he mumbled. "Jon's."

Lee leaned forward. "How'd you do it?"

"It was an accident," he said, looking up at Lee with a look of such total misery that Clint almost felt sorry for him. "I never meant to destroy the plant. I set the notes on fire. I thought the fire was out when I left."

Jon hesitated on his way out of the barn. He looked as if he wanted to hit Brad again. Jake put an arm on the boy to prevent him from moving. "Easy, son."

"And you made sure everyone thought I did it," Jon said. "And you threatened me *and* Christy to make sure I wouldn't talk."

"But someone did," Lee stated. He waited for Clint to answer.

"Tina," he said. "She was the one who wrote the letters. She was terrified to tell us herself. She's been afraid of Brad and the things he'd do when he was jealous, so she wrote the letters, hoping that Jon wouldn't get in trouble. When Brad ran them off the road the night of the prom, Tina was scared to death. She pretended to go back to him so no one would get hurt."

Lee tugged on Brad's arm to help him up. "Come on. We're going to call your parents and then you're going to tell me exactly what happened."

As Lee walked the boy out the door, Amanda stopped him. "My grandfather will want to know what's going on."

Lee nodded. "Tell him I'll be in touch with him first thing in the morning, right after I talk to the insurance company. This should speed things up."

Amanda smiled. "Thank you. That will be the best news he's had for a long time."

The women, accompanied by the other teenagers, started to leave the barn. Clint followed them and called Marina's name. She stopped, framed in the beam of light from the barn door, and turned to him.

Clint walked over to her as Britt hustled the teenagers

toward the house. He waited until they were alone before he put his hands on her shoulders, before he spoke. "I'm glad it wasn't Jon," he said.

Marina backed away from his embrace. "You should have believed him, Clint. You should have believed *me*."

Shocked, he stood still and looked down at her. She still thought he'd turned her son in to the police. She thought he'd turned against her. She hadn't trusted him enough to know he would rather die than hurt her, that he would always be there for her. And for Jon. "I did what I could to help you both."

She shook her head. "I'm sorry. This isn't going to work." She started to turn away from him. "I have to go take care of my son."

He stood there and watched her walk across the yard. There didn't seem to be anything else he could say to make a difference. She'd reluctantly let him into her life and she'd easily kicked him out of it.

"Clint?" Jake came up to him. "That was pretty good detective work. How did you figure it out?"

Clint shrugged. "Just a feeling I had about these kids."

"But what made you go to Tina?"

"She was the other kid who always seemed to be in the center of trouble, just like Jon." He looked across the empty yard, hoping that Marina would change her mind and come back to talk to him. "I lucked out. Tina was more than ready to talk. Brad had scared her to death, but then she told me what the kids planned tonight." He shook his head. "I've got to hand it to them. It worked out, though not the way they expected."

Jake nodded. "Yeah. It would have been easier if they'd come to you or me first. Are you all right? You look a little shook up."

"I'm going home."

"Come on in for coffee. Or something stronger. I think we could all use—"

"No," the Texan said. "Thanks, but I don't need anything." *Except a woman who loves me enough to trust me to do what's right for both her and her son.* He tried to smile, but couldn't. He was tired of kids and school and women and even Tyler. Especially Tyler.

Without another word, he turned and walked out into the darkness.

"WHAT'S JON GOING to do this summer?" Amanda filled the watering can and proceeded to water the plants that hung in the office window.

"He had a choice between working for your grandfather and working at the farm." Marina took a stack of papers to the copier machine and started the process of copying three real-estate contracts. "Even though the plant is still being rebuilt, Mr. Ingalls thought he could use him as an assistant. I guess there's still computer entry work to do."

"My grandfather was impressed with your son. What did Jon decide?"

"He picked the farm. Said he wanted to get in shape." She pretended to be interested in the papers that stacked up in the bin. "I think Christy was a bigger attraction, though."

"Ah." Amanda smiled. "The power of love."

Marina didn't want to talk about love. She didn't want to *think* about love. She didn't want to be reminded of how big a fool she'd been. She took the papers over to her desk for stapling. "I guess so. He's a different kid lately. It's like the weight of the world is off his shoulders."

Amanda finished watering the plants and hesitated at Marina's desk. "Meanwhile, you're the one who's suffering. Do you want to talk about it?"

"About what?"

"You haven't been yourself for days, not since that night

at Christy Hansen's. I hate to see you so sad. Is there anything I can do?"

"No." She tried to smile. "But thanks for asking. I'm fine, really." And she would be fine, too, once she'd grown accustomed to being alone again.

Amanda didn't return the smile. "Maybe I shouldn't say this, but you might want to know." She took a deep breath. "There's a rumor going around town that Clint Stanford is going to resign as principal as soon as school gets out. I heard…that he's thinking about moving away."

Marina swallowed the sudden lump in her throat. "Does anyone know why?"

Amanda shrugged. "Not that I've heard."

"I see." She turned back to her work. So he was going to leave. She hadn't seen him since that night at the farm. For three days he hadn't called or come to visit. It was as if he'd disappeared. And, Marina figured, if that was the way he wanted it, then that was the way it would be. She didn't want him, certainly didn't need him, even if her heart was breaking because she missed him so much. He'd made her feel safe, he'd made her laugh. He'd walked all over her heart in those cowboy boots of his.

"I'm really sorry it didn't work out," Amanda said, before going into her office.

Marina couldn't reply. She finished her work, and when five-thirty came she said goodbye to Amanda and walked home. She could hear Jon laughing when she crossed the front yard. She went around the side of the house and saw him in the grass with the five puppies climbing over him. The puppies were quickly growing into fat black balls of fur with dark eyes and little pink tongues, but they still didn't stray too far away from their mother. Tex kept a careful eye on them, but now she was asleep near Jon's thigh.

"Hi," Marina said, wishing she had a camera. The boy and the dogs would be all grown-up too soon.

"Hey, Mom." Jon sat up and carefully brushed two puppies off his chest. Marina laid her purse down and picked up the puppy that toddled over to sniff her shoes.

"Don't you dare pee on me," she told him, and then she laughed. His little face wrinkled as if he'd understood her.

"He probably will," Jon warned.

Marina set the little dog on the lawn by Tex and watched him try to walk over to join the other puppies. "Don't let them chew on your sneakers."

"Doesn't matter. They're old."

She looked at his feet. "You're right. Why didn't you tell me you needed new shoes?"

"Mom." Jon gave her a patient smile. "I bought some new ones Saturday. And Christy says I'll need a pair of work boots for the farm, too. You don't have to worry about it, though. I saw some at Gates."

"Oh." Yes, definitely growing up. Buying his own shoes, earning his own money. What was next? She was afraid to think about it, so she asked a question that was certain to get an answer. "Are you hungry?"

"Yeah. What's for dinner?"

"Whatever's in the refrigerator. Leftover spaghetti and leftover meat loaf."

"You want me to start heating it up?"

"Sure. I'm going to change before we eat." She made her way around the puppies and went into the house. It didn't take long to change into shorts and a T-shirt, but Jon had the food out on the counter and the table set by the time she returned to the kitchen.

"Mom?"

"Mmm?" Maybe she should open a can of corn.

"Are we ever going to talk about it? You haven't said anything all weekend, except to ask if my face hurts."

"Talk about what?" But she knew what "it" was. And she didn't intend to discuss it. Instead she turned around and opened the refrigerator.

"Why are you mad at him? Mr. Stanford was only doing his job."

Not when he was making love to me, he wasn't. Marina kept her head in the refrigerator. "He thought you set the fire."

"Jeez, Mom." Jon was clearly exasperated. "The whole *school* thought I set the fire."

She grabbed the catsup and turned around, pushing the door shut behind her. "I told him you couldn't have done something like that."

"So? Who's gonna believe a mother?"

The man who loves her. "No one," she said. "No one at all."

"Mr. Stanford tried to help me, Mom." Jon put his hands on his hips and gave her a disgusted look. "He gave me a lot of chances to tell the truth and I didn't. I blew it. I should have trusted him to help me out, but I didn't and that was stupid."

She tried to smile. "Yes. That's true."

"I'm getting smarter," her son insisted. "Next time something goes wrong, I'll ask him for help."

"I heard he's moving away."

Jon's chin dropped. "Moving away? Who told you that?"

"Amanda told me today. She said it's all over town."

"You're gonna let him go?"

"I don't think that's up to me, Jon." She turned to the meat loaf and grabbed a knife. She would slice it cold, and they could make sandwiches—

"Mom!"

"What?" She put the cutting board on the counter and slapped the meat loaf onto it.

"Quit doing the meat loaf thing and listen to me." She

turned around and waited for him to continue. "You've got to listen to me, Mom. Mr. Stanford didn't turn me in to the police. That was Mr. Nielsen's deal. And it was Stanford who figured out that Tina would know the truth. He went to her house and got her to talk. She told me that Stanford figured out she'd been sending him the letters. He went to her house that night and convinced her to tell the truth so I wouldn't get into trouble."

"He did?" Marina had wondered why he'd turned up at the barn, but she figured the police had told him where to meet them. "What letters?"

"She'd been writing anonymous letters, trying to get me off the hook without hurting Brad. Despite everything, she still didn't want him to get hurt. And she told Mr. Stanford what we'd planned at the barn."

Marina's heart lifted. "I didn't know all that. Why didn't you tell me?"

"I've tried. You wouldn't talk about it, remember?"

She remembered. Now it was time for some revelations of her own. "Mr. Stanford—Clint—asked me to marry him last Friday night."

Jon's mouth dropped open. "No sh—kidding?"

"That was before..." Marina hesitated. "I didn't answer him."

"Well?" Jon looked absolutely fascinated. "What are you going to say?"

"Nothing, not now. We haven't exactly...talked for the past few days. I couldn't stand that he'd turned you in to the police. I didn't think I could forgive him for that." Clint hadn't called her. She hadn't called him. She'd assumed it was over. She was positive it was over. After all, she'd *told* him it was over. And he'd taken her at her word, of course. She'd tried desperately not to cry her heart out at night for being such a fool as to fall in love.

"That's only because you didn't know the whole truth,"

Jon stated. "I wouldn't mind having him in the family. He came through when we needed him. He never stopped trying to help," her son added, his voice quiet. "Don't you understand?"

She understood. Finally.

THE JEEP WASN'T in front of his house. There was no answer at the phone at the cabin, which meant he could still be at the school this late in the afternoon. She'd barely slept all night, she'd been pretty useless at work today and had begged off early. Amanda had been happy to let her go home.

Marina turned around and drove by the high school. Sure enough, the white Jeep was parked in the faculty parking area.

She parked her car, took a deep breath and went into the school. The hall was empty and smelled of fresh paint. There was no one around, though she heard a radio playing from somewhere nearby. Marina walked to the office, half expecting to see Mrs. Donelly at her desk, but the room was empty. The door to Clint's office was open, so Marina peeked inside, to see him at his desk, piles of papers stacked in front of him.

He looked up when she knocked on the door frame, but his expression was guarded. "I didn't expect to see you here. Is this school business?"

"There are a couple of things I needed to talk about." She entered the room, sat down across from his desk and wondered how on earth she was going to get through this.

"And they are?"

"Well…" She hesitated, searching for the right words. She chickened out. "I hear you're moving, and I want to know what you plan to do about Tex and the puppies. You can't leave me with all these dogs."

He looked at her blankly. "Moving? I'm not moving."

"You're not?"

"No. Except out to the lake next month. I have another week's work here at school before I take my vacation. Where'd you hear something like that?"

"Never mind." Amanda, matchmaking again, had most likely invented the rumor. She would have hoped it would make Marina come to her senses.

Clint cleared his throat. "Jon said Christy and Amanda are taking two of the puppies, and I'll start trying to find a place for the others. Jon wants to keep Tex. I'll pay to have her neutered, of course."

"You and Jon have talked?"

He shook his head. "Not exactly. Just on E-mail. That's electronic mail, via computer. I'm getting pretty damn good at it, too." Clint still hadn't smiled. "What was the other thing you wanted to talk about?"

Marina cleared her throat. "I owe you an apology."

His eyebrows rose. "Yeah?"

"About the fire. You were only trying to help and I didn't believe you and for that I'm sorry." She took a breath. "Truly sorry."

He still didn't say anything, but he stood up and came around to stand in front of her. He picked up her hand and placed a careful kiss in her palm. "Does this mean you're going to marry me now?"

"You're asking me again?"

"No." He shook his head and her heart fell. "I'm still waiting for an answer from the last time I asked, sweetheart."

Marina stood up and went into his arms. She wrapped her arms around him and held on as tightly as she could. "I was an idiot."

"You could have had a little more faith in me," he murmured. "I wouldn't hurt you or Jon for anything in the world."

"I'm not good at leaning on anyone," Marina admitted, looking up into his eyes. "I guess I've been alone too long."

"Not anymore," he said.

No. Not anymore. "I'll get better, I promise."

"Does that mean you're going to marry me?"

She smiled. "Yes."

He closed his eyes briefly. "Good," he said, his voice husky. He bent down to kiss her until she was breathless. "I've been waiting to hear you say that."

"But you didn't call. You didn't come over."

"You gave me my walking papers that night, sweetheart. Then Jon warned me not to call right away. He said to give you time to cool off. So I took the kid's advice, but it wasn't easy. I was giving you the rest of the week and then I was coming after you."

"Texas persistence?"

"Yes, ma'am. I wasn't going to let you get away." He looked down at her simple leather flats. "One more thing," Clint said, lifting his head and smiling into her eyes. "If you're going to be The Cowboy's wife, we've got to get you a decent pair of boots."

Hometown Reunion

continues with

FANCY'S BABY

by Pamela Bauer

Gossip about the fire is on the back burner once Kika
Mancini, talent scout, rolls into Tyler; everyone's hoping to
be a star. But Kika is looking for one particular baby—
Nick Miller's—who's perfect for her client. Finding Nick
is a bonus, because he's perfect for *her,* even if
he is about to cost her her job.

Here's a preview!

FANCY'S BABY

"I'M GOING TO Tyler, Wisconsin, Dad, not New York City. And I'm going in search of a baby, not a man."

So Kika had said on her way out the door, but it was a man who caught her eye at the Milwaukee airport. As she dragged her wheeled suitcase through the terminal, she spotted him in a crush of people deplaning at one of the gates.

He was tall with short dark hair, deep set eyes and a wholesomeness that made her think she could cast him in a dozen parts as the "guy who gets the girl." He looked familiar, but it was only when he smiled at one of the flight attendants that Kika recognized him from the Tyler Tots Playschool video.

In a glance, she determined he'd just arrived on a flight from Los Angeles. He was probably an actor, not a real day-care father. He certainly had the good looks to be one of the Hollywood crowd. Could he be on his way to Tyler, too? He looked up and their eyes connected for the briefest of moments.

He was a hunk, all right. Automatically, Kika's lips parted in a smile. He looked away, but not before she had noticed a flicker of interest. She continued on her way, dragging her suitcase behind her.

She'd just lined up at the rental-car counter when she sensed someone coming up behind her. It was him. He was even better-looking up close. Her eyes were drawn to his left hand. No wedding ring.

Of course, that didn't mean he wasn't married, but at least

there was no obvious Keep Off sign. Unashamedly, with a professional eye, she looked him over, taking in the details she'd failed to notice at the gate. Like the fact that he smelled good.

Always thinking of work, she took a mental inventory of clients who might be interested in what this guy had. She'd give him a business card and tell him to get in touch with her. With the ease of someone who had years of experience flirting, she allowed her gaze to linger on him, a hint of a smile on her face. She could find him plenty of work. Before she could act, however, he spoke to her.

"If you're not careful, you might lose something." His voice was as impersonal and polite as a cab driver's.

Kika glanced down to see that her suitcase had come partially unzipped and a pair of red bikini briefs threatened to fall out. With an embarrassed grin, she bent down and pulled the zipper shut around the underwear. "Thanks."

He nodded and glanced at his watch, clearly indicating he had no interest in further conversation.

He obviously didn't want to be bothered, and that was fine with her, because she really had no reason to flirt with him anyway. All she knew about him was that he'd been in a children's video.

The clerk returned with the keys to her car and she was half way to the parking lot when she heard the guy from L.A. calling, "Wait!"

She turned, thinking her father had warned her about this, but he was holding her compact umbrella saying, "You dropped this." He pointed to the sky, where jagged lightning broke the summer darkness, and added, "You'll probably need it. It looks like rain." Thunder rumbled in the distance as they moved toward the cars.

She grinned, gratefully this time. "Thank you. Again."

And this time there was an answering smile on his face.

It made dimples appear and caused Kika's insides to do a funky little dance.

Yet they didn't speak again, not even when Kika found ''her'' car, opened the trunk and tossed her overnight bag inside, while he unlocked the car next to hers.

After slamming the trunk, she automatically glanced in his direction. He was pulling a jacket out of his suitcase. Before he closed the leather bag, she noticed he had a pair of handcuffs and a blindfold inside. She quickly looked away.

No doubt married, an actor and kinky. The guy had three strikes against him. Relieved that he hadn't responded to her flirting, Kika climbed into her rental car and drove out of the lot. He was right behind her.